Formula for a Felony

International Thriller Book 4

J.T. Kelly

CHAPTER 1

An early nor'easter blew winds and rain that swelled local waterways during the past week. Fortunately, the sun would soon make an appearance, giving way to a hot and sticky Friday morning.

Lanky Rob Wyte had stretched and laced up his new Brooks running shoes. He loved getting in a few miles through Paint Branch Park near his condo before going to work. His earbuds played Rimsky-Korsakov's *Scheherazade*. Dew saturated the ground and leaves. A light fog was slowly evaporating.

Making the turn along the trail next to the creek, it wasn't surprising to see how rapidly the water was flowing after the extended downpour. Something caught his eye. *What the hell?* He slowed to get a better look. *Is that a man's legs sticking out of the stream?* Rob leaned over the bridge for a better view, then gradually crept closer to the muddy bank near the stream. His eyes didn't deceive him. Two legs were indeed visible. Occasionally, there were glimpses of hands rising above the flowing water. The runner stared for several moments. Sweat had already coated his skin. A rush of cold air chilled him.

Taking a few steps back from the creek, he took out his earbuds. His trembling fingers reached for the cell phone in the pack around his waist. He punched in the numbers.

"Yes, 911 response. How can I help?" a young woman answered.

"Uh...I'm in the park...there's a b-body...in the creek," Rob sputtered as he continued to gape at his shocking discovery.

"Oh my. Give me your name and exact location," she answered. Rob offered her as much information as he could. She told him she'd alert the police. He provided his phone number so they could reach him.

Rob returned to the bridge. Other runners and walkers hustled by without stopping to witness the horror in the water below. His cell phone rang. "Is this Mr. Wyte?" a police detective inquired as he sped toward Rob's location in Silver Spring, Maryland.

"Yes...it is," the jittery runner replied.

"This is Detective Art Hillery. We got your whereabouts but need more details."

"Okay," Rob answered, then gave a description of his position in the park, on the bridge overlooking the swollen creek.

Minutes later, a siren broke the stillness of the morning. Rays of sunshine poked through the branches. Flashing lights from the squad car were soon visible. After parking nearby, two cops marched briskly toward Rob.

"Mr. Wyte?" a police officer barked as he neared.

"Yes?"

"I'm Detective Hillery, and this is Officer Onger," the muscular, plain-clothed man announced as he introduced himself and his slightly pudgy partner. "Okay, what's this about a body?" As soon as he asked, Hillery and his partner spotted the legs protruding from the creek. "A-ha!" He and Onger nodded to each other. "How close did you get to the body, Mr. Wyte?"

"Uh...not real close. It was barely light out when I first saw it. I...went closer...probably ten feet...to make sure my eyes weren't playing tricks on me."

"Okay, we'll need to borrow your shoes to verify the footprints," the detective ordered, as he scanned the immediate vicinity for other imprints."

"Gee, these are brand new," Rob stammered.

"You'll get 'em back," Hillery paused. "Onger, call forensics and start taping off this area."

The detective pulled booties over his shoes and ambled from the bridge to the bank leading to the stream. He grabbed a flashlight from his coat to see if he could detect footprints or any other clues. It wasn't long before forensic technicians arrived and started photographing the area and the partially submerged body. A pair of pathologists soon reached the scene. Following a consultation with Hillery, they carefully lifted the body from the rushing water. The man appeared to be a thin, balding, well-dressed person in his late fifties. They weren't immediately sure how he died. After examining his front, they turned him over to inspect the man's back. The pathologists quickly identified a red puncture wound in his neck, just below the hairline.

"Bingo. Looks like foul play, Detective," the lead examiner opined, as he looked at the other police officers. "We'll need to perform an autopsy to verify, but I'd say he's been dead for at least twelve hours."

"I haven't seen any other shoe prints in the mud other than those belonging to Mr. Wyte," Hillery said. "Could be whoever did the job hauled the body through the creek a fair distance. Have the forensics team search the bank for a hundred yards in each direction. Maybe something will turn up."

The pathologist began checking the body for identification. He fished out a keycard from the Garden Inn in his back pocket, placed it in an evidence bag, and handed it to Hillery. "This is the only thing I can find on him. The guy looks familiar but I can't place him."

"Okay, see what else you can dig up here. Let me know if your team finds any other footprints," the detective ordered. "Onger, let's head over to the Garden Hotel." Before leaving, Hillery snapped a few photos of the corpse with his cell phone.

The two cops took possession of Rob Wyte's new running shoes to document the footprints and promised to return them. "Please come to the station today for a statement, Mr. Wyte. Got to cover all the bases," Hillery insisted.

* * *

THE TWO MARYLAND police officers approached the hotel's front desk and asked to see the manager. The concierge directed them to the office of Brent Aker. They greeted him and introduced themselves. "We're investigating a crime and have this key card from a person of interest. Are you able to identify who it is?"

"Hmmm. Well, let's see what we've got." After scanning the card, the manager had an answer. "It appears this person had a room for one night. It was Amon Busch. You know, I think he might be the Food and Drug Administration Commissioner."

Hillery's and his partner's eyes widened with the sudden news as they glanced at each other.

"FDA Commissioner, huh?" the detective responded.

"Do you have video surveillance of the lobby and hallways we can review? As mentioned, this crime is under investigation, so we'd appreciate your help in maintaining confidentiality."

"Certainly, Detective. Come with me to our video security room," Aker offered, then led the two policemen to another office loaded with video monitors. He logged into the system and began loading up the previous day's digital video. Speeding through the visual feed, he stopped and rewound to show Amon Busch checking in – about 10 p.m. the previous night, then taking the elevator to his floor. The manager switched to a view of the hallway that showed Busch entering his room.

"Okay, good. That's our man," Hillery agreed. "Let's run through the tape to see if anyone joins him."

The manager continued to speed through the video until he came to a scene with a sexy young woman exiting the elevator and arriving at Busch's hotel suite. She knocked and soon went in.

"Let's see what time he and his friend depart," the detective urged.

Aker put the video in fast-forward mode. After more than an hour, the investigators saw the woman leaving. Several minutes later, Busch left, suspiciously glancing around the hallway, then taking the elevator.

"Check the lobby again," Hillery requested. There was no sign of Busch. "Hmmm. You have an underground parking lot, right?"

Aker switched the feed and zoomed to the corresponding time with the elevator. Suddenly, they spotted two men wearing dark glasses, hooded sweatshirts, and ball caps escorting Busch to a waiting car with blackened windows. The two muggers tossed the FDA Commissioner inside. They quickly hopped in the car and sped away.

"Oh my God!" Aker moaned, as the three stared at the video monitor.

"Back it up...need to see that again," the detective ordered.

They couldn't get a good look at the kidnappers – or their vehicle's license plate. All they could tell was that the car was an older, dark-colored Lincoln Town Car. "Would it be possible to get a copy of this video for our case, Mr. Aker?"

"Sure. If you can wait a few minutes while I pull the different video feeds together, I'll put it on a disk for you," the manager agreed.

After the two cops returned to their office, Hillery phoned the forensics department. "Hillery here. Did you get any other footprints along the creek?"

"Yes. Our men located two sets of prints heading into and then out of the creek bed – about twenty-five yards from where we located the body. Their trail didn't continue on the path for any distance. We'll get footprint records for both and have them for you at the station," the lead forensics tech replied.

The detective then called the pathologist about the post-mortem. "Any update on our body? Might have him ID'd as Amon Busch, the *former* FDA Commissioner. There was good surveillance video of the crime at the hotel."

"We're running a tox screen now to see what the attackers injected into his neck. Must have been a pretty potent dose of something lethal. I've got my money on either cyanide or potassium chloride," the pathologist determined.

"Let me know when you get the results back," Hillery requested.

"Okay, this should give you all the scenes of Mr. Busch, his girlfriend, and the two thugs," Aker stated, as he handed them the DVD.

The police officers thanked him and left.

"Have to wonder if that female visitor had anything to do with the hit?" Onger asked his partner. "I'll run a search on her to see what comes up. We'll find out who she is soon enough."

"Good call. I'll make an announcement as soon as we've reached his next of kin and the FDA."

CHAPTER 2

P rior to his demise, an unknown source delivered threatening voice messages to Amon Busch's cell phone. He didn't know who was behind them, but they were extremely unsettling. A synthesized deep voice insisted that the FDA restrict the number of markets approved for the prolific drug RGB101.

"This is your last chance to do the right thing, Mr. Busch. Consider this your final warning. Powerful forces are against the approval of RGB101 as a medication in the markets being considered by the FDA." Each time one of these calls ended, Busch leaned back with sweat beading on his balding head.

RGB101 was a product owned by NuPharma of Boston. The company's owner, Jack McCabe, had witnessed the nearly miraculous benefits of his drug on numerous occasions. The medication was known to counteract problems with the immune system, colds and flu, pneumonia, respiratory illnesses, heart disease, and diabetes. It had even

FORMULA FOR A FELONY

proven to counteract the deadly effects of poisonous ricin and the Ebola virus. Remarkably, RGB101 also allowed people to live healthy lives, well past the age of 100 by maintaining their cellular health.

Amon Busch knew that competing pharmaceutical companies were intensely covetous of this drug's range of applications and its proprietary formula. He suspected that some of them would stop at nothing to see it disappear.

Busch was unaware that two hitmen had been monitoring his daily routine. They knew when he arrived at his office in the morning and when he returned to his home at night. The men tracked him during visits to restaurants, outings with associates, and the occasions he took in a ballgame. The men were also aware of the times he rendezvoused with his lover. His life operated like clockwork. The assassins could easily pick a time to make their move.

On the night of the ambush, the FDA Commissioner arrived at the designated hotel to meet with his confidential companion. He tried to be inconspicuous by frequently switching locations. By the time Lucy arrived, he'd already ordered her favorite wine and greeted her with a glass. It wasn't long before she slowly undressed and the foreplay began. She always urged him to take his time to enjoy their evenings together. Despite her insistence, the passion quickly erupted and continued for the rest of the hour.

After Amon paid Lucy and watched her depart, he checked the room to make sure he had all of his belongings and prepared to leave. Suspicious of anyone in the hallway, he peeked both directions from the doorway, then briskly walked to the lone elevator. When he entered, two men were inside, facing away from the entrance. After it closed, they turned toward Busch. One man grabbed his arms, the other plunged a hypodermic needle into the back of his neck. Amon began to yell, but one of the men covered his mouth. They took the elevator to the garage where a large Lincoln was waiting. The two men pushed their hostage inside and it sped away. The toxic poison took only moments to do its job.

FOLLOWING the discovery of the body, Detective Hillery delivered the heartbreaking news to Busch's inconsolable wife. He then met with stunned FDA executives to provide the horrific details. The story broke the next day in media outlets around the world. No one could imagine how something so shocking could happen to such a respected government leader.

Unfortunately, Hillery's murder investigation was at a dead end. They located Busch's lover, but the woman's story checked out and the cops released her. The footprints that were found at the muddy creek weren't leading anywhere, and they hadn't been able to locate the Lincoln Town Car. As promised, the police returned the Brooks running shoes to Rob Wyte, the person who discovered the body.

After investigating Busch's personal effects, the police located his cell phone and listened to the menacing messages. There was no way to detect where the calls originated, but they had the motive. NuPharma Corporation's product was on someone's hit list. Busch hadn't cooperated and paid the price. Hillery had to alert NuPharma's owner, Jack McCabe.

The detective's phone calls to NuPharma eventually reached Jack at his summer cottage on Lake Maxinkuckee in northern Indiana. "Hello, Mr. McCabe, this is Detective Art Hillery with the Maryland Police Department."

"Oh...yes!" Jack responded with stunned surprise as he glanced over at his wife, Sara, who was enjoying a puzzle with their son, Amos. "I saw you on TV recently announcing the terrible story of the FDA Commissioner." Sara looked up with a concerned expression.

"Well, that was something no one would've expected," Hillery agreed. "I wanted to let you know we retrieved Busch's cell phone and listened to a frightening call demanding that the commissioner stop your product's approval into new markets."

"My God, Detective! Who could be behind such a threat?"

"We're still in the middle of our inquiry, Mr. McCabe, but with a clear motive, I want to make sure you take the proper steps with your security. No telling what these people could be up to."

"Yes...I understand," Jack replied with his eyes narrowing. The thought of potential violence against him and his family was terrifying. "I appreciate your alert and will take every precaution."

After the call ended, Jack sunk back into his living room couch and stared out at the lake. Sailboats raced by in the distance. "What in the world was that all about, honey?" Sara questioned with alarm. When Jack relayed the information from the detective, she pulled Amos closer to her. "Oh, no! What are we going to do?"

"Have to think this through, but don't like the sound of it. Got to put our team on notice." Jack punched in the number to his attorney, Christopher Masse. "Hello, Chris, I just got off the phone with the detective who's been investigating the FDA Commissioner's murder."

"Goodness! Really? What'd you find out?"

"Someone was sending threats to Busch on his phone. They ordered him to stop the approval of RGB101 into new markets. Got to find out who could be behind this. Also, we need to beef up security. The detective warned me that another attack could be possible."

"Well, damn! I don't like this at all, Jack," Masse replied, as he sat in his Indianapolis office tapping his pen on a legal pad. "Have you contacted Milt yet?" The attorney referenced the brilliant chemist Dr. Milton Lennium, the head of NuPharma's operation. "I'll reach out to a private security team to cover the Boston facility and key executives. I also know a group that will keep an eye out for your family and home here in Indy."

"Thanks. I'll contact Milt and fill him in," Jack said and ended the call. When McCabe reached Lennium's private office number, the chemist answered. "Milt, hope you're sitting down. Got some troublesome news. The detective who's been investigating the FDA Commissioner's killing called. He explained that an unknown source made threats for him to keep *us* out of new markets...or else."

"I...I can't believe this, Jack! Have to wonder if we're also on their list?" Lennium stammered.

"Chris is going to bring in a security team for the facility and to protect you personally."

"Good to know," Lennium answered. "I'll start a screen on all of our recent hires, especially the new chemists. Have to ensure that we protect the formula for RGB101."

"You're right. We don't want another heist like we had a few years ago by Promethia Degal." They'd hired Degal directly from MIT as a promising chemist. Eventually the company learned that she stole the product's composition and threatened to sell it to a rogue pharma company unless NuPharma paid her $25-million. With the fast work of Interpol in Europe, they averted the blackmail scheme.

McCabe's next conversation was with his local caretaker and personal bodyguard at the lake, Hans Kriechbaum. Jack strolled out onto the long white pier where Hans finished repairing the motor on the family's speedboat. "Hello, Hans, how's it going?"

"Hi, Mr. McCabe. Think I've got this back in order. It apparently had an electrical short, but it's as good as new."

"Thanks for getting it working again," Jack continued, as he shielded his eyes from the glaring sun in the west. "I wanted to let you know that we may have a problem. The detective investigating the murder of the FDA commissioner called. Turns out there were threats on the commissioner's life if he didn't block approval of RGB101 into new markets."

"That's incredible, Mr. McCabe!" Hans replied, as he climbed out of the boat and onto the pier. "Hope that doesn't mean we're in the killer's crosshairs now?"

"Can't say for sure, but we'll need to be on alert for anything. Before I head back to Indy, I'll reach out to Detective Lewis Tenant in Culver. Want to see if he'll keep an eye out and be available in case you need help."

While walking back to the cottage, Jack phoned the bearded Tenant and described the potential threat. "Unbelievable, Jack! There are just too many crazy people out there. I saw the news about the commissioner's assassination on TV. Terrible."

"Hans will watch our cottage but wanted to let you know in case he needs assistance. We just don't know what kind of danger there could be. We're beefing up security in Indianapolis and also at our plant in Boston."

"You can count on me, Jack," Tenant responded as Deputy Jerome Atrich looked over at his partner after taking a sip of steaming coffee.

"Well, Lew, what in the wide world of Lake Maxinkuckee was that all about?" the elderly Atrich inquired as he cocked his head and rubbed his nose.

"Looks like our friend Jack McCabe may have another serious problem threatening him and his business. There's someone who wants to stop his prized product from taking a bigger share of the pharmaceutical market."

CHAPTER 3

The pharmaceutical industry netted billions in profits every year. In most cases, its revenues were higher than other leading industrial corporations combined. While many drug companies continued to research and develop medications to help cure illnesses, a few simply revved up their marketing machines to bolster their incomes. Instead of relying on a new product, they changed a minor ingredient and called it *new*. Then they promoted it as a breakthrough innovation. Patent owners also played games to delay when competitors could create a generic of their drugs. Once it became a generic, hefty profits quickly disappeared.

Added to these practices was the leverage some big drug companies had over the U.S. House of Representatives and Senate. Lobbyists offered many members of Congress hundreds of thousands of dollars every year to boost their campaign coffers. In return, the donors demanded that the politicians support their pet projects. Most of these involved voting for appropriations and laws that favored the drug companies' special interests.

One of the most powerful yet secretive pharmaceutical lobbying organizations that influenced the direction of government legislation and FDA approvals was the Consortium. It was led by a man whose vast wealth enabled him to control not only political leaders, but CEOs of a number of major drug companies in the United States and Europe. His considerable investments in these enabled him to maintain his unquestioned dominance. His name was Karsen Ojin. Born in Germany of a Chinese mother and German father, Ojin grew up with wealth from his father's real estate holdings. Through his mother's political connections, he gained ties with powerful Chinese businesses.

Maintaining his fitness was an important routine for Ojin so he regularly sparred with his brilliant Japanese assistant, bodyguard, and lover, Fon Tazi, who held a black belt in karate. "Again, Tazi!" Ojin barked after Fon knocked him to the ground. He jumped back up and squared off for more contact.

"Yes, K! I'm ready," Fon replied, as she repositioned her uniform, known as a dogi or gi, and returned to her stance. 'K' was the name his inner circle connections called him. The white-haired, sinewy, fifty-four-year-old Ojin was in excellent condition, but he would never be a match for the fleet-footed, forty-something Tazi. Sometimes she would let him get in a kick or a punch, but she could easily block or pivot to avoid any actual harm. The exercises typically continued for nearly an hour. At the end, they were both dripping with a healthy sweat. Afterwards, Tazi disrobed and joined a nude K in his lavish steam bath. During these occasions, they continued their physical contact in a much more pleasurable manner. When they had both satisfied their desires, Tazi assisted her boss with his bath and laid out his day's clothing. As was her custom, Fon wore a skin-tight, ninja-style black body suit without the head covering. It made her feel like she could jump into action whenever the situation called for it.

"Contact the members of the Consortium for a conference call today at 11 a.m. EST in the U.S.," Ojin ordered after dressing. "We need to discuss the next steps in our efforts to eliminate the competition."

"Certainly, K," Tazi replied, as she poured Ojin a steaming cup of tea while he settled in behind his massive wooden desk in the ornate office. "I assume this will be on the private video connection feed."

"Of course. And please ask the chef to bring my morning meal."

His headquarters was in a 12th century refurbished castle, nestled above the city of Trento in the Italian Alps. Inside, enormous fireplaces with elaborate sculpted mantles remained lit. Heraldic banners hung from the walls. Painted frescoes displaying battle scenes adorned the ceilings. The ancient castle sat on a rocky cliff above a lush forest. Stone walls surrounded the structure's exterior reflecting its history as a fortress. Armed men stood guard throughout.

Tazi bowed, smiled, and left Ojin to prepare for his day. He booted up the high-speed computer and clicked on the three large monitors in front of him. He first checked his investments in the international markets. If his returns were satisfactory, he emitted a contented grunt. When revenues declined, he growled. Then Ojin scanned through the world news to determine his next options.

There were four key members of the U.S. contingent of the Consortium, including two pharmaceutical CEOs and two U.S. senators. The latter sat on the appropriations subcommittee that influenced the healthcare market and matters associated with the FDA. These members included:

- Barron Lidst, of ReMedin located in New York City.
- Rubin Bisch, of PharMax in Tampa Bay.
- Sen. Emon Barras, from Philadelphia.
- Sen. Stuart Pitts, from Los Angeles.

In Europe, the group included four pharmaceutical CEOs:

- Rome's Imelda Broglio, of Drogari.
- Vienna's Byrn Zaer, of Medika.
- Paris's Kahn Cordant, of Curatif.
- Brussel's Regis Volt, of Genez.

The members of the Consortium almost always found it inconvenient to meet with Ojin when he called an impromptu meeting. Most of them had schedules that were already filled, but with the financial leverage K held over each of them, they invariably adjusted their schedules to his. No one wanted to risk Ojin's ire.

The meeting began promptly at 11 a.m. ET time with the members secretly logged onto their computers. "Thank you for attending today's gathering," Ojin began as he scanned the faces of his group. They nodded individually and mumbled a greeting. "Now that we've dealt with Amon Busch, the former FDA commissioner, what can we expect from the new man in charge?"

"Everything I've been able to gather leads me to believe the acting commissioner, Samuel Mirch, will align with our wishes, K," Sen. Barras responded.

"Yes, I spoke with him briefly, and he appears to be aware of the importance of keeping the playing field fair for everyone concerned," Sen. Pitts echoed.

"Certainly we cannot allow RGB101 to gain a monopoly in the markets the company hopes to enter. It already holds an unfair advantage," Rubin Bisch chimed in as others nodded. "That damned drug dominates so many areas, it's difficult for our products to compete. We'll be ruined if it enters more sectors of the healthcare field."

"Your men did an excellent job on Amon Busch. We may need to continue to play hardball with the new man at the FDA if there's any sign we can't trust him," Imelda Broglio continued. "I have to protect my market share in the diabetes field or I'll have to make significant reductions in my operations."

The participants echoed their agreement with murmurs.

"Our *cleaners* are on retainer, so we're ready to move forward with another *scrub* if we're forced to respond," Ojin concurred with a sneer. "In fact, we've started to monitor Mirch's daily activities in case he needs to be sent a message."

"Excellent, K!" Regis Volt interjected with gusto. "What about the people who run NuPharma and its owner?

What's his name, Jack McCabe? Someone in power needs to be taught a lesson about fair play, don't you agree?"

"Yes, but let's see how our influence with Busch goes before we commit another um...hit," Ojin insisted. "If we don't succeed with our relationship with Mirch, we'll take the next step with him or McCabe."

Each member continued to provide input about their goals. The pharma companies described their failing profits since the news of RGB101 began chipping away at their individual market shares.

Fon Tazi observed the discussion incognito. She would provide her own feedback to K when the meeting concluded and communicate with him during the meeting if she had a suggestion. Toward the end of the discussion, she gave K an idea through an earpiece he was wearing. He reiterated her recommendation to the group.

"Sen. Barras, I'd like you to initiate an antitrust complaint against Jack McCabe," Ojin ordered. "Invite him to a Senate hearing and have him explain why Congress shouldn't charge him with unfair practices and a violation of monopoly laws."

"Of course, K! It might be a stretch, but I like that approach. I'll get some of our media friends on board to start a campaign against his company," Barras replied, as he nodded his approval. The others demonstrated their agreement with head bobs and enthusiastic mumbles.

When the video meeting concluded, Tazi joined her boss next to his desk to discuss the comments from the Consortium members. "Shrewd idea, Fon!" Ojin complimented his talented assistant.

"There are two men who continue to track Mirch," Tazi

replied. "They tell me he leads such a boring life, there's not much to report. Should we consider watching the McCabe fellow in case we decide to take action against him?"

"Excellent! You continue to impress me, my dear!" Ojin bellowed as he stroked Fon's upper leg. She smiled in return.

Minutes later, Tazi reached her man in the United States and ordered him to track Jack McCabe at his homes. "I understand he has two properties. There's a primary residence in Indianapolis and a vacation cottage in a small lake community next to Culver, Indiana. Report back to me when you've got your people in position.

"Of course, Ms. Tazi," answered Yao Min, the husky, bald-headed Chinese enforcer with a small, black goatee. "We'll need to bring on a few additional people to cover both areas, but it's not a problem."

"Do what's necessary to accomplish the assignment, Yao," Tazi responded. "Keep me informed on your team's progress. K doesn't want any slip-ups. Understand?"

"Certainly. I can assure you we will not fail him," Min acknowledged.

After the call, Min hired the extra cleaners he needed to keep track of Jack McCabe. Atticus Roshus would cover the Indianapolis area and he sent Mona Strauss to monitor his activity in Culver. They were both experienced in managing covert operations and staying under the radar. Neither would be detected by the target – or the police.

CHAPTER 4

Jack McCabe, his wife Sara, and their six-year-old son Amos loved cruising on Lake Maxinkuckee in their refurbished Chris-Craft. As the sun set they neared the dock. Jack idled the motor and steered the speedboat as it drifted closer to the pier. Amos was on his lap and helped guide the craft toward the boat lift.

"A little to the right, Amos, you've almost got it," Jack encouraged the boy as he continued to learn the nuances of maneuvering the vessel to its destination. The boat slightly bumped the dock but then floated below the canopy above the lift arms.

"Great! You did it!" Sara yelled happily. She jumped out of the boat onto the pier then turned on the electric lift to raise the craft above the water.

"I can't wait to ski tomorrow, Dad!" Amos shouted. "I'm getting better and want to slalom next time."

"If you think you're ready, we'll try it," Jack responded.

"We should go early to make sure the water is calm and there aren't many other boats out."

"Okay! Perfect!" Amos agreed eagerly as he watched his mother complete the lift operation.

Jack grew up spending summer months at the lake and inherited the family cottage. Shockingly, an assassin murdered his parents while they were on a snow skiing trip in Innsbruck, Austria. Unexpectedly, Jack also inherited NuPharma Corporation from Adamis Baum, the wealthy leader who ordered his parents' attack. Interpol officers eventually slayed the terrorist at his estate in Rome. In an ironic twist, Jack learned that he was Baum's closest living relative. As a result, Jack became an instant multi-millionaire.

When the family returned to their cottage after the boat ride, Jack checked his cell phone for messages. There was one from his attorney, Christopher Masse. "Jack, call me. Something very strange came up that we need to discuss."

Jack punched in the number. "Hello, Chris," he began, eager to hear about the problem.

"Don't know who's behind this, but a senator's office requested our presence at a subcommittee hearing on competitive drug practices."

"What the hell?" Jack snorted. "Someone's pushing their buttons to force this kind of inquisition. Who's the senator in charge?"

"Ronald Amock from Vermont is the chair of the appropriations committee that influences the Food and Drug Administration. Two other senators apparently argued their position – Barras from Pennsylvania and Pitts from California."

"Did you contact Milt yet?" Jack asked, referring to Dr. Milton Lennium, the chemist who ran NuPharma's operation.

"Yes, and he's beside himself. Seems borderline criminal if you ask me," Masse offered. "For now, we'll have to do their bidding and attend their inquiry next week. I'll begin putting our defense together."

"I'm glad you strengthened our security after the murder of the FDA commissioner, Chris. I've discussed the situation with Hans here at the lake. He's devoting more time to watching our property."

"Good to hear. Your Indy home should also be well-protected now too. I assume you'd like to fly to D.C. from Indianapolis. I'll arrange for Milt to meet us there so we can review all the details of the senate probe."

"Yes. I'll reach out in the next few days. Thanks for the heads up, even if it wasn't something I wanted to hear," Jack stated with a frown.

When Sara joined him, he described the information that his attorney provided. "Oh no, Jack!" Sara moaned. "What kind of people would do something like this to a respected company like NuPharma?"

"Good question!" he replied, shaking his head. "Chris is putting our rebuttal together. We have to see it through, especially if we want RGB101 to enter the markets where we know it will be effective in healing people."

"Can you wait until after tomorrow when Amos gets another opportunity to ski?" Sara hoped. "He's really eager to show us he can slalom."

"Sure, we'll head back to Indy tomorrow afternoon."

* * *

THE NEXT MORNING, the McCabes rose early and were ready to give Amos a chance for a one-ski trial. The sun had risen and the lake was as calm as they'd hoped on the southwest corner. Wispy clouds tinged in orange hovered overhead. Few boats were visible except for some stealthy fishermen. The family sped to the placid part of the lake and Amos jumped in the water with his life jacket on. A regular ski was soon on his left foot and the slalom ski was on his right. Jack hit the throttle to propel his son above the surface. As Amos glided behind the speedboat, Sara was in the back of the Chris-Craft yelling for the young skier to slip off the left ski and attach his foot to the slalom while holding the ski rope. Amos looked from his left foot to his right, then dropped the left one, quickly sliding his foot into the back part of the right ski. Jack picked up the speed to keep him above the water. Sara screamed, "You're doing it, Amos! Yes!" Amos stayed on the slalom for nearly thirty seconds but took a spill when a wave threw him off balance. Jack immediately slowed the speedboat and circled back for Sara to pick up the dropped ski. She soon floated it to her son.

"Let's do it again!" Amos yelled to his parents. He worked to get the left ski back on and was ready for his second effort. Once he got up on the two skis, Amos soon dropped the left one, slipped his foot into the slalom sleeve, and was racing along on the single ski again. Sara applauded the boy as Jack glanced back with a wide grin. This time, Amos stayed up for several minutes before finally letting go of the ski rope and sinking gently into the water. His parents roared their approval from the boat.

After circling back, they hauled in the skis and Amos climbed on board. Sara wrapped a towel around his shoulders. Jack and Sara were ecstatic with Amos' skills and praised the beaming boy.

A few hours later after having a snack, they packed up their Audi, ready to head back to Indianapolis. As they pulled their vehicle up the driveway and turned south on East Shore Drive, they were unaware that an unfamiliar woman had been spying on them. The Consortium had assigned Mona Strauss to monitor Jack's movements while he was at his Lake Maxinkuckee cottage. The spy pretended to be a jogger, wearing shades and a ball cap, with her black hair tucked up inside. As soon as they drove away, she'd attempt to sneak into the house and plant audio listening devices.

When they arrived in Indianapolis, Jack unloaded their luggage. As they settled into their Meridian-Kessler home, he phoned Christopher Masse.

"I've got tickets to D.C. for the two of us. Milt will meet us at the hotel," Masse reported. "See you at the Indy airport." Jack was unaware that there were *two* opposing forces monitoring his household. Masse had hired security men to watch over the McCabe house. They typically stayed in their car, often driving around the Indianapolis neighborhood looking for anything suspicious. Unknown to security, another person was also keeping an eye out. The Consortium brought on a man named Atticus Roshus who wore several disguises. Occasionally, he walked around the block with his dog on a leash. At other times, he rode his bicycle.

No one would know that he had a sidearm stuck inside his belt. The team watching McCabe's place suspected nothing.

* * *

AFTER THEIR FLIGHT touched down at Ronald Reagan Washington National Airport, McCabe and Masse took a taxi to their hotel and met up with Milton Lennium in the café. "I still can't believe these senators are attempting to press an antitrust complaint against us," Lennium groaned as he took a sip of coffee. "What's their case?"

"They don't have a snowball's chance in hell of proving anything nefarious," Masse groused. "I've got a litany of examples that show how RGB101 has saved people's lives from a variety of illnesses. We'll also expound on the miraculous way it's cured people who had contracted severe viruses and toxins."

"As I recall from our studies, it's also proven to be effective in battling certain cancers," Jack stated, as he looked at his associates, who nodded. "There was also that outbreak in Africa where our medication stopped a cholera outbreak in its tracks."

"That's right, Jack," Lennium responded. "Contaminated food or water caused the disease. Both children and adults became dehydrated with high fever, diarrhea, weight loss, rapid heartbeat, and other deadly symptoms. Fortunately, we flew a supply of our drug to the region in time to contain it."

"We're expecting to get an FDA green light for our product to manage heart disease and as a way to combat problems associated with diabetes," Masse added. "There's someone who's behind this damn inquiry. I'm not sure who yet, but we'll find out."

* * *

THE NEXT MORNING, the three took a taxi to the Capitol Building. After passing through security, the NuPharma men were ushered into a committee meeting room where senators sat behind a stately rostrum. In the center was the chair, Sen. Ronald Amock. Nearby sat Sens. Emon Barras and Stuart Pitts.

After being sworn in, the visitors sat at the witness table facing the inquisitors. "Thank you for coming today," Amock greeted and paused as he looked around the room then back at the testifiers. "The purpose of our FDA inquiry is to determine if NuPharma Corporation is abiding by the guidelines of fair trade in the drug markets it seeks to enter. If you would, please introduce yourselves for the record before you give a testimony. Tell us why your product shouldn't be limited in its applications. We need to uphold the integrity of the pharmaceutical marketplace, you understand."

"My name is Christopher Masse, attorney for NuPharma. For the record, I would like to submit documentation that illustrates the effectiveness of our product, RGB101, in the markets for which we seek entrance." Masse handed a stack of bound submissions to an assistant who distributed them to the senate panel. They took several minutes to review the contents and mumbled comments to each other, shaking their heads and gesturing.

CHAPTER 5

S en. Emon Barras broke in with his eyes squinted towards the visitors, "Mr. Chairman, I'd like to ask a few questions, if I may."

"The chair recognizes the senator from Pennsylvania," Amock responded.

"Mr. Masse, in a quick review of your documentation here," Barras announced, as he waved the bound folio in front of him, "you maintain that your drug, RGB101, has proven its effectiveness in the treatment of heart disease as well as diabetes. Sir, I'm sorry, but I find these claims to be somewhat of a stretch. Please tell this committee how you've come to these conclusions."

"I would like to defer to our chief chemist, Dr. Milton Lennium, who supervised the clinical trials for these two markets," Masse replied, as he nodded to Milt.

"Senator, there were extensive trials that proved beyond question the curative results of our studies. With more than 2500 patients in each market in the phase three trials,

29

our drug had a success rate above 95%," Lennium explained as he glanced at the rostrum and his associates.

"We will certainly want to investigate those results in more detail, Dr. Lennium. Personally, I find this data to be questionable," barked Barras. "How can one formula do so much?"

Sen. Amock interrupted Barras. "Now I have to disagree. These results appear to be legitimate, Sen. Barras."

Secretly knowing that Amock had also taken money from the Consortium lobby, Barras sneered and retorted, "With all due respect, are you sure about that comment, Sen. Amock?"

Just then, Sen. Pitts raised his hand to be recognized.

"The chair recognizes the senator from California," Amock fumed, as his eyes narrowed at the criticism from his colleague.

"Certainly we need to conduct research into the current health of this study group, Dr. Lennium," Pitts snickered. "Surely you don't expect us to believe that your drug cured 95% of the patients' heart and diabetes diseases?"

"What's unique about our product is that it provides molecular healing, which enables it to rebuild the cellular breakdown in the heart muscle. The results are indisputable," Lennium explained, then continued. "We had a very similar result with our diabetes trials and–"

Pitts interrupted Lennium, "Now, please, Dr. Lennium. You don't expect us to believe you've got some kind of wonder drug that can actually do all the things you say it does?"

"Actually, yes!" Lennium rebutted. "Our drug

strengthens the immune system to help the body fight infections and viruses. It builds up the insulin-producing beta cells in the pancreas." When he finished, Sens. Pitts and Barras shook their heads in disbelief. Lennium glanced at McCabe and Masse who smiled back at his authoritative responses.

After more questions and answers from the senators, the chair concluded the inquiry by recommending a third-party investigation of the trial subjects. "I think we can all agree that your product has certainly proven its value in these new healthcare markets, gentlemen. I'd like to thank you for your participation in our review and hopefully we can expedite your product's approval."

Pitts and Barras continued to shake their heads and looked at the chairman with disgust.

As Jack, Milt and Chris packed up their briefcases and were leaving the meeting room, they overheard loud arguing among the senators. Looking back, Jack could see Barras and Pitts browbeating the chair, Sen. Amock.

"You're going to regret rolling over to NuPharma," Barras barked at Amock. "Did you forget who helped bankroll your last election campaign?"

"Well, we have our principles to consider, Senator. I don't like your accusation one bit!" Amock responded angrily.

"Guess we can tell who's behind this investigation," Jack commented to his friends after they left the Capitol Building.

"We know there are very influential lobbyists who provide sizeable donations to politicians," Masse agreed. "I'd be willing to bet those two senators are heavily indebted to somebody high up in the hierarchy of a phar-maceutical clique."

"No question, Chris," Jack concurred. "And that was a masterful job explaining our product's benefits, Milt! You hit a home run in there."

* * *

AFTER THE MCCABES left their Lake Maxinkuckee cottage, the Consortium's secret agent, Mona Strauss, continued to spy on their residence. The next day, she jogged along East Shore Drive shortly after sunset. Reaching Jack's address, she stopped and put her hands on her knees like she was catching her breath. Then the woman pretended to be checking her pulse. Looking around, she couldn't see anyone nearby. Mona continued glancing back and forth down the street, then crept closer to the cottage. She assumed the doors would be locked, so she tried several windows. Having no luck, she climbed up one of the columns supporting the back porch. When she reached the second story, she began checking the windows. In no time, Mona located one that was unlocked. She pulled it open and crawled inside.

McCabe's personal security guard, Hans Kriechbaum, was also a nighttime jogger. Mona didn't see him heading down the road and then the driveway. He arrived just in time to see the woman wiggling through a second-story bathroom window. Rather than scream at the trespasser, he quietly darted to the back door, unlocked it, and went inside. The lights in the house were off. Pulling the small Ruger EC9S sidearm from his running pack, Hans crept along the wall of the kitchen to the dining room. He peered up the steep stairway. No one was in sight. He took one step at a time, aiming the pistol in front of him.

Upstairs, Mona had put on a headlamp and pulled small audio bugs from her waist pack, placing them inconspicuously inside light fixtures. When she completed the bathroom, she slipped into the hallway, looked each way, then proceeded to a bedroom, seeking ideal places to hide more electronic bugs.

When Hans came to the top step, he craned to peer around the hallway. He suddenly heard a slight noise coming from one of the bedrooms. Inching his way toward it with the gun pointed forward, he arrived at the bedroom door. Even though there were no lights on, the headlamp gave Mona away. He could see her inside.

"Halt! Don't move!" Hans shouted.

Mona quickly turned while grabbing her own small pistol and prepared to shoot. Hans dropped to the floor. Mona fired wildly but missed. Hans pulled the trigger several times and drilled the invader in the head, propelling her backwards. Waiting momentarily, he switched on the overhead light. Sprawled on the carpet in front of him was a woman he'd never seen. Blood puddled on the low shag carpet below her skull. He stared at the body in shock. One bullet pierced her forehead. The other knocked out the headlamp.

Hans ran to the fallen robber to make sure her weapon was no longer a threat. Feeling for a pulse and finding none, the young man dug through her waist pack. Inside, he found what he suspected were some sort of tiny surveillance devices. There was also a cell phone. A few moments later, he contacted Detective Lewis Tenant of the Culver Police. Tenant answered his phone at home.

"Yes, Tenant here." The person's name showed up on his caller ID. "Hello, Hans. What's going on this evening?"

"You won't believe this, Detective. I spotted someone crawling into a second-story window at the McCabe cottage. I followed her inside. She was planting audio surveillance devices. I yelled for her to stop, but she fired her weapon. I shot back. Now she's dead."

"Oh my God! Good thing you were on duty. I'll reach an ambulance, and we'll be there shortly." After he ended the call, Tenant dialed his deputy, Jerome Atrich. "Jerry, hope you're still up. Got a call from Hans at the McCabe place. There was an intruder, and he ended up gunning her down when she fired at him. He said she was planting some sort of surveillance equipment."

"Holy cow, Lew!" yelled Atrich. "We haven't seen any problems at the McCabe cottage for several years. Thank goodness Hans was there to catch the intruder... Surveillance devices, huh? Who in the Sam Hill would do something like that?"

"Guess we'll have to figure it out. I'll pick you up at the station."

After meeting his deputy, Tenant drove them to the McCabe place with their siren blaring and lights flashing. Turning into the driveway, they found the ambulance already at the scene. Two EMTs were walking inside the back door as Hans directed them to the location of the body.

When the police greeted the former Army sharpshooter, he told them he only touched the woman to see if there was a pulse. "I didn't start looking for the devices the woman planted, but she certainly put a few upstairs already," the young man reported.

"Good thing you were close by, Hans!" Tenant said, as he and his deputy made their way inside. "Show us the bathroom window she crawled through."

Reaching the second floor, Hans led the police to her entry spot, then to the bedroom next to it. The EMTs were already inspecting the body.

"She's got a phone along with the bugs, Detective," Hans explained as they peered at the woman stretched out in front of them. "I saw those but didn't handle them."

"Okay, good to know," Tenant replied. "Jerry, stake out the area with crime-scene tape. I'll put the woman's items in an evidence bag and search for what she might have planted."

"Poor Mr. McCabe," Hans remarked. "I'll let him know. He won't like this foul play one bit."

Moments later, the phone in Jack's car alerted him, as he drove back from the Indianapolis airport after his trip to D.C. "Yes, Hans! What's up?"

"Got some disturbing news, Mr. McCabe. I caught a woman sneaking into your cottage. She was planting some sort of audio bugs. She fired at me, but now she's dead. The police are investigating."

CHAPTER 6

Jack sputtered, as he tightly gripped the steering wheel of his car, "What the hell? This can't be happening, Hans!"

"Sorry to say it did. I'm glad I was out jogging and caught a glimpse of the woman as she was sneaking into a second-story window. She had a phone, so maybe the police can determine who sent her."

"Yes, hopefully they'll track her calls," Jack responded, as he tried to control his pounding pulse. "You say she had some sort of audio bugs, huh? Damn...I think I may know who's behind this invasion."

"Really?" Hans paused. "On another subject, I hope you had a successful visit to the Capitol, Mr. McCabe."

"It went well. Our attorney and chemist gave a great presentation to the senators. When we left, several of them were arguing. We could tell which ones were dead against us."

"So you think someone in government is behind this?"

"Can't say for sure, but something smells fishy. We know pharmaceutical lobbyists spend a fortune donating to people in Congress. There's a piece to this puzzle among that group," Jack said. "This is all so upsetting, but thank you for being there for us, Hans! You're a lifesaver. Are you still with Detective Tenant? Please ask him to call me."

Hans described his conversation with McCabe. After Tenant completed his search for the surveillance devices and the EMTs had bagged and departed with the woman's body, he called Jack. "I'm sure you're eager to learn anything new about your break-in," Tenant began. "I'm very sorry this happened, Mr. McCabe. Just awful....I think I've located all the bugs the woman placed. The people in the morgue will fingerprint her so we can find out who she is and if she's got a record. I'm sending her cell phone to forensics to see if they can identify any of the phone numbers. Chances are they're from burner phones, so we may not have an immediate idea who hired her. This case looks big. I'm going to contact the FBI to see if they can help us."

"Good idea, Detective," Jack responded from his home. "My attorney and I suspect that someone involved in the pharmaceutical industry has colluded with a few of the senators at the inquiry we attended."

"I'll be darned. If you're right, there's no telling where this investigation's headed. I'll keep you posted on anything that turns up."

* * *

THE FIXER for the Consortium in the United States, Yao Min, was getting concerned. He hadn't heard from the woman he hired to monitor Jack McCabe in Culver. She should have planted listening devices inside his cottage on Lake Maxinkuckee. Several days had passed and his nerves were on edge. He called Fon Tazi, Karsen Ojin's right-hand enforcer on his burner phone. "Yes, Ms. Tazi. I haven't been able to reach my cleaner in Culver. There haven't been any signals from the planted bugs at McCabe's. I'm beginning to think someone spotted her and took her out."

"I thought you were confident of this person, Min!" Tazi growled. K will not be pleased. I'll discuss it with him and let you know our next steps."

Right before Tazi heard from Min, Ojin received a call from Sen. Emon Barras. "I hate to be the bearer of bad news, K, but our subcommittee hearing with the NuPharma people did not go well."

"How could this happen?" Ojin fumed. "Who dropped the ball?"

"Unfortunately, Sen. Ron Amock was very conciliatory toward them. I have to say that his positive response to their presentation may have swayed the other senators to grant an approval of their entry into the new markets. There'll be a follow-up study of the patients from the clinical trials. But, if they validate the data, NuPharma's as good as confirmed."

"Amock must pay for his disloyalty! The pharmaceutical companies aligned with us will be furious, and my investments will be in the tank," Ojin thundered. "I'll get back to you."

Shortly after her call with Yao Min, Fon Tazi joined her

boss. "The current is moving swiftly against us at the moment, Fon. I've just learned that Amock screwed us at the NuPharma inquiry. We can't let him get away with it. Contact our man in D.C. to arrange for Amock to have a serious *accident*. We must remove him from his position as the chair on the senate subcommittee.

"Of course, K!" she responded with a wicked expression on her otherwise lovely face. "I've already taken the initiative to have Amock monitored near his home. Our people there know where he goes and when there'd be a good time to make something happen."

Ojin smiled and nodded to his assistant.

"There's more, I'm afraid," she continued. "I spoke with Yao Min, and he hasn't heard from the cleaner we sent to Lake Maxinkuckee to track Jack McCabe. And there've been no signals from the bugs she was supposed to hide in his house. We haven't planted any in his Indianapolis home yet."

"What? No! How could this happen?" Ojin thundered. "Set up the anonymous calls to his cell phone. He needs to get a clear message that we won't tolerate his plans to enter any new markets."

"Yes, K, we'll get everything in motion."

Fon soon called her other point man in Washington. "Hello, Cho? Tazi here. We need to take the next step with Sen. Amock...but it needs to look like an accident. Any ideas?"

"Oh, yes, Ms. Tazi," Cho En Dai answered. "Let's see. Amock likes to take long walks in the evening. There's a very steep stairway between Prospect Street and Canal Road that he uses for exercise. You like old movies?"

"Sometimes. What the hell are you referring to?"

"Ever see the horror movie *The Exorcist?* Amock takes those stairs during his walks. They are very treacherous. Someone could have a terrible fall...if not careful."

"You're saying that Amock could have a serious accident there?"

"Yes. If he trips, it could happen, Ms. Tazi. Very steep."

"Do what you have to do to," she replied with a sneer.

Tazi's next call was back to Yao Min. "Ojin is furious about the lack of progress with NuPharma, especially its owner, Jack McCabe. Set up the phone calls to threaten him to stop his plans to enter the new drug markets he's exploring. There can be no slip-ups. Make sure the calls aren't traceable. Understand?"

"You want the same type of message we sent to former FDA Commissioner Amon Busch?" Yao Min asked as he made notes.

"Of course," Tazi responded. "Let me know when they begin."

"Yes, Ms. Tazi," Yao Min acknowledged.

AFTER HIS CALL WITH TAZI, Cho En Dai knew what he had to do to stage an accident with Sen. Amock in D.C. He and his partner, Din Shu Pu, both wiry and athletic, did a masterful job on Amon Busch. They didn't leave a trace then and wouldn't for this job either. Cho met with Din to plan their approach. It had to look like an accidental trip and fall. Usually there weren't many people on the precipitous stairway next to Canal Road at night.

They could follow him and quietly approach from behind and push him as he walked down the steps. Cho also wanted to trip him. Din would sneak into the building next to the stairs and access the window. Cho would drill a small piton or stake into the stone on one side of the stairs and tie an unseen cord to the loop on the end. Then he would stretch the cord across the step and wrap it around the stair post next to the window. As Amock neared the step, Din would raise the cord and pull it tight. Cho would simultaneously push the senator from behind to intensify his fall. They hoped the sharp incline would be enough to cause a fatal injury.

The evening of their attack, they set up the stairway with the trip cord before Amock arrived. Cho and Din each wore ball caps pulled down over their heads and donned fake beards and dark-framed glasses. As expected, Amock came speed-walking along the street and turned to go down the stairs. Cho was on his phone nearby, then quietly followed the senator. He told Din to be ready. The senator almost skipped down the stairs. Just before he reached the step with the cord, Din pulled it tight. Cho closed the distance and pushed the unsuspecting man forcefully from behind. The cord caused Amock to lose control. He flew several feet in the air before landing hard on his shoulders and neck. Then the senator tumbled down the rest of the long flight of stairs. Cho pulled the piton from the stone. Din reeled the cord through the window, then closed it and left the scene. Cho rushed up to the top of the stairs and disappeared.

Amock's body stretched out awkwardly on the ground with his head twisted unnaturally at the bottom of the stairs. It wasn't long before a shocked passerby spotted the grisly scene and gasped. Seconds later, he composed himself, pulled out his cell phone, and dialed 911.

A police siren echoed in the night and came to a stop on the street below the steps. Officer Maria Ott and her partner approached the still shaking witness who'd called it in. They took a statement and inspected the distorted body. "Call for an ambulance, then cordon off this area for a block," Ott ordered her partner. "Looks like this guy had a nasty fall."

The ambulance arrived and the EMT soon checked for a pulse. "Poor guy," one of them stated. After checking through his clothing, the tech located a small wallet and handed it to Ott.

With gloves on, the officer scanned the contents. "Holy hell! This is Sen. Amock." She quickly got on the phone and called her precinct. "Got a major news story here. Better prepare for a media frenzy. We found the body of Sen. Ronald Amock at the bottom of the *Exorcist* stairway on M Street and Canal Road."

The next day, descriptions of the macabre death of the noted senator from Vermont filled the news. Reports claimed that the relatively young and handsome Amock would certainly be missed. Privately, Sens. Barras and Pitts confided to each other that they weren't surprised their colleague met an early demise.

CHAPTER 7

The news of the man's death shook Jack McCabe. He seemed so full of life when they saw him at the senate hearing just a few days ago. "Can you believe the story about Amock, Chris?" Jack asked his attorney after phoning him at his office. "It's incredible!"

Masse snorted in disbelief, "First the FDA Commissioner and now a senator who favored our application into the new markets?"

Meanwhile, back in Culver, Detective Lewis Tenant recalled how FBI Agent Miles DeLong helped solve The New Global Order case. Terrorists bribed a medical expert who worked at the Centers for Disease Control in Atlanta to steal samples of an Ebola Zaire virus. DeLong and two of his people, Barbara Dwyer and Andrew Friese, eventually determined how the man stole the samples. Later, the FBI arranged to get doses of RGB101 to cure the criminals who accidentally contracted the Ebola virus.

After learning that the woman who broke into Jack

McCabe's lake cottage had a shady past, Tenant reached Agent DeLong to see if he'd provide help. "Hello, Detective!" DeLong answered when the call came in and Tenant introduced himself. "I recall you're a friend of Interpol Chief Sam Aritan. What's going on?"

"Yes, we worked with Interpol during several investigations," Tenant acknowledged. "You might remember the name Jack McCabe. He now owns NuPharma Corporation that has the drug known as RGB101."

"Let's see," DeLong thought for a second, "Yeah, sure! That's some powerful medicine. And Jack's now the owner?"

"Yes, in a very unexpected twist of fate, it turned out that Jack was the closest living relative to the terrorist leader Adamis Baum who had purchased the pharmaceutical company in a hostile takeover."

"Of course! It's all coming back to me. So what's happening with Mr. McCabe that you needed to contact the FBI?"

"I'm sure you're familiar with the murder of the former FDA Commissioner and the accidental death of the senator in D.C.? A Senate committee ordered Jack to attend an antitrust inquiry regarding his prized drug. NuPharma had petitioned the FDA to enter the heart disease and diabetes markets. The company conducted clinical studies with patients and the results were overwhelmingly positive. The former FDA Commissioner and the senator were in favor of an approval for both markets. Now they're both dead."

"I have to agree the connection between the two tragedies appears to be very suspicious," DeLong responded, as he narrowed his eyes.

"Yes, and Mr. McCabe's cottage on Lake Maxinkuckee near Culver, Indiana, was broken into. A woman was discovered planting audio bugs in the house. McCabe's security man spotted her entering and stopped her before any damage could be done."

"No kidding. What do you know about the woman?"

"We matched her fingerprints to a criminal background. We're trying to find out who hired the woman through her phone, but we haven't had any luck so far. I'm hoping your resources can help us."

"Yes, we can provide assistance, Detective. Sounds like you believe there's a link between the woman and the deaths of the commissioner and the senator."

"Yes, sir, we do. It would be one thing to have a simple break-in, but for this woman to be planting surveillance devices. That's pretty darn sophisticated."

"I don't disagree, Detective. Tell you what, express ship the phone to me, and I'll see what I can find out."

Tenant thanked him and ended the call.

"Sounds like you've got a good contact there, Lew," Deputy Jerry Atrich proposed, as he finished eating a chocolate-covered Long John.

"Yep. We'll see what comes of it. Do me a favor and get that cell phone from forensics and express it to this address," Tenant said, handing his deputy the address from DeLong.

* * *

AMOS MCCABE HAD ALREADY LEFT for school. Jack and Sara were both in the mid-40s. Jack was tall with early stages of premature gray hair. He kept in good shape by running outside or on a treadmill. Sara stayed in excellent condition with yoga and her stationary bicycle training programs. Sara managed their advertising and public relations firm, McCabe and Bellamy. Besides NuPharma, Jack kept track of a major petroleum-products company, McCabe Industries, that he inherited from his grandfather.

Suddenly, Jack's cell phone rang. When he answered, a deep, synthesized voice demanded, "It's time for you to do the right thing, Mr. McCabe. Consider this a warning. Powerful forces are against the approval of RGB101 as a medication in the markets being considered by the FDA." Then it clicked off.

"Oh my God, Sara! You won't believe what just came through on my cell."

"W-What in the world, Jack?" she stammered. After all the mysterious and frightening events that had been going on, she hated to find out.

"It was a weird-sounding voice telling me to back out of the new markets...or else!" Jack gulped.

"No...It can't be! We better get someone to find out who's behind this."

Jack thought for a few seconds, then phoned his attorney, Christopher Masse. "Something very troublesome just happened. An anonymous phone call warned me to pull RGB101 off the heart disease and diabetes markets...or else!"

"I'll be damned, Jack!" Masse responded with disgust. "We've got to get to the bottom of this. I'll double up on security and contact the police. We need to make sure there's no one that comes near your place. On second thought, you might consider moving out for a while until we figure out what's going on. Also, buy new burner phones for you and Sara. Get rid of your current phones."

"Hate to do it, but we'll just have to contact everyone to let them know how to reach us," Jack agreed reluctantly. "We should keep Amos at home with us too."

Overhearing the conversation with Masse, Sara quickly left to pick up her son at school and collect his studies. She would be home-schooling him for the foreseeable future.

Jack contacted his security man Hans Kriechbaum at Lake Maxinkuckee to alert him of the heightened threat. Next, he phoned Detective Lewis Tenant in Culver. After explaining the message he received, Tenant told Jack he'd spoken with Agent DeLong of the FBI, who offered to hack into the woman's cell phone. Her contacts could lead them to whoever was behind the warnings.

Sara soon returned with Amos. Jack filled her in on the plan to move to a condo and that he was going to buy new burner phones. He wondered if someone bugged their cell phones. For all he knew, his house could be under surveillance. Since the threat came from his cell phone, he knew the criminals could reach him any time. It didn't take Jack and Sara long to pack up their necessary items and locate a condo nearby. They'd lie low while the police investigated the threatening phone call.

Walking a dog near Jack's house was the Consortium's hired hitman, Atticus Roshus. He hadn't bugged Jack's place, but it was easy enough to get his cell phone number. Roshus was not aware that Jack planned to temporarily move out of his Meridian-Kessler neighborhood. The only thing he noticed was the two McCabe vehicles had left and returned. Eventually they left again. Yao Min informed him that the threatening calls were starting. He suspected that's what caused this recent flurry of activity.

As soon as Agent Myles DeLong received the cell phone that belonged to the deceased Mona Strauss, he took it to his specialists for examination. As suspected, her calls came from burner phones, so there were no names or addresses associated with them. However, he put a wiretap on several numbers. His technicians soon started recording conversations. The name Yao Min soon came up. He had several discussions with a woman by the name of Tazi, who appeared to be giving him orders. She told him to continue pressuring Jack McCabe. "We can't let him get away with this," she insisted.

"Okay. Now we're getting somewhere," DeLong said to his assistant, Barbara Dwyer. "Conduct a search for this Yao Min to see what comes up. He's located somewhere in the United States. Don't know if we'll find this Tazi person. Our analyst thinks she's in Europe."

Dwyer initiated an investigation of the U.S. suspect. She soon found a match for Yao Min, who had underworld connections and spent time in prison for counterfeiting and blackmailing. Even though there wasn't a current address, they had a photo to work with.

Agent DeLong knew he needed help. Since the Tazi woman lived in Europe, he contacted his old Army buddy, Chief Samuel Aritan, the head of Interpol's counterespionage and intelligence operations. In addition to his group headquartered in Innsbruck, Austria, Aritan had teams in Belgium and Italy. The bearded, cigar-smoking chief had spent time with DeLong on several tours of the Middle East wars, so they were well-acquainted.

"Hello, Chief! Glad I caught you in your office. It's Agent DeLong from D.C."

Aritan recognized the voice on the phone right away. "You can't fool me, Myles!" the chief boomed and laughed. "You had me at hello, as they say. To what do I owe your call on this beautiful day?"

DeLong chuckled and filled him in on his latest concern. "We've got a bit of a mess here. I'm sure you remember Jack McCabe."

"Of course, Jack's done a lot of good things since he became the owner of his inherited pharmaceutical company. In fact, he helped out several police officers in Amsterdam who came in contact with ricin poisoning. He flew some of his product there to save them."

CHAPTER 8

C hief Aritan continued to describe recent experiences with Jack McCabe. "On another occasion, we helped stop the theft of his drug's formula by one of his previous employees. A team from our Rome office tracked down the perpetrator and his accomplice before they could do any harm."

"Sounds like you've had several opportunities to be in touch with McCabe," DeLong responded as he jotted notes on a pad in front of him. "As you can imagine, his prized drug is able to cure so many ailments that he petitioned the FDA to approve it for two new applications – heart disease and diabetes."

"Well, that's not surprising," Aritan said, as he blew a smoke ring from the corner of his mouth.

"The problem is there are forces allied against him. In fact, he recently received a threatening phone message to stop his foray into new drug markets – *or else*! He's gone into hiding until this thing has been resolved. Earlier, a senate committee invited Jack to a hearing to evaluate his product's possible antitrust practices. In the past few weeks, the former FDA Commissioner and a senator friendly to NuPharma have both turned up dead."

"Well, I'll be damned, Myles!" Aritan nearly coughed. "This has all the earmarks of a criminal collaboration against Jack and his company."

"Yes, and there's another thing that's taken place," the FBI agent continued. "A woman tried to sneak into McCabe's lake cottage. The caretaker spotted her and ended up taking her out. She was starting to plant listening devices."

"I'll be a sonofabitch!" Aritan barked. "From what you're telling me, a person involved in this cabal is somewhere in Europe."

"Bingo! We were able to wiretap some phone numbers from the woman's phone. One of them came from the European continent. All we know is it belongs to a woman named Tazi. She was calling the shots to a guy in the States named Yao Min. We're having a problem locating him."

"I'll tell you what, Myles. Send me the recordings and phone numbers and I'll have our top technical person see what she can figure out."

"Great. I've got your email so it's heading your way. Appreciate your help."

Aritan soon received the information from DeLong and forwarded it to his specialist in Rome, Sarah Graff. "Got the information, Chief. I'll get right on it," the young techie promised. Graff sported a spiky punk hairdo and had several facial piercings. The thin young woman was adept at getting through virtual private networks and tracking the location of phone calls.

Several hours later, Graff suspected that the calls from Tazi came from an area near the city of Trento in the Italian Alps. "Chief, it's Graff. I narrowed down the location of the calls from the person named Tazi." She explained her analysis and then described the spot the team could begin searching.

"Good work, Graff. Looks like a job for Officers Fresco and Sterrio from the Rome office. Is one of them available?"

"Yes, sir. Please hold." Moments later, Kara Sterrio got on the line.

"Hello, Chief! Good to hear from you. What's the latest?" Sterrio asked.

"As I told Graff, we've got an international case involving our old friend, Jack McCabe. We're trying to track down a woman by the name of Tazi who's had several conversations with a man named Yao Min in the States." Aritan began. "Graff told me the calls came from somewhere near Trento in northern Italy."

"That's our part of the world, for sure," she commented.

"Yes. It appears there's a collaboration among pharmaceutical companies and a few senators in the U.S. to battle against Jack's product." Chief Aritan continued to describe the recent murder and death in connection with Jack's request to expand his markets.

"Sounds like more than a coincidence, Chief," Sterrio responded as she made notes. "What do we know about this Tazi woman?"

"So far, she's off the radar," Chief replied, as he relit his Nicaraguan cigar.

"I'll get together with Fresco and Graff. We'll find out more," Sterrio offered.

Alberto Fresco was the head of the Rome Interpol operation who partnered with Sterrio on investigations as often as possible. They were more than a great team. They were lovers. Both in their 40s, Sterrio was considered statuesque with classical Roman features and long, dark hair. Fresco was muscular with a dark Italian complexion.

After her call with Aritan, Sterrio met with her partner and described the challenge ahead of them. "I've asked Graff to see what she can find out about this Tazi woman," Sterrio explained.

"Good. Looks like we'll be paying a visit to the Italian Alps. Are you ready for a road trip?" Fresco asked with a grin.

"Always up for a little mountain scenery. Let's get our weapons and gear packed up and be ready to head out tomorrow," she agreed.

Later that afternoon, Graff visited Sterrio with an update on the mysterious Tazi. "Looks like her name could be Fon Tazi. I located a photo of her from her time with the Japanese Air Force and the Olympic team. She was a gold-medal winner in martial arts. I'm still searching and will update you as soon as I get more."

"Interesting, thanks. One more thing. Can you research the backgrounds of European pharmaceutical companies? Get their locations, CEOs, and primary markets. I know there's a big one in Rome."

* * *

THE WIND WHIPPED along the top of Karsen Ojin's castle as the sun descended behind the Italian Alps. The leader of the Consortium and his assistant and lover, Fon Tazi, strolled next to the castle wall and peered out between the merlons, the stone projections where defenders fired their weapons.

"Our efforts to change the course of NuPharma's foray into new markets haven't had the impact we intended, Fon," Ojin remarked disgustedly, between sips of wine from his goblet.

"Now that Sen. Amock is out of the way, either Sen. Barras or Pitts should be able to maneuver into the chair of the healthcare subcommittee," Tazi remarked. "If it's not too late, it's possible they can delay the FDA approval for NuPharma."

"Jack McCabe got the message we sent, but now he's disappeared. Your man Roshus hasn't done much good. What else is there?"

As she brushed the wind-swept black hair from her face and took a drink from her own goblet, Tazi contemplated their next move. "It appears that NuPharma has increased its security, but we could consider kidnapping its main chemist, Dr. Milton Lennium. This would accomplish two objectives. One, we can force McCabe's company to reverse its plans for expansion. And two, we might be able to force Lennium to provide the formula for RGB101."

"My, my, Fon! You never fail to amaze me," Ojin responded with a wicked grin. "It sounds perilous. Do you think your people can pull off such a daring scheme?"

"I'll speak with my contact and let you know soon, K," she replied with a wicked grin.

Ojin became instantly stimulated and set his wine down on the wall. "You inspire me, my dear," he shouted, then jumped into a karate attack position.

Tazi smiled and took up her own defensive stance, feigning kicks and punches at her boss. They both laughed, as he blocked her thrusts. It wasn't long before they made their way to the ornate steam bath for an evening of relaxation and sexual satisfaction.

Later that night, Tazi grabbed a recently purchased, prepaid burner phone to call her contact in the D.C. area, Cho En Dai. "I have a new assignment for you. You're familiar with the NuPharma operation in Boston, correct?"

"Yes, we've been there to observe NuPharma on several occasions," Cho responded.

"Do you think you could kidnap its leader, Milton Lennium? This needs to be carefully executed. We cannot afford any errors. Once you have him hidden away, you'll begin a torture treatment involving restrictions on food and water mixed with blaring music to break him down. You'll need to locate a place where you could accomplish this without being disturbed?"

"Hmmm. I see, Ms. Tazi. This will indeed require careful planning. Let me discuss your request with my partner, and I'll report back to you with our plan. I know that there's security surrounding the company's building and Lennium's home, so it will be difficult...and very costly."

"Money is not a problem, Cho," she answered. "Let me know what you're going to do."

After the call, Cho and his partner Din Shu Pu met for

dinner to discuss the details of their operation. The first thing they had to do was travel to Boston and begin reconnaissance of the area and determine where they could hold their captive.

* * *

AFTER FLYING to Logan International Airport and renting a dark van, Cho and Din staked out the NuPharma operation to monitor Lennium's movements. They easily spotted the security team that accompanied him whenever he left the headquarters. Following a safe distance behind the vehicles in the entourage back to his home, the two hitmen instantly spied two additional armed guards stationed at Lennium's home. They would pose a problem, but not an insurmountable one. It appeared that the chemist was either at his home or in the NuPharma building. Regardless, this would require a stealthy and highly technical approach.

The next day, the two criminals located a remote warehouse in the South Boston area. Wearing a disguise and using a false identity, Din Shu Pu met with the rental agency rep and signed up for a six-month lease.

CHAPTER 9

During the following week, the two Asian hitmen watched to see who else came and went from the Lennium house. They noticed minimal activity other than when Mrs. Lennium left for errands or shopping. A security detail always accompanied her. There were no children at home that they could see. At the NuPharma building, daily deliveries of supplies and shipments from FedEx, UPS, and others arrived. Certainly getting inside the building would require a security clearance. Should they risk bribing someone to find out?

If they were to break into Lennium's home, they would need to determine an optimal ingress and egress. To get inside, they'd have to incapacitate the chemist and his wife long enough to escape with the man's body. But how? Cho purchased a drone with a video camera to see what possibilities existed on the roof. Just as dawn was breaking, the two hoods launched the drone and watched a TV monitor from inside their van. The small drone hovered above the Lennium home and scanned the roof.

"A-ha!" Cho shouted when he spotted several skylights that came into view. He carefully lowered the drone to determine how they were attached to the roof. There were no latches, so they were permanently sealed. They'd have to cut through one to enter. The drone flew closer to the different skylights to get a better view inside. If Cho took this approach, he'd have to know the best one to enter. He finally saw one that appeared to be above a second-story hallway. "That one will work," he said to his partner, as they viewed the video.

"Here's an idea," Din offered excitedly. "I read about the new Eurocopter with noise-cancelling Blue Edge blades that makes almost no noise. I think we can rent one at Logan Airport, but they aren't cheap. I could drop down on a cable to get inside after we incapacitate the guards stationed outside."

Din Shu Pu's idea of using a low-noise helicopter to fly above Lennium's house, take out the guards, then enter to capture him intrigued his partner. Cho had piloted many choppers during his time with the Chinese Air Force. He called Fon Tazi to give her the details. His plan thrilled her even though she wondered if it would be too difficult to execute. After conferring with Karsen Ojin, she called Cho back with a green light to proceed.

"Won't they demand special training to fly the new chopper, Cho?" she inquired, still having her doubts.

"My helicopter license here in the U.S. is still in effect, even though it's under a fake name. If they can provide some instruction, I should be in good shape to fly this new bird."

Cho wore one of his disguises when he visited Logan Airport to discuss renting a Eurocopter for an evening. The representative described the features that would require a minimum of preparation through an online tutorial. The website provided complete instructions on using the controls. The rental fee was exorbitant, but that was of no concern. Cho reserved the chopper for the middle of the week when the weather was expected to be mild.

While his partner was at the airport, Din rented a heavy duty cable hoist that could be fastened to the top of the helicopter door. After arriving at the commercial section of the airport, Cho paid the fee and strolled to the chopper. Din drove the van to the tarmac and moved the hoist inside the craft, then hid the van behind a hangar. After parking, he sprinted to the helicopter carrying a backpack. He found Cho acclimating himself with the controls. Before lifting off, Din changed into his black ninja-style apparel. They both wore skin-tight gloves.

When they were airborne, the low-decibel sound of the blades amazed the two assassins. It was indeed an extremely quiet aircraft. Inside his backpack, Din carried a silenced rifle that would need to be assembled, equipment to cut through the skylight, a small pistol, and several syringes with powerful tranquilizers. The flight to Lennium's location took them nearly twenty-five minutes. They knew how to find his house from aerial photos.

Hovering high above the home, they instantly spotted the four guards patrolling the property. The weather was muggy with minimal wind. The security team had parked its vehicle on the street. Even with its low-noise level, several of the men noticed the helicopter overhead and started pointing up to the sky. Flying at 1,000 feet, Din grasped his assembled rifle with a silencer attached and took aim. He would need to be quick and efficient. Hoping the guards wouldn't scream, the assassin went for head shots. *POP*, the first guard went down. Then *POP, POP, POP*. Each of the security men dropped to the ground.

Cho gradually lowered the craft's altitude and remained stationary above the skylight they targeted. Din was ready with the handheld remote control for the cable hoist that he attached to his belt. He momentarily hung from the chopper to ensure it would hold, lowered the cable down to the top of the roof, then hopped off.

Quickly locating the glass-cutting device in his pack, he quietly sawed through the skylight and set the glass section to the side. It was at least nine feet to the floor of the hallway below the skylight. Din stepped back onto the hook at the end of the cable and pressed the remote control to lower himself through the opening. Once inside he hopped off and waited to see if there was any movement. It was quiet. He could quickly access the syringes. The small pistol was in his free hand. Slowly edging down the hall, he checked one bedroom then another. Reaching a third one, he could make out two bodies beneath covers in the bed. As silently as possible, he moved closer.

Suddenly, one sleeper snorted and rolled over. The glow from a nightlight was dim, but he could see it was a woman, Mrs. Lennium. Din crept to the bed. Grabbing a syringe, he plunged it into her neck. Her eyes grew wide momentarily, her mouth agape. She tried to scream, but no sound came out. Din made his way to the other side of the bed. With the other syringe in hand, he pierced the neck of Dr. Milton Lennium. The man tried to wake and flailed his arms for a few seconds. Then he was still.

Din made sure he tucked the syringes and weapon neatly inside his waist pack. He saw eyeglasses on the nightstand and stuck those in as well. Pulling on Lennium's arms, he lugged and lifted him onto his shoulder. Fortunately, the chemist wasn't a large man. Testing his balance, Din turned and plodded back to the hallway. When he reached the cable, he stepped on the hook and hit the remote control. It was a narrow opening, but he and his captive made it through and ascended up to the helicopter. When he neared the door, he rolled Lennium off his shoulder, then climbed inside.

Cho hit the controls, and they flew higher above the roof and quickly gained altitude. They'd picked out a spot in another industrial area to land where Din had parked the other rental van. As soon as they were on the ground, Din detached the hoist, grabbed his backpack, and darted to the van. When he was inside, he tore off his head covering, started the engine, drove closer to the helicopter, and opened the vehicle's side door. Running to the chopper, he grabbed the tranquilized Lennium, hauled him to the van, and rolled the man inside. Before Cho took off, Din carefully wiped down the area in the back of the helicopter and left. As soon as Din moved the van farther away, Cho lifted off, and headed back to Logan Airport.

When Cho En Dai returned to Logan, he wiped down the cockpit and strolled casually back to the leasing desk. A night rep was on duty. Still in disguise, Cho told him it was a joy to fly and would return for another flight. After leaving, he picked up his pace and reached the van where Din had parked earlier. Once inside, he sped away from the airport grounds and drove to the remote lot where he left Din. He soon joined his partner, and they drove to the leased warehouse with the sedated Lennium in the back. They would return their first rented van later.

* * *

As DAWN BROKE, Mrs. Trish Lennium rolled over to touch her husband. *He's up already,* she realized. Trish felt suddenly ill. Her head ached like she had a fierce hangover. Getting up slowly, a nausea came over her, forcing her to sit back on the bed. "Miltie!" she cried for her husband. There was no response. Finally, she stood up and got her balance. "Miltie!" she yelled again. Trish went to the bathroom then looked at herself in the mirror. *My God, I look awful,* she thought.

Trish made her way to the stairway landing and turned off the motion sensor on the first floor. If her husband had awakened before her, where was he? Why didn't he turn it off? Checking the other upstairs rooms, he was nowhere to be found. Suddenly, she stepped on glass on the hallway carpet. She screamed. Spotting her bleeding feet, she saw tiny glass shards. Looking up, she saw the hole in the skylight. She screamed again. *What the hell!* "Miltie!" she hollered again. Trish went back to the bathroom to clean and bandage her feet. "Ouch!"

Gingerly descending the stairway, she looked around. No sign of her husband. She searched every room. Then she glanced outside. To her horror, she spotted a body next to one of the rose bushes. Trish screamed and covered her mouth. Slowly, she unlocked her side door and made her way to the edge of the wrap-around porch. Blood had pooled next to the man's head. "Help! Help!" She shouted and glanced around the exterior of her house. No security guards were visible. Darting back inside with stinging feet, she made it to her cell phone. She called the number for security.

"I-it's Trish Lennium! Y-y-you've got to send someone!" she sputtered in a panic. "One of the security guard's head is bleeding. He's not moving. And I can't find my husband." After giving her address, the security responder said she'd send someone immediately and phone the police.

Trish put on her slippers and made her way outside to the lawn. Looking left and right, she crept to the location of the bleeding guard. She spotted another one on the grass! Gasping and covering her face, Mrs. Lennium continued walking around her house. She gulped. There was another one. "Oh my God!" After seeing a fourth guard with blood puddled by his head, she hurried back inside, found her favorite sofa, and plunked down on it with tears streaming. Trish was in shock.

It wasn't long before she heard sirens. A police car and an ambulance soon arrived. The security company also sent a team to investigate the frantic call.

The doorbell rang. Trish jumped from the couch and moved toward the front door. Slowly opening it, a police officer said his name was Detective Veldon Crow and asked if he could speak to her.

"Uh, yes, Detective." After introducing herself, she led Crow to the living room and invited him to be seated.

"Mrs. Lennium, my people have cordoned off the neighborhood. I'm very sorry you had to experience this terrible ordeal," Crow explained. "Is Mr. Lennium here? I'd like to speak to him as well."

"Oh, my! He's disappeared!" Trish sobbed again. "When I got up, I couldn't find him. And there's a hole in a skylight upstairs!"

Crow's eyes narrowed. "What the...can you show me, please?"

Trish rose and made her way up the stairs. When she reached the landing, she pointed down the hall to the location of the glass shards and skylight. Crow glanced around as he walked to the spot. "Hmmm. Very strange..." Crow mumbled out loud and continued scanning left and right, up and down. "Mrs. Lennium, when was the last time you saw your husband?"

"I-I think when we went to bed. This morning I started to wake up, I reached for him, but he wasn't there. I yelled, but there was no answer." She then lead the detective to her bedroom. "One other thing. I felt terrible when I first woke up. Like I had a...hangover. My head was throbbing, and I was dizzy. It still hurts. But I haven't had a drink in days."

"Excuse me, ma'am," Crow interrupted. He then used his comms to call one of his people to meet inside. "Need to examine the house. Looks like a possible missing person."

"Oh, my!" Trish squealed and sobbed. "What could have happened to my husband?"

"It's too early to tell, Mrs. Lennium. I'm very sorry to say, but with the hole in the skylight and the guards apparently murdered, it's possible someone kidnapped him."

Two additional Boston police officers arrived outside the bedroom door. One of them barked, "What d'ya got, Vel?"

"Mrs. Lennium's husband is missing. There's a hole in a skylight down the hall. She and her husband were probably drugged. We'll need a blood sample, ma'am. Also, do you have a recent photo of Mr. Lennium?"

CHAPTER 10

Jack, Sara, and Amos McCabe had secretly moved to a condominium, hoping to avoid attacks by forces determined to stop his drug from expanding into new markets. They'd purchased burner cell phones and limited the people they spoke with in order to stay under the radar. Jack's new cell rang. "Hello, I've got terrible news!" attorney Christopher Masse informed him. "Someone's kidnapped Milt!"

"Oh, no! How?" Jack cried in disbelief.

"The Boston police called. Someone murdered the four guards outside his house and snuck inside. They apparently sedated Milt and his wife before leaving through a skylight. The cops don't know exactly how the abductors did it but think they may have used an aerial device or helicopter."

"This is horrible, Chris!" Jack exclaimed, as he tried to imagine how awful it was for Milt. In fact, he could recall because people associated with The New Global Order kidnapped him in Europe and later exchanged him for one of their people. Jack could easily remember the suffering he experienced.

"Yes, I know the FBI is involved in the case and has expanded its search in Europe. They've identified northern Italy as a likely origin of the calls to criminals in the U.S. Your old friends at Interpol are investigating."

"I have to think that the same organization that hired the woman who snuck into my lake cottage is behind Milt's kidnapping. Who else would have a reason to do such a terrible thing?" Jack responded as he realized he was likely still in their crosshairs. "What do you suppose they hope to accomplish by holding Milt hostage?"

"My worst fear is that they torture him and try to learn all they can about the formula for RGB101," Masse answered, shaking his head. "I'm not sure how well he'll hold up in such a situation. I know I'd be less than heroic."

"They'll certainly try to break him down," Jack surmised. "Hopefully, the police can locate him before he's murdered...or gives in to their demands. I feel terrible for Milt *and* Trish. It's insane!"

"I'm going to get back to the police officer who called me. He needs to know that FBI Agent Myles DeLong is investigating related crimes," Masse offered. "He and his team might add their knowledge to Milt's kidnapping."

* * *

AFTER ATTORNEY CHRISTOPHER MASSE reached Detective Veldon Crow in Boston, he explained that someone had perpetrated other crimes associated with NuPharma Corporation. Masse also provided the contact for the FBI agent who was now involved. "You may have heard about the murder of the FDA Commissioner in Maryland. Then there was an *accidental* death of a senator who was in favor of NuPharma's drug gaining approval to expand to new markets. Plus, someone broke into the vacation cottage owned by CEO Jack McCabe and tried to plant listening devices," Masse described.

"Sounds like an organized campaign against McCabe's business, Mr. Masse. I appreciate knowing about the other crimes," Crow responded as he jotted notes on a pad in front of him. "I'll reach out to Agent DeLong so we can join forces."

After several attempts, Crow got in touch with DeLong and described the recent kidnapping of the head of NuPharma Corp. "How awful, Detective!" DeLong responded. "What do you know about the people behind this?"

"We quickly reached the conclusion that the kidnappers used some sort of helicopter. We researched the local airports to determine if a person rented a chopper on the day of the crime. The only one that occurred on that day was at Logan International. Someone leased a new aircraft called a Eurocopter. It has super quiet rotors which may have allowed it to fly above Lennium's home nearly unnoticed until it was too late. We checked the video stream at the rental office and have the person's name, *Joe Andes*, which matched the license. There was surveillance video, but it was hard to see the man's face since he wore a bucket hat and had a beard and black-framed glasses."

"Have you sourced the helicopter license to get more information about the man?" DeLong inquired.

"There's a photo on the license, but we haven't tracked down its origin yet," Crow replied. "We're working on that angle. The personal address Mr. Andes gave was not legit, so we're stuck."

"I see, Detective. I'm going to send one of our people to assist you. Agent Andrew Friese has had experience with NuPharma Corp.," DeLong explained. "One other thing you should know. We've tracked phone calls to a person in Europe who has ordered people in the U.S. to do her bidding. Her name is Tazi. Our contacts at Interpol have a team trying to locate her."

"Wow! This is even more complex than I would have imagined," Crow responded. "I'll look forward to meeting with Agent Friese."

HITMEN CHO EN Dai and Din Shu Pu arrived at the South Boston warehouse with their captive, Dr. Milton Lennium. Although they'd tranquilized him during the kidnapping, he was regaining consciousness. Cho and Din wore black ninja outfits and headwear. They lugged Milt from the van and dragged him inside the facility with his two feet scuffing the ground behind him. They entered a large room with a chair that was anchored to the floor. After sitting their victim down, they bound his feet and hands and blindfolded him. The prisoner tried to speak, but Din shoved a wad of cloth in his mouth and wrapped duct tape around his head. All Milt could do was mumble an attempted scream for help, which no one heard. Before they left, Cho put headphones on him and turned on a CD that played Wagner's *Flight of the Valkyries* at full volume. Milt's head dropped to his chest, as his body shook.

They continued this torture for the next four hours. At some point, Milt must have fainted or lost consciousness. After taking the headphones off, Din threw a bucket of water at his head. Cho used a synthesizer to disguise his voice and barked, "Dr. Lennium, we want you to know that this is your new reality – pain and suffering. There's no way for you to escape, and no one knows where you are. You will receive minimum food and water. There will be two options from which you can choose. I will reveal them to you soon. Cho put the headphones back on Milt's head and turned up the volume. The chemist tried to scream, but it was fruitless. After two more hours, Cho removed the headphones and threw another bucket of water at his prisoner.

"Here's what I offer you. Option one, provide us with the formula for RGB101." Cho waited.

Milt shook his head and moaned.

"Option two, order your company's CEO to stop its plans to expand into new markets."

Milt shook his head and moaned some more. Cho waited another minute.

"I will give you a chance to choose between option one and option two. If you wish to choose option one to provide the formula, nod your head."

Milt's head twisted left and right as he groaned.

"Okay, then. Do you choose option two to cancel your expansion into the new markets?"

Once again, Milt indicated *no* with more moans.

"Very well." Cho put the headphones back on the

chemist's head and turned up the volume on the symphony. Milt's head could only twist around in agony. They continued this persecution for another four hours.

During the torment, Din left to get some food while Cho remained to watch. The man occasionally became more alert and tried to wail for help.

Later in the evening, Din removed the headphones and threw another bucket of water at Lennium's head. After several minutes, Cho recited the same options and waited for him to respond positively. The scientific leader of NuPharma continued his bravery and withstood the suffering. Cho and his partner's patience was wearing thin.

They changed the music and blasted the heavy metal song *Master of Puppets* by Metallica at full volume. It played repeatedly for the rest of the night. Milt's head was exploding, and he'd already wet himself from the torture. Din and Cho had had enough for one day. They locked up the door to the warehouse and returned to their hotel. On the drive, Din asked his partner how long they should continue Lennium's torture. "I say we keep it up for several days. If we don't have the results we want by then, we'll contact Ms. Tazi to determine the next steps." In the morning, they planned to return their other rental van before driving to the warehouse.

Tears continued to stream down Milt's cheeks as he gritted his teeth and shook his head, trying to dislodge the headphones with the blaring music. They didn't budge. He kept telling himself that he had to be brave and willing to die for his company. *But is the company worth dying for,* he moaned to himself. *What if I give them the formula but omit a key ingredient?* He didn't know if he was strong enough to withstand the pain much longer.

* * *

FBI AGENT ANDREW FRIESE joined Detective Veldon Crow at the Boston police station. "Okay, Detective," Friese began, "what sort of leads do you have on the Lennium kidnapping?" Crow had a folder in front of him and spread out photos of the house where the attackers killed the guards and entered the house. He described their assessment of the helicopter and learning about Joe Andes who rented a chopper on the night in question.

"So far, we're coming up empty for fresh evidence. We couldn't find any fingerprints, or hair or skin samples," Crow admitted as he filtered through his documents and photos.

"Where did Joe Andes gain his helicopter license?" Friese asked. "I would think they'd have some record of him. A photo or something."

"He got the license in D.C. several years ago," Crow explained, "but the photo on the license is not the best. He's an Asian fellow in his late thirties. He must have secured a fake ID because there's no record of him. The man obviously forged his license."

"He must have been wearing some sort of disguise when he rented the chopper," Friese proposed. "Hard to tell it's the same person."

CHAPTER 11

Even though Jack's family moved to an unknown condo in Indianapolis, his attorney, Christopher Masse, maintained security at the McCabe home. Guards frequently parked along the street to keep an eye on his property.

At the same time, the Consortium's Fon Tazi ordered Yao Min to have their wiry, middle-aged spy, Atticus Roshus, break into McCabe's house to plant listening devices. She assumed the family would move back to their home eventually. With the McCabes away, this could be an ideal opportunity to get in and out unseen.

Roshus had scouted the property for weeks but hadn't ventured close to the actual house. From his experience in covert operations, however, Atticus knew that there was likely an electronic alarm system that he would need to dismantle. Wearing bib overalls, a tool belt, and a floppy hat, he arrived in a pickup truck. It pulled a rented trailer carrying a riding lawn mower and other tools. How would anyone know he didn't belong there? After parking, he picked up his edging tool and began working on the lawn next to the sidewalk, then he worked on the area next to the driveway. He occasionally snuck a peek to see if anyone was watching him. As he continued moving closer to the house, he realized his plan could work. No one had paid any attention to him.

When he neared the back corner of the home, he spotted the electrical line that fed into the home. His edging device also worked as a trimming tool for small limbs. It would serve his need to cut the wire. From his position away from the street, there didn't appear to be anyone in sight. He swung his cutting tool up, extended it out to reach the power line, and snipped it. Quickly moving the tool back to an edger, he continued working on the lawn. A few minutes later, he rushed to the side door and jimmied the lock with his tools. As he expected, there was no alarm sound when he entered. Atticus waited for a moment, then darted from room to room, planting surveillance bugs.

Parked on the street near the McCabe house was an unmarked security vehicle. Inside sat Officers Rory Tund and Ron Umpus. The two retired cops were now on the hefty side. Both of them enjoyed the low-pressure demands of their job. They'd just finished devouring their sack lunches from a nearby fast-food restaurant. Rory and Ron had been discussing the sad state of the local NFL team, the Colts. Rory thought they needed a new coach. Ron thought the general manager had made too many poor decisions.

They noticed the yard man when he arrived and were

surprised no one told them he was coming. "Did you know anything about this guy showing up?" Tund asked his partner.

"Nope. It's a new one on me," Umpus responded. Just then, Tund's cell phone rang. It was a security office monitoring person. "Hello, headquarters here. There's been a power outage at the McCabe house. We're not getting a signal from the alarm system. You need to check it out."

"Ten-four. We're on it," Tund replied, as he hung up and looked at Umpus. "Might have an issue at the house. No alarm signal." They both opened their car doors and rolled out. Walking up the long driveway to McCabe's Victorian-style home, they looked ahead to where the lawn guy was last seen. He was nowhere in sight. When they reached the side door, they noticed the edging tool on the ground.

"Something's fishy about this guy, Rory," Ron commented, then strolled to the back of the house where he saw that someone had snipped the power line. Pointing at the wire, he whispered, "There's definitely some illegal hi-jinks going on. I'm calling the local police."

As Ron phoned it in, Rory investigated the interior. Slowly entering the unlocked door, he crept into the kitchen, then ambled gradually down a hallway. He tried to listen for any noise that might give away the intruder. There was a creaking sound from the floorboards upstairs. Pulling his sidearm, he checked to make sure it was loaded, then pointed the weapon in front of him as he moved forward toward the stairway.

Atticus Roshus had visited all the rooms downstairs and was half-way through the upstairs when he heard noises below. *Crap, what the hell's that?* He started looking for a window that he could crawl through to escape. There was one that easily opened in a back bedroom leading to the first-story roof. Atticus could jump to the ground from there. Just then, he heard sirens blaring on the street.

Guard Ron Umpus hustled toward the front of the house and saw two police officers marching toward him. Ron quickly gave them the lowdown and told them he'd check the back of the house. One cop went inside, the other ran to the front. Atticus Roshus had wiggled through the upstairs window and was nearing the edge of the roof. He was ready to jump. *Damn!* Seeing the guard, he scurried to the far side.

From outside, Ron spotted the lawn man on the roof and yelled, "He's here! In the back of the house!" Rory heard his partner's voice as he looked out the open window in the second-floor bedroom, then glimpsed the invader running across the shingles.

"Halt!" Rory screamed, but the man kept moving. The guard hustled to another bedroom and spotted him through a window. He arrived there as fast as he could, pulled it open and yelled again, "Halt!" Rory aimed his weapon at the man's leg. He pulled the trigger. Atticus screamed, grabbed his knee, and fell violently off the roof. The officer outside rushed to see the man writhing in pain in the midst of landscaped plants. Ron, Rory, and the other cop hurried to see the wounded trespasser with his blood splattered on white hydrangea flowering bushes.

"Nice shot, pard," Ron boomed in praise of Rory. "Bet you didn't think you'd be firing your pistol when you woke up this morning." They all grinned, as the first police officer pulled the offender away from the flowers and cuffed him. As the cop frisked him, he soon noticed the audio bugs in his tool belt.

"Well now, what's your game, mister?" the cop asked as he pulled out his wallet to read the name *Atticus Roshus.* After grabbing Atticus' cell phone, the officer stood him up and helped him hobble to the front of the house.

"Yard man, my ass!" Rory fumed. "You've got a lot of 'splaining to do, Mr. Green Jeans." In no time, an ambulance arrived and the EMTs attended to the bleeding criminal.

After Roshus was taken to the station and booked for breaking and entering, word was sent to McCabe's attorney, Christopher Masse. When he finished alerting Jack, Masse phoned FBI Agent Myles DeLong and described the attempt to plant audio devices in the McCabe home.

"Good to know the security guard didn't end the life of this guy. Hopefully, we'll get him to talk and find out who's behind all these attacks." DeLong responded. "I'll send Agent Barbara Dwyer to Indianapolis to interrogate him. The problem is, if it's Yao Min who ordered it, we haven't been able to find him."

DR. MILTON LENNIUM had endured a second day of torture at the hands of Cho En Dai and Din Shu Pu, the two assassins hired by the Consortium's Fon Tazi. They continued blasting more heavy metal music through the headphones on Milt. Iron Maiden's *Run to the Hills* was among the latest punishments. Milt didn't know if his hearing would ever be the same after going through this incredible agony. The kidnappers had only given him a minimal amount of food and water, so he was rapidly wearing down.

After the chemist refused to give in to their demands, Cho decided to phone Tazi. "We haven't made any headway with Lennium. Should we get rid of him now or do you want to try something else?"

"I see. Let me speak with K, and I'll get back to you," she answered, wondering what it would take.

Fon strolled from her small, secluded office to Karsen Ojin's massive study. He was busy scanning through his many investments. Even though much of it went to pharmaceutical stocks, he had diversified into other industries and crypto-currency. He had a sour look on his face as he tipped up a cup of steaming tea when Fon entered.

"K, our men have been breaking down the NuPharma chemist, but so far he hasn't given in. Should we kill him and dump his body?"

"Hmmm," Ojin thought as he glanced at his assistant and lover. "I'd rather use him as a bargaining chip. Try to contact someone in authority at NuPharma. Offer to return him in one piece if they agree to back off of their plans to enter the heart disease and diabetes markets. If they refuse, have our men dispose of him."

"Very well, K," Tazi replied as she left to contact Cho En Dai. Upon reaching her man, she instructed him to do as Ojin directed. She didn't know if NuPharma would agree, but it was worth trying.

Cho wasn't immediately sure how to contact Jack McCabe since he appeared to be off the grid, but he knew the cell phone number of his attorney. When Christopher

Masse answered, a deep, synthesized voice announced, "Milton Lennium is near death, but we will release him alive on one condition: NuPharma must cease its plans to expand into new markets. I expect your decision in 24 hours." Then the call ended.

"Holy crap!" Masse groaned as he stared out his office window. Moments later, he phoned Jack. "You won't believe the call I just received. One of those strange, deep voices offered to return Milt if we stopped our plans to enter the new drug markets!"

"I'll be damned!" Jack shouted, as he looked at his wife Sara and son Amos playing nearby. "Of course! We'll do what we have to do, at least until the police have captured the people behind it."

"No question about it," Chris replied. "Thank God he's okay! Hope they haven't treated him too harshly, but I'm sure they've tried to put him through hell." Next, Masse phoned Lennium's wife to give her the good news.

"Oh, good heavens! He's alive!" Trish cried.

Masse's next communication was to FBI Agent Myles DeLong, who was eager to track the phone call back to the kidnappers. "Agent Barbara Dwyer should be arriving in Indianapolis shortly to interrogate Atticus Roshus. I'll arrange for her to connect your phone with a device to track the origin of the call."

"Excellent!" Masse replied.

CHAPTER 12

The athletic-looking redhead, Agent Barbara Dwyer, arrived in Indianapolis and soon reached the police station to meet with prisoner Atticus Roshus. After a half hour of grilling, the surly Roshus continued to stonewall. His attorney was present, but the spy wouldn't reveal the source of his orders. Dwyer's research showed that he had a record of covert activities in the past and spent time behind bars. She knew he wouldn't be an easy nut to crack.

Roshus' cell phone provided a link to Yao Min's number, as she suspected, but Min remained elusive. Dwyer then contacted attorney Christopher Masse to set up the call-tracking device for the kidnappers. She met Masse at his downtown Indianapolis office and attached his phone to the equipment that could get past a virtual private network. The agent advised him to stall for more time when the call came in so she'd have a better chance of determining its origin.

After 24 hours, the phone call finally came through. The

deep voice announced, "Yes, we have Lennium and will release him alive if your company agrees to cease plans for expansion to other drug markets. What's your decision?"

"I'm going to need proof of life before I agree to anything," Masse responded as Dwyer sat nearby, monitoring the call on her laptop. "I have to know that he's okay."

Cho En Dai cursed under his breath and walked into the warehouse space where they kept the chemist in bondage. Cho ripped the tape from Milt's face and pulled the rag from his mouth, but the captive's eyes were still covered. Masse could hear a scream in the background. Cho instructed Lennium to tell Masse he was okay, then he put the phone on speaker.

"I-I'm alive...Can hardly b-breathe...N-need help..." Milt stammered with drool dripping from his mouth.

Cho went back to his other room to complete the call. Masse could hear Lennium yelling for help in the background. With the synthesized voice back, the assassin continued, "I hope you're satisfied that the man is alive and well. I must have a decision. Either you agree or Lennium dies. It doesn't matter to me."

Masse recognized Milt's voice even though it was strained and much weaker than he'd ever heard it. "Yes! We agree to stop our entry into the new markets. When will you release him to us?" Chris implored. Barbara Dwyer gave him a hand signal indicating that she'd almost reached the source of the call. The agent could see the location showing the Boston area and closing in.

"I will call again to let you know where we'll leave him," Cho barked.

"But how will we know we can count on you?" Chris asked.

"You don't have any choice. Instructions will follow soon." Then the call ended.

Dwyer gave a thumbs up. "Very good, Mr. Masse," she exclaimed. I think we might be close to a location. I'll contact Agent Friese.

"Andy? It's Barb. We just got off the phone with the kidnappers and think there's a possible source. See what you can find on Industrial Drive near the railroad tracks in South Boston. Sorry, that's as close as I could get. They said they'd call back with a drop-off spot, but maybe you can find them before they make a move."

"Great, thanks! We'll see what we can do," Friese responded as he sat near Detective Veldon Crow.

"Did you get something?" Crow inquired eagerly.

"Should be close. Get your people. Looks like Southie," Friese ordered as he sprung up and led the way to Crow's squad car.

"Okay, Cho, do you have a deal for this guy?" Din asked when he returned to the office.

"Yes. I'm looking at some possibilities of where we can dump him. Readville Park nearby has a storage shed close to the street," Cho proposed as Din nodded in agreement.

Rain splattered the windshield as the police reached Industrial Drive. Friese rode next to him. Another squad car with two cops tailed them. They arrived at the area and drove down the street past a parking lot for refuse trucks and several storage facilities. They scrutinized a few possibilities, but most of the buildings appeared to have legitimate businesses. A couple of warehouses had leasing signs posted. Crow pulled off the road and parked in front of one. After inspecting it and another property, they decided those weren't good bets. Getting back in the vehicle, they cruised by more potential locations but didn't stop.

Suddenly they arrived at a location they couldn't see from the road. A damaged chain-link gate with deteriorating concrete blocks on either side of it partially barricaded the entrance. Mature trees and unkept foliage lined a gravel driveway back to an unseen building. "Let's check this out," Friese proposed. Crow nodded and pulled off the road while Friese got out in the downpour and opened the squeaky gate. He returned to the car and they slowly motored until they could see a building thirty yards ahead. A black van was parked in front of a large garage door. Next to it was an entrance door. Crow alerted the cops in the other squad car. All four of them were going to make their way to the facility on foot to see what was inside.

Grasping their sidearms, Crow and Friese led the two other Boston police officers. Creeping closer to the rusted, aluminum-sided warehouse, Crow signaled that he'd check one side and for Friese to inspect the other. There were few windows, so they didn't know what the interior perspective would be. The storm continued.

Stomping through puddles, Friese soon located a window that was mostly covered in black paint. Squinting inside, he could see a large space with a concrete floor dotted with puddles. Sitting with his back to the window was a man seated in a chair. The FBI agent quickly noticed he wore headphones and appeared to be bound. *Well, I'll be damned*, Friese thought to himself. Using his comms device, he told Crow there was a person inside tied to a chair.

"Holy shit!" Crow responded quietly as he looked inside another window that was also mostly blacked out. He spotted two men sitting at a table. One of them was on a phone. "Can't see 'em well, but there's two of 'em."

They returned to the front of the warehouse to determine their incursion strategy. "I'd like to get to the bound man first. Have to assume it's Lennium. Want to make sure he's protected so the kidnappers don't try to use him as a shield or something," Friese recommended.

"Good call," Crow agreed, then directed the two other police officers to split up and observe through the blacked-out windows. "If the men inside use their weapons, knock through the glass to provide backup." Crow would wait for the signal from Friese that he'd found a way in, possibly from the back of the building.

Agent Friese's clothes were drenched, as he moved behind the building. There was a canopy covering a rear entrance. There were no other windows, so he couldn't tell what was directly inside. The door was locked. Pulling lock-picking tools from his jacket, he eventually dismantled the bolt and slowly opened the door. There was no alarm. Creeping inside, he saw a doorway to the large space where the man was tied up. He alerted Crow and the other police that he was inside. "Give me five minutes to get Lennium free," he advised.

Friese cautiously stepped toward Milt. With a pistol in one hand, he held his FBI identification in the other. He gently pulled the headphones from the prisoner, then lifted the covering from his eyes. There were no lights on, but Lennium blinked to adjust to the environment. Friese showed his ID and signaled he'd untie him. Much of it was tape, so he used his knife to slice through it on his legs, then his torso and hands. There was a rancid odor coming from the prisoner who'd urinated on himself several times. Friese helped the chemist stand up, but he was wobbly, so the agent nearly carried the tortured captive toward the back of the warehouse. When the two reached the rear entrance, Friese alerted Crow and the police that they were out.

"Be ready, men," Crow ordered. He kicked the front door once. It didn't budge. He shot the lock then kicked again. Crow stood back to see what response he'd get from the two inside. The cop looking through the window saw the hitmen jump and search for their weapons. The officer busted the glass and yelled for Cho and Din to stand down. Cho grabbed his weapon and sprayed bullets at the window. The officer ducked. Din ran to the open space where they kept Lennium. He emitted a low-level scream and curse. Raising his weapon, Din fired at the front entrance. The cop at the nearby window busted the glass and pulled the trigger. Din was too late with his response. The bullet hit the assassin in the shoulder, propelling him backward. He landed hard on the concrete floor.

Cho darted to the room. Detective Crow and the officer outside had their guns aimed at him. "Drop your weapon. Turn around and put your hands high on the wall," Crow barked, as he closed in on the assassin. The other two cops ran inside. "Call for backup and ambulances. Not sure what shape Lennium's in."

While Crow kept Cho covered, one of the officers grabbed Cho's wrists and cuffed him. Frisking the two, he located cell phones and wallets with identifications. "Keep these two covered." Crow then entered the office space to search for evidence. He found a box and placed anything suspicious inside it.

As one of the cops looked through Cho's wallet, he spotted the helicopter license. "Chopper pilot, huh?" the officer asked Cho sarcastically. Cho glowered and shook his head.

Ambulances and police sirens soon filled the air. The vehicles found their way to the warehouse where a soaked Agent Friese was still supporting Dr. Milton Lennium. The EMTs jumped out from one of the ambulances and rushed to help Milt inside. They immediately gave him fluids and planned to take him to a local hospital to check his vitals. Aside from his complaining about not hearing well, he seemed healthy.

The other ambulance techs attended to Din Shu Pu and put a tourniquet around his shoulder. Surgeons would remove the bullet as soon as possible.

The police who arrived would set up the facility as a crime scene for further investigation. The officers who came with Crow took Cho En Dai to the station for booking.

Agent Friese and Detective Crow grinned at one another. "We've got solid evidence against these two," Friese stated confidently. "Maybe we'll find out they're connected to the murders of the D.C. senator and the FDA commissioner."

CHAPTER 13

Sun settled behind the mountains near the high-perched castle in northern Italy. Karsen Ojin strolled through one of the halls admiring the heraldic banners hanging from the walls. His lover, Fon Tazi, met him as he stopped by a roaring fireplace to warm his hands. Ojin adored his fortress but it became chilly at night. Even though there was updated central heating, it was frequently cold after sunset.

"I should have heard by now that NuPharma agreed to cease its expansion plans, but so far, nothing," Fon reported. "If my men failed, we may be at a standstill."

"Damn!" Ojin snapped as he turned to look at her. "We still need to send a strong message. What else can we do?"

"Jack McCabe is off the radar, so he's out – at least for now. Don't know how much influence our senate subcommittee will have to delay approval for McCabe's drug," Fon groaned. "The only thing I can think of doing is finding a hacker to falsify the validation of his clinical trial patient database. If we can achieve that, the approval would be delayed and RGB101 may have to begin its trials again."

"My God, Fon! You never fail to come up with a brilliant idea!" Ojin thundered, then hugged her. "Contact the Consortium members and set up a meeting for 11 a.m. ET tomorrow. I need to let them know we are hopeful that a delay by NuPharma is forthcoming."

"Of course, K," she grinned. "Yao Min will surely be able to find the right person to do the job."

Later, Fon called Yao using another pre-paid cell phone. She instructed him to locate a good hacker to falsify the clinical studies data to make the patients appear to still be suffering from their heart or diabetes diseases. Yao thought he knew just the right person for the job.

THE NEXT MORNING at 11 ET, the Consortium meeting came to order. Its members had logged into the private video channel to join. After welcoming them, K reluctantly gave them a blow-by-blow description of the failed efforts to stall NuPharma's entry into the new markets. "However, we have a new tactic," he continued. "We'll access the FDA database and modify the validation of the patients' health statistics to show that RGB101 is not a viable product."

There was a strong murmur of approval by those in attendance, including:

- Barron Lidst of ReMedin located in New York City.
- Rubin Bisch of PharMax in Tampa Bay.

- Sen. Emon Barras from Philadelphia.
- Sen. Stuart Pitts of Los Angeles.

In Europe, the group included four pharmaceutical CEOs.

- Rome's Imelda Broglio of Drogari.
- Vienna's Byrn Zaer from Medika.
- Paris's Kahn Cordant ran Curatif.
- Brussel's Regis Volt at Genez.

"Excellent, K!" Sen. Barras cheered.

"Bravo!" Imelda Broglio chimed in.

"Sen. Barras, I am hoping that you and Pitts will control the healthcare subcommittee," Ojin barked with a scowl. "Once the work is done on the database, I expect you to come down harshly on NuPharma for its shoddy clinical trial effort."

"Yes, K! As soon as your man has done his magic, we'll make a real show of it," Pitts sneered. "Hopefully the FDA firewall doesn't preclude the um...intervention."

Later that evening in the castle, Ojin and Tazi dined together. They both favored seafood and sushi. Sharing a bottle of Chardonay, the couple was pleasantly content, but Ojin was feeling particularly feisty after what he hoped would be a solid score against his opponents at NuPharma. Rather than retire to their usual location for affection, they moved to K's large bedroom that had a magnificent view of the Italian Alps. Ojin had ordered one of his staff to prepare a roaring fire in the stone hearth. He and Fon soon luxuriated without clothing and absorbed the embers' warmth on a massive pillow. The intensity of the flames was all they needed to soon enjoy each other's physical heat.

* * *

WHILE OJIN and Tazi consummated their passion, Interpol Officers Alberto Fresco and Kara Sterrio were in the midst of their own intimacy not far away. The lovers always enjoyed the assignments in the field to rekindle their love affair. The investigation had led them to the beautiful city of Trento to seek the origin of a phone call to the United States.

Recorded by an FBI wiretap, Interpol hacker Sarah Graff identified the call to the phone of Yao Min from a woman named Tazi in this general area of Italy. Fresco and Sterrio were searching but hadn't determined the woman's exact location. At this point it was like finding a needle in a haystack.

Additional research from Graff generated a photo and described a woman who'd been an Olympic gold-medal winner in martial arts for the Japanese team. Fon Tazi had also been a pilot in the Japanese Air Force. So far, that's all they had to work with.

Interpol Chief Samuel Aritan also asked Graff to identify the top pharmaceutical companies and their CEOs in Europe. He would assign his team to visit them to determine if they had any knowledge of the attacks in the United States.

* * *

THE NEXT MORNING after a light breakfast with cappuccinos, Fresco and Sterrio split up to explore the area. Fresco would pay a visit to the Trento police station. Sterrio would peruse the city in hopes of spotting Tazi in the parks or outdoor shops, seeking a person who matched the photo Graff provided. Sterrio found Trento to be breathtaking and picturesque, as she strolled by piazzas, past fountains, and through gardens. There were people everywhere, but no one resembled her target.

When Fresco stopped into the police station, he was introduced to the chief of police. Gino Ganti was a large, engaging man who immediately impressed the Interpol officer with his size and outgoing personality. The Interpol officer described the woman they were looking for and asked if Ganti would provide assistance if it was needed.

"Of course, Officer Fresco," Ganti beamed. "Please come into my conference room. I'd like to know more."

Fresco explained the killings and kidnapping that took place in the U.S. as well as the two people captured trying to plant electronic listening devices in the homes of the NuPharma CEO. "The FBI wiretapped a criminal's phone and recorded a conversation with a woman named Tazi. Our specialist identified this locale as the source of the call. My partner is exploring the city today to see if she can spot the woman based on this photo." Fresco presented the image of Tazi. Ganti wanted to make a copy for his team.

"I'm sorry, but I'm not familiar with her name or a person who matches the photo," Ganti responded.

"Another piece of background," Fresco continued, "is that Tazi was an Olympic champion in martial arts, so she would be formidable in hand-to-hand combat."

"I see," Ganti nodded and narrowed his eyes.

"Are there residences outside the city where someone with considerable wealth might live?" Fresco asked his new acquaintance. "We believe that for someone to try to influence the U.S. Senate and the FDA, there has to be a strong connection to the pharmaceutical industry. The individual would have to have a financial stake in the international pharmaceutical market. It must be someone with considerable resources."

"That makes a lot of sense, Officer," Ganti agreed as he made notes in front of him. "There are many luxury residences in the mountains and near the city. I'm afraid I wouldn't know where to begin ferreting out such an individual."

"Interpol planned to investigate European pharmaceutical companies about possible relationships with the hidden force behind the U.S. crimes," Fresco explained.

As their meeting wrapped up, the Interpol officer told Ganti he'd keep him apprised of any new developments.

Fresco and Sterrio met up for lunch and discussed their mornings.

"So far we're striking out on our search for Tazi, Alberto," she said. "I was thinking we could access a property database that shows residences around the city. Certainly we agree that the person would be affluent enough to have an upscale residence. Maybe we can determine those that are among the most luxurious and identify the owners."

"I like that idea, Kara," he agreed, "and it's possible that Tazi works for the real kingpin. If we get the names of the owners, we can run them through the Interpol search engine to see if any has a criminal record. Maybe Graff can help us learn about the sources of their wealth."

"Sounds like a plan! Let's head out to the local government building to search the *catasto*, which is the land registry that provides ownership records," Fresco stated.

As soon as they arrived, they met with a representative named Mr. Destra who led them to a computer room.

"You're welcome to review our *visura catastale*, the land registry. It identifies properties, values and owners. As you probably know, it's used for maintaining ownership records and assessing taxes," Destra explained.

"Wonderful," Sterrio acknowledged as she smiled at Destra and Fresco. "This is exactly what we need."

As she began her search, the partners made notes of the more upscale locations and their owners. *Tazi* was not coming up, but there were approximately thirty other names they could research. After a half hour, Sterrio made a digital copy that she emailed to herself and printed out a list to investigate. "I'll email the list to Graff and ask her to conduct a criminal background check," she told her partner.

As soon as Sarah Graff received Sterrio's email she wrote back to say she'd get started on it immediately. The next day, she completed her assignment and sent the information needed to investigate potential criminals in the Trento, Italy, area.

CHAPTER 14

F on Tazi had instructed Yao Min to hire a crack computer hacker to get inside the FDA database to change the results of the recent NuPharma clinical trials. She was specifically interested in the ones that dealt with RGB101's performance in the heart disease and diabetes markets. Yao had used several hackers in the past, but one was head and shoulders above the others. His name was Frankie Leece.

"Hello, Leece. Yao here," he began. "I've got a job for you if you're available."

"For you, I've always got time," Leece responded while he continued to tap in computer code on his keyboard.

"I hope this isn't too much of a challenge, but I'm sure you'll tell me if it is," Yao chuckled.

"I'll be the judge of that, my friend," Leece grinned.

Yao went into detail describing the pharmaceutical company's clinical trials. The FDA was completing its phase three verification of nearly 95 percent positive results from patients in both markets. There were at least twenty-five hundred subjects in each control group. Yao wanted Leece to change the results to show that less than 25 percent of the patients were cured of their diseases.

"Assuming I can get past the FDA's firewall and other cybersecurity barricades, I should be good, Yao," Leece replied confidently. "If you're willing to pay the same price for my work, I should have the results you need in a few days."

"Yes, your price is good, no problem," Yao answered. "I'll phone you in two days."

As he sat behind an array of monitors with a phone headset on, Frankie was content to live in a modest, unkept home. Empty pizza boxes, food cartons, old magazines, and soda cans littered his workspace. Even though he was a savant as a hacker, his personal hygiene and the cleanliness of his immediate environment received little attention. Staying laser-focused on his current project drove him.

As for Yao Min, he was a chameleon. He suspected that the authorities would wiretap the calls he received from Fon Tazi and other clients at some point. The only way he could be confident of staying one step ahead of the law was to have multiple residences and rotate among them regularly. Yao traveled by train from one city to the other and had vehicles ready in each location. He had residences under false names at each place. The criminal also used various pre-paid cellular phones or burners. He kept his clients abreast of this tactic. They each had personal codes to use on his dark website. The codes alerted the client to a specific phone number to call based on the date they needed him.

Yao was also a master of disguises and wardrobes. He used a series of hairpieces and wigs, hats, beards and eyeglasses. For each location he lived, he'd use a different appearance that kept him unrecognizable from one city to the other. Since he had no family in the United States, he could remain relatively unknown.

The fifty-year-old Yao was born in New York City as an only child. His parents struggled financially and after they passed away at a relatively young age, Yao had to fend for himself. While he was working his way through the City College of New York, he became acquainted with members of the Chinese underworld. Over time, his criminal lifestyle grew. Eventually, he made connections with people who needed someone who could get certain jobs done – efficiently and anonymously. His name reached Fon Tazi. She contacted him, and their relationship blossomed.

Initially, Frankie Leece had difficulty cracking into the FDA database. Eventually, however, his cyber codes and programming expertise enabled him to develop a work-around to access the NuPharma files through a backdoor. It was a time-consuming task to change all the clinical results, but he achieved the modifications he was sure would please his client.

When Yao Min called back, Frankie assured him that the files reflected the negative results he requested. "The NuPharma people are going to be in for a big surprise," Leece boasted with confidence. "Whatever they thought their outcomes were, they're completely different now. This was a tougher job than I expected, but it's done. You and your people will be pleased."

"Excellent, Frankie!" Yao Min cheered. "Is there any

way of looking at the work you did? Or will we have to wait until there's another senate committee hearing when they announce the results publicly?"

"You'll be happy to know that I posted the results on your dark website, Yao," Leece stated proudly. "Review the data for yourself."

"I'll definitely verify your work immediately and, assuming all the patient data's been changed, share it with my client."

After the call, Yao logged into his website and located the electronic folder Leece had placed. As soon as he opened it, several graphic and statistical presentations displayed the new results on his laptop. Unfortunately for NuPharma, they showed RGB101 had failed miserably in both the heart disease and diabetes studies. Certainly, Fon Tazi will be quite impressed.

THE ILLEGAL WORK done to the FDA results thrilled Tazi and her boss after Yao broke the good news. Karsen Ojin spread the word among the members of the Consortium. He encouraged the U.S. Senators Barras and Pitts to reconvene the hearing with NuPharma to announce the disappointing findings. Certainly, they could now deny the pharmaceutical company's entry into the new markets.

Attorney Christopher Masse soon received a formal request for him and any of NuPharma's key executives to attend a senate meeting the following week. The FDA had completed its assignment of verifying the clinical trial results.

"Jack, it's Chris. I just received an invitation to attend another senate meeting to learn the FDA's validation of our clinical studies."

"So they've completed it?" Jack answered skeptically. "I hope the senators are prepared to make a formal apology for their prejudiced view of our product. We still don't know how they're connected to all the crimes that the murderers committed. Thank God Milt survived the latest attempt to sabotage our company. I'll always think of him as a hero for standing up to their torture."

"He's feeling better after being released from the hospital, but his hearing still hasn't completely recovered."

"Damn, that's terrible! I hope the hearing aids he's using continue to help until he gets back to normal. Those kidnappers are going to pay for what they've done. Hopefully, the police and FBI will link them to the other crimes that took place."

"So far, there's no evidence connecting them to the murder of the FDA commissioner and the *accidental* death of the senator. I'm hoping they'll be able to break one of them down and find out who's behind the kidnapping."

"I assume you want to maintain the confidentiality of your location until the FBI and police have captured the people behind these crimes?" Chris asked Jack.

"Yes. I'd like to attend the senate hearing, but I don't want to give anyone a hint to my whereabouts. If Milt's up for it, maybe he can join you."

"I'll confer with him to see if he's comfortable going. He has the most knowledge of our results in case there's any discrepancy in the data."

After their call, Masse phoned Lennium. "Hope you're feeling much better, Milt."

"Hey, Chris. I'm pretty close to normal now except for my hearing, but I'm still having trouble sleeping at night. The nightmares won't stop," Lennium responded. "I've been working with security by my side 24-7."

"The senate group has requested that we attend a follow-up hearing to review the FDA's verification of our patient trials. Are you willing to accompany me?"

"I'd like to go, but I'm still nervous about being in public after what I went through. You have all the data from the doctors who attested to the patients' improvements. There shouldn't be any question about the effectiveness of RGB101."

MASSE and one of his assistants flew to D.C. and took a taxi to their hotel near the Capitol Building. The attorneys carried all the data in a binder. Masse reviewed the results during the flight. With the health of nearly every patient confirmed, he didn't expect there to be any question about the results.

In his late forties, Masse was tall with premature gray hair that he combed back. His black-framed glasses and expensive suits gave him an air of sophistication. As he strolled into the senate meeting room, he felt confident that the senators would be brief and to the point. They should easily confirm RGB101 for entry into the two new markets.

After the chair concluded the initial order of business,

Sen. Barras took the floor to present the results from the FDA. "I'm sorry the executives from NuPharma couldn't attend, Mr. Masse. We have some important data to share with you and the public."

"I understand," Masse responded. "Unfortunately, they couldn't join me. Dr. Lennium is still recovering from the trauma he experienced at the hands of outlaws. The police captured them, and we hope to find out who's behind the vicious kidnapping and torture the doctor suffered. During his confinement, he was pressured to reverse NuPharma's intentions of expanding into new markets or lose his life. The alternative was for him to provide the formula for our medication. He stood up to their cruel demands."

"Yes! How dreadful," Barras expressed in feigned horror, shaking his head. "Good to know the authorities have apprehended the criminals."

"Hmmm. Indeed." Masse responded, peering back at the senator with narrowed eyes.

"I'm sure you're interested in learning about the results of the FDA's verification of your studies," Barras inter-jected. "Their efforts were no doubt quite time-consuming and exhausting. Please provide Mr. Masse and his assistant a few copies so they can read along with my statement." An aide rushed to the rostrum, took the folders from Barras, and handed them to Masse. Chris opened to see the nega-tive statistics and was dumbfounded. "As you can see, the details the FDA uncovered appear to differ greatly from what you told this senate committee not long ago, Mr. Masse." Barras let his comment sink in.

"Where in world did this data come from?" Masse

nearly shouted. "This is totally incorrect, and I refuse to accept the authenticity of these findings."

"Mr. Masse, I warn you that you're treading on very thin ice," Barras rebuked the attorney. "The medical team carefully examined and validated the new data. As the chair of this committee, you and your company may be subject to criminal contempt for the fraudulent results you previously presented."

CHAPTER 15

S tunned by Sen. Barras's inflammatory comments and his *revised* clinical data, attorney Christopher Masse was speechless for a few seconds, but then responded, "I challenge the validity of these *new* results. Licensed physicians examined the patients in our clinical studies and signed affidavits attesting to their improved health. We do not accept your amended findings. I request the people involved in conducting the verification process appear before this senate committee to attest to the actual findings."

"Are you questioning the FDA and its procedures, Mr. Masse? That ice you're treading on is getting thinner by the moment," Barras responded harshly. "I'm recessing this meeting until we have determined our next steps. However, until further deliberation, consider your application to enter the new markets to be denied." Barras then slammed his gavel to close the meeting.

Rather than say something that might further jeopardize NuPharma's application, Masse bit his tongue, grabbed his materials, closed his briefcase, and stormed out of the meeting room. As he was leaving, he glanced back at the rostrum and saw Barras and Pitts smiling and nodding at each other in triumph.

When he left the senate meeting room, Masse collected his thoughts and soon phoned Jack and Milt on a three-way call. "You won't believe what they're trying to do. An updated FDA patient summary showed that RGB101 only healed 25% of those in the study groups. They sabotaged the clinical results. I don't know who's behind it, but I smell a rat."

The news incensed Jack and Milt. "How do they think they can get away with this crap?" Jack steamed. "We've got sworn signatures from physicians attesting to our successful results."

"Someone got to the FDA or its data and compromised the validation process, but I can't imagine how," Milt fumed.

"I told them I wanted the FDA examiners to appear in a senate meeting so they'll be questioned under oath. We'll sue the FDA if necessary. This is outrageous," Chris thundered. "For now, the senate committee has denied our application, but it's not over by a long shot."

* * *

Continuing the investigation in their Trento hotel, Officers Kara Sterrio and Alberto Fresco scanned spreadsheets displaying owners of high-end properties in the area. Computer hacker Sarah Graff had identified this general location as the source of the phone call from the myste-rious Fon Tazi to Yao Min in the United States.

They'd also searched the Interpol website to find any records of crime among the property owners. Even though all the estates were quite valuable, one stood out in more ways than one. Perched high above Trento was an ancient castle owned by a person named K.S. Ojin. Later, the name Karsen Ojin also came up on an Interpol search as someone who'd been charged with securities fraud. Unfortunately, the courts never convicted him. The property records described Ojin's castle as centuries old. Only one steep road carved out of the mountain accessed the fortress.

"What are the odds there's a person named Fon Tazi living with Mr. Ojin?" Fresco asked as Sterrio smiled and shook her head in agreement. "I'll ask Trento Chief of Police Gino Ganti to come along with some of his officers for support. No telling what we'll face once we arrive."

"Good call. Should we attempt to phone the place or send up a drone to get some video of what's up there?" Sterrio asked her partner.

"I like the idea of getting video," Fresco agreed. "We should be able to see how many guards are protecting the property. If Ojin's involved in this dirty business, he'll have hired guns nearby."

"I'm going to contact Sarah Graff to see if she'll research Ojin to determine where his money's invested," Sterrio proposed. "What are the chances he's dumped a ton of money into pharmaceutical stocks?"

"Great idea!" Fresco concurred. "I'll reach out to Ganti to see if he has access to a video drone or if he knows where we can rent one."

"Sarah," Sterrio began. "I've got another project for your special skills. We found a person by the name of Karsen Ojin who owns a castle on the mountain overlooking Trento. It's got to be quite a place. The law tried to convict him of securities fraud in the past, but nothing stuck. I'd like you to find out where he invests his money. There must be pharmaceutical companies in Europe and the U.S. where he's financially involved."

"Right," Graff responded, as she sat in front of a bank of monitors in her Rome office. "As you know, Chief Aritan asked me to identify the pharmas in Europe, which I've done. I'll also check out ones in the U.S. It shouldn't be too difficult to get inside their portfolios to see the names of the major investors."

"Excellent! If we can find ones where Ojin has poured in large amounts of cash, we'll have another reason to pay him a visit."

"Sure, it'll be interesting to find out."

"It just occurred to me that there are some other people we might want to research. Chief Aritan told us there are two senators on the healthcare committee who are possibly aligned with the crimes that have taken place. Sen. Emon Barras from Pennsylvania and Sen. Stuart Pitts of California made disparaging remarks to Jack McCabe and his people at the first senate hearing. I'd like to find out if they've received significant donations from a pharmaceutical lobbying group and who's behind it."

"Wow, this is going to be a challenge, but I'm up for it, Kara," Graff beamed.

After her call, Sterrio phoned Chief Aritan and filled him in on the latest in their investigation. "Sounds to me like you're getting closer to the people behind these crimes in the U.S.," Aritan barked as he tapped a Dominican cigar on an ashtray. "As soon as Graff has determined if this Ojin character is a major shareholder in certain pharmaceutical companies, I'll have our people pay them a visit. I can also send the information to our FBI connection regarding the pharmas in the U.S. who may be complicit in the conspiracy."

After her call, Fresco announced, "I've got a drone ready to go, Kara. Ready to look at what's going on at the castle?"

"Love to," Sterrio answered as she prepared to leave.

"Chief of Police Ganti has a drone we can pilot from his office. Let's head over there."

Ganti welcomed them when they arrived and instructed one of his people to launch the small video drone outside. Ganti and the Interpol officers would monitor and steer the bird from inside a control room. He gave Fresco instructions on how to use the joystick to move the drone in any direction. Minutes later, a Trento police officer launched the drone outside, and it propelled up. Ganti pressed a button to record the video as it flew.

Fresco was awkward with the controls at first, but he soon got the hang of guiding the drone above the trees along the route of the carved-out road. The castle was soon in full view. Fresco circled around its ancient walls, then soared slowly by the towers to the property's courtyards. Armed guards were present everywhere. Workers outside tended to landscaping and other duties. There was one area they couldn't see well because a large canopy covered something below it. During the flight, they spotted various people inside the castle. Fresco couldn't get a good view of them because of the reflections on the windows.

"I think I counted at least ten guards scattered around the property," Ganti commented. "When you're ready to visit them, I'll bring my people to back you up."

"Great. I'm sure they'll be valuable," Fresco commented after he steered the drone back to the base. "No telling what kind of battle we might encounter. Let's get ready to pay the castle dwellers a visit."

BACK IN ROME, hacker Sarah Graff was busy following the money. She learned that Ojin's investments in Europe were substantial in four pharmaceutical companies. Once she broke into their company websites, she located lists of the owners. The amounts Karsen Ojin had invested were staggering. He didn't have a majority stake in the pharmas, but he was close to it. His control would have been enough to allow him to be very influential at board meetings.

The pharmas in Europe consisted of Drogari in Rome, Medika in Vienna, Curatif in Paris, and Genez in Brussels. By now, she also had the name of the chief executives at each of them.

When Graff completed her review of the European companies, she analyzed the pharmaceutical companies in the U.S. Ojin's name did not come up in most of them. However, there were two in which his stake in the companies was similar to those in Europe. There was ReMedin in New York and PharMax in Tampa Bay. *Well, this guy has certainly spread his wings in the drug industry,* Sarah thought as she smiled to herself and took a sip of an energy drink.

She completed her research by making a PDF of her findings and emailing a copy to Chief Aritan and Officer Sterrio. She wrote, saying, "Your suspicions were on the money. Karsen Ojin has invested millions of U.S. dollars into six different pharmaceutical companies – four in Europe and two in the U.S. I've also looked into the two senators you asked about. They both had major contributions from a pharma lobby, but I haven't been able to determine where all the money's coming from. It may have originated from the six pharmas but I'll verify before I've completed my investigation."

As soon as Aritan reviewed the intel from Graff, he forwarded a copy to FBI Agent Myles DeLong in D.C. He then called his old Army buddy. "Hey, Myles. Sam here in Innsbruck."

"Howdy, Sam, what's new?" DeLong responded.

"You should receive an email that contains information about six pharmaceutical companies. Two in the U.S. have significant investments from a person named Karsen Ojin," chief explained. "The guy has some skeletons in his closet, but the courts have never convicted him of anything. Two of my officers are about ready to pay him a visit in a castle he owns in the Italian Alps."

"Good work, Sam!" DeLong responded, as he made notes at his desk. "We'll follow up with the U.S. companies. Thanks!"

CHAPTER 16

S en. Emon Barras sent a secure message to Karsen Ojin
advising him of the results of the senate meeting with
NuPharma. The changes to the FDA database did the trick,
showing a minimal number of patients with improved
health. However, as expected, the attorney for NuPharma
demanded that the senate panel summon the clinical physicians for questioning. NuPharma was not going to accept
the new results without a fight.

Ojin shared the communication with Fon Tazi. "We
need to get to the FDA physicians," he confided, narrowing
his eyes. "If we anonymously threaten the lives of those
doctors and their families, they'll be ready to play by our
rules."

"I'll contact my man to get the list of the physicians and
how to reach them, K," Tazi responded with a smirk.
"Either they comply...or die."

Shortly after her conversation with Ojin, Tazi phoned

Yao Min and gave him the instructions. As soon as he learned the names and numbers of those involved in validating the NuPharma results, he was to begin his deep-voiced phone threats. "It might take several calls to get their attention, Yao," Tazi insisted.

In the meantime, Ojin sent an encrypted message to Sen. Barras detailing the plan to blackmail the docs who verified the clinical studies. "Arrange for a follow-up senate hearing with NuPharma but give it two weeks. We'll need time to put the fear of God in those medical people."

Another ideal job for Frankie Leece, Yao thought after he hung up with Tazi. Leece connected the call to his headset when it came through. Getting the names and numbers of those involved in the FDA verification process wouldn't be difficult for Leece.

"I don't see a problem, Yao. I'll let you know when I've completed the job and place the info on your dark website," Frankie assured him as he tossed a handful of nuts into his mouth.

The clinical trials for RGB101 in the heart and diabetes markets followed the FDA protocol. Phase one studies were conducted in a medical center where the physicians and nurses tested the medicine on less than a hundred healthy volunteers to determine proper dosing, learn how easy it was metabolized, and evaluate if there were any side effects.

Phase two trials involved 250 participants for each market. When the drug demonstrated it was beneficial, effective, and the risks were minimal, it moved on to the next phase.

During phase three, they tested about 2,500 people with each disease. In phases two and three, the trials also involved a control standard where a select group of the participants was given a placebo or inactive pill to compare the results with the active drug. If the actual medication demonstrated the benefits it promised without undue risks, they approved the medication for the marketplaces.

The four doctors overseeing the two studies were easy for hacker Frankie Leece to identify. The two in charge of the heart disease trial were Drs. Morgan Talliti and Conrad Verm. Those overseeing the diabetes group were Drs. Axel Mattick and Hamas Zaird.

Yao Min wrote the names and numbers from Frankie on his website and began the calls. Dr. Talliti was first up. He knew she was married and had two small children. When she answered, the deep voice came on. "Doctor, you will only receive one warning. Powerful forces are against the approval of RGB101 as a medication in the market you supervised for the FDA. When you appear at the senate hearing, you will testify that the drug had minimal success in the trial – in fact, less than 25%. If you fail to do as ordered, you and your family will die." The call clicked off.

Stunned by the message, the doctor trembled and dropped her mobile. *That can't be real!* she thought. Shaking, she reached down to pick up her phone.

Next came Dr. Verm, who was in his late forties. He and his wife had three teenage boys. After he heard the message, he was horrified. "What the hell was that?" he growled out loud.

Dr. Mattick got the next call. He and his wife, both in

their fifties, had two grown children. His reaction was just as visceral as the other docs. *Son of a bitch! What can I do to stop these prank calls?* he asked himself.

The fourth physician was Dr. Zaird, who had a small infant with his bride. Having moved to the States from the Middle East, he didn't believe it could be real. He phoned his friend, Dr. Mattick and told him about the frightening call.

"Yes, I got one too!" Axel Mattick replied. "Can't believe it's legitimate."

"Who would do such a thing?" Zaird asked, shaking his head. "I have to say it's very alarming."

"I'll phone our colleagues who managed the heart disease study," Dr. Mattick offered. He rang Dr. Morgan Talliti. "Hello, Morgan, Axel here. Both Dr. Zaird and I received phone messages that threatened our lives if we didn't give a false testimony at the senate hearing."

"I-I got the same thing, Axel!" she stammered. "What's this all about? I haven't spoken with Conrad. I'll get in touch with him and call you back."

"Hello, Conrad, it's Morgan. Did you receive the horrible phone call about the senate hearing?"

"Yes! In fact, I was going to contact you," Dr. Verm responded.

"Drs. Mattick and Zaird got the same thing!" Morgan informed him. "What should we do?"

"Why don't we sit tight to make sure it's not a hoax," Conrad proposed. "The hearing is in two weeks. If one of us gets another one of those crank calls, let's get together to determine how we'll handle it."

FORMULA FOR A FELONY

* * *

THE NEXT DAY, Karsen Ojin sat at the desk in his massive study and spoke with the members of his Consortium on their private video feed. A raging fire burned in the hearth. He described the threats the physicians who supervised the NuPharma trials were receiving. "I expect the docs to comply – or die." He smiled, remembering Fon Tazi's clever way with words.

"We have to hope they take the warnings seriously," Sen. Stuart Pitts said, as the others nodded and grunted in agreement.

"The physicians will receive more than one message," K added as he scanned the faces on the monitor. "They may not take them seriously at first, but hopefully they don't test us."

"Things are going so well now in our market," explained Byrn Zaer of Medika from Vienna. "If NuPharma is approved, our heart disease medicine may have more competition than we'd like."

"Of course, we'll all suffer if our threats fail," Ojin replied. "I may need to give the docs an example of what might happen if they disobey. Hang in there." After more discussion from members of the group, Ojin ended the call and Tazi joined him after monitoring the communication.

"We could cause a family member to suffer before the next hearing. It wouldn't have to be a murder, but something to get their attention," Fon said.

"Yes, I agree," Ojin nodded. "See if your man can arrange for one of the spouses to have an accident. Find out if a wife or husband is a jogger. Unfortunate things happen, don't they?"

"They certainly do, K!" Fon agreed. "I'll see what our man can do."

Tazi reached Yao Min and described the situation. She recommended that Dr. Talliti's husband, Fabio, who they learned liked to jog early in the morning, would be a good person to make an example of. "He doesn't need to be killed – only injured. Then make a follow-up call letting the docs know Fabio's injury wasn't an accident."

Yao knew someone he could trust to handle a job like this. He'd counted on Abe Arrent for similar situations in the past. He knew the man would not go overboard. Arrent had the details and scouted young Fabio Talliti. It was easy to see he liked to jog in the mornings before work on the Sligo Creek Golf Course next to the family's condo in Silver Spring, Maryland.

Abe decided he'd hide behind a large grass bunker near the cart path Fabio ran on. As soon as he was in sight, he'd hit him with tranquilizer darts. Early golfers would discover the sedated man later in the morning. *Easy peasy,* Abe thought.

Early the next morning, Abe was in position before the jogger started his run. Fabio soon came into view. Abe aimed his rifle and fired. Fabio was instantly stunned, screamed, and rolled off the golf cart path onto the dewy grass, as he grabbed his leg. Abe fired a second dart into the runner's other leg. Fabio's body jerked. Then he was still. The shooter stuffed the rifle into a golf bag and hurried away in the opposite direction. He pulled his hat down as he swiftly departed.

An hour later, an elderly twosome teed off, slipped into their golf cart and rode along the cart path. Suddenly, one of the men yelled, "What in the world?" Laying awkwardly in the dewy grass was the body of an unconscious man.

The cart driver wanted to continue on and not get involved. His partner had other ideas. Sliding from the cart, the man crept slowly toward the victim and immediately spotted darts in both legs. He reached down to feel for a pulse. "I'm calling 911." Pulling out his cell phone, he dialed, then announced what he'd discovered.

The sound of sirens soon filled the morning air. An unmarked squad car followed by an ambulance stopped on the nearby Sligo Creek Parkway, with their flashers still spinning. Two men hustled toward the open-mouthed golfers.

"I'm Detective Art Hillery and this is Officer Onger. How long ago did you discover the body?" he asked, glaring at the fallen jogger and the shocked golfers.

"Spotted him several minutes ago," the golfer acknowledged. "Looks like someone shot him with darts. I felt for a pulse. He's alive."

Officer Onger took their names while Hillery bent down to inspect the man lying in the grass. He put on his gloves, reached into the fallen man's waist pack, and pulled out a small wallet.

Just then, two EMTs marched toward them with equipment and a gurney. One bent down to check his vitals. "Looks to be breathing okay. Possibly tranquilized based on the look of these darts."

"Guy's name is Fabio Talliti. Lives across the street," Hillery announced after sifting through the wallet. "Thanks for calling it in, guys." The two gawking golfers nodded and glanced at each other and the cops. "Who in the world would want to fire tranquilizer darts at a guy out for a morning run?"

Onger only shrugged.

CHAPTER 17

The EMTs rushed Fabio Talliti to a nearby hospital. ER physicians removed the darts and kept them for the police investigators. Based on the man's address, authorities discovered he was the husband of Dr. Morgan Talliti of the FDA. As soon as the hospital reached her, Morgan dropped what she was doing and hurried to be by Fabio's side. The man was regaining consciousness when she arrived, but he was still groggy from the tranquilizers. Morgan told him she was there to help any way she could, rubbing his arm and kissing him.

The police officers noticed when the doctor arrived. After giving her time to be alone with her husband, they got her attention. When she stepped out of the hospital room, Detective Art Hillery introduced himself and told her how sorry he was for this strange attack. "It was fortunate that a couple of senior golfers teed off early and discovered your husband," Hillery explained. "This is quite an unusual occurrence, Doctor. Do you know any reason why someone would want to hurt your husband?"

Morgan Talliti had a sudden epiphany of what could be behind such a strange assault. With fear setting in, she wasn't sure she should reveal her suspicion. "I-I'm really not sure, Detective. If I can think of something that makes sense, I'll reach out to you."

"Okay, we would appreciate any information that might shed some light on this. Here's my card. Please don't hesitate to contact me. Thank you."

Morgan walked back into her husband's room and sat next to his bed, stroking his hand, trying to think. Just then, her cell phone rang. She answered. The synthesized, deep-throated voice announced, "Dr. Talliti, you now see what can happen if you fail to comply with our demands. We could have easily murdered your husband. This is your final warning. Tell the other docs what happened – or you'll *all* pay!" The call clicked off.

Oh, my lord! This can't be happening! Morgan thought, as tears welled up in her pale-blue eyes, then streamed down her cheeks. The young woman sat in a trance for a minute, trying to compose herself. *Got to alert the others,* she told herself.

Fumbling for her phone, she punched in the call to her colleague, Dr. Verm. "Conrad, someone shot my husband with tranquilizer darts while he was jogging this morning. I'm at the hospital. He's okay."

"Oh, my! Thank God for that, Morgan! I'm so sorry. You don't suppose–"

"Yes! Minutes ago I received a call from *the deep voice* telling me they could have easily murdered him!"

"What the hell? I-I can't believe this is real," Conrad sputtered. "You sit tight. I'll contact Mattick and Zaird. We've got to be in agreement with this threat. I'll get back to you."

Dr. Verm connected Drs. Mattick and Zaird on a three-way call. "An attacker shot Morgan's husband with tranquilizer darts while he was running this morning. Fortunately, he's okay."

"Son of a bitch! I can't believe this," Dr Mattick responded with a furrowed brow. "Could this have anything to do with–"

"Indeed! It does!" Conrad jumped in. "After the attack, Morgan got one of *those calls* telling her they could have killed him just as easily."

"Oh, no! No!" Hamas Zaird interrupted. "We don't have any alternative...do we? We must go along with their demands...or we could face more terror...even death. Have to think of our families!"

The three physicians continued to discuss their options, but none seemed reasonable. If they went to the police, or even the FBI, their lives could be in imminent danger. When the next meeting occurred, the four of them agreed to falsify the facts.

* * *

LATER THAT DAY, Interpol Officers Kara Sterrio and Alberto Fresco strapped on body armor for their visit to the castle. The Trento Chief of Police Gino Ganti and seven of his deputies did the same.

Before traveling up the road to the castle, the chief asked Fresco how he wanted to play it when they arrived.

"Here's what I'd like to do," Fresco proposed. "You and three of your men approach the main entry. When someone answers the door, inform him you're there to collect unpaid property taxes, and you need to speak with Karsen Ojin or Fon Tazi. Your other four men split up and surround the castle, looking for entry points. Keep your comms open for updates and watch out for the guards on the wall. From the drone video, we noticed a section of the castle that didn't look protected. Sterrio and I will scale the wall there. Once we're inside, we'll let you know our progress."

Ganti drove a squad car. One of his men took another. Sterrio and Fresco let them take the lead. The road was indeed steep and wasn't wide enough for more than one vehicle.

* * *

UNAWARE OF THE IMMINENT ATTACK, Karsen Ojin and Fon Tazi strolled outside along the castle walkway with goblets of wine. They always marveled at the spectacular view of the Alps. The chef was busy preparing their evening meal. Earlier, Tazi received a call from Yao Min informing her that his man fired tranquilizer darts at the husband of one of the FDA clinical-trial docs, as instructed. Then, he called the woman to remind her that this attack showed the threat was very real. Tazi conveyed the message to Ojin.

"Excellent, Fon! Hopefully, they'll be quaking in their surgical boots after that!" Ojin laughed.

"Yes, K! We'll just have to wait to find out if they've

complied with our demands." Tazi agreed and smiled as the wind whipped through her raven hair. Moments later, one of the assistants informed them that their evening meal was prepared. The two responded and left the walkway.

Beyond the walls, Ganti and his men, plus the two Interpol officers, neared the fortress. They stopped their vehicles before they could be seen by the armed guards atop the castle wall. Fresco and Sterrio pulled over to join the others. The Trento chief of police reminded four of his men to approach through the trees.

As Ganti led three of his deputies closer to the castle, the guards at the top of the castle spotted them. "Halt! What business do you have here?" one of them yelled.

"We're Trento police," Ganti shouted back. "We'd like to speak with Karsen Ojin or Fon Tazi about unpaid property taxes." Four of the deputies and the two Interpol officers were out of sight, creeping through the trees to their positions.

"Wait there," the guard yelled back. "I'll alert Mr. Ojin." Ganti and the three deputies edged closer to the large entry door.

Fresco carried a rolled-up rope with a grappling hook attached to the end. When he and Sterrio arrived at the area they thought was unguarded, the couple paused for a moment to listen. When Fresco was confident there was no one near, he began twirling the hook above his head, then flung it up over the edge of the castle wall. Pulling the rope tight, the hook caught. He yanked on it to make sure it was secure. They waited a few minutes to be certain the noise didn't attract a guard. Nodding to Sterrio, he grasped the rope to climb up. His partner covered him.

At the front of the castle, an armed guard opened the entry door and announced to the police that Mr. Ojin was confident he was current on his taxes.

"According to our records, there is a past-due amount that needs to be addressed," Ganti announced and pulled out a fake document that he waved in the air. "I must deliver this to Mr. Ojin or Ms. Tazi personally."

"Wait here," the guard said, and closed the door.

As Fresco reached the top of the facade, he peered over. No one was in sight. He pulled himself up, hopped onto the walkway, then signaled for Sterrio to come up. She grasped the rope and began scaling the wall. Fresco stayed low and scanned the area for any guards. Moments later, Sterrio joined him. He alerted the other police that they'd breached the wall.

Inside, the news from the police instantly interrupted Ojin and Tazi's supper. They stared at each other after getting word of the officer's request to see *either* of them. "I don't like this one bit, Fon! Sounds like a raid. We don't have a tax problem and they shouldn't even know about you."

"Should we consider making a run for it?" she asked, feeling the tension erupt.

"Pack up your things. Let's take the chopper. I sense a potential attack," Ojin whispered. They scurried from the large dining table, ran to their private rooms, and stuffed clothing and other belongings in backpacks. Tazi hurried to the large canopy. She yelled for an assistant to help retract the cover over the small, hidden helicopter. Before he joined his lover, Ojin rushed into his study, pulled out the hard drives from his computers, grabbed his laptop, and hurried to meet Tazi.

As Fresco and Sterrio moved into the main part of the castle, two guards confronted them with gunfire. The officers ducked and returned a barrage of their own, taking out the hired guns. Searching the castle, the pair came to Ojin's empty study. Suddenly, the Interpol officers heard the whir of the helicopter blades outside. Glancing at each other, they dashed toward the sound. Several assistants moved away at the sight of the police. Two other guards were in position near the chopper and sprayed bullets at Fresco and Sterrio, who jumped behind pillars to avoid being hit. In the distance, they recognized Tazi piloting the helicopter. It quickly lifted off from the pad. The Interpol officers could do nothing but fight more defending guards.

The Trento police officers exchanged fire with the remaining guards on the wall and inside the castle. Gino Ganti killed the guard at the front door after the man raised his weapon to shoot. Then Ganti and his men edged inside, preparing for more gunfire. The other police deputies who'd circled around the walls took out several guards on the walls.

Near the escaping helicopter, Fresco killed one guard, but another bullet hit Fresco in the arm, propelling him to the ground. Sterrio glanced at her partner, stared back at the shooter, aimed, and put a bullet in the guard's head. She dashed over to Fresco, who was grabbing his left arm.

"I'm okay. Get Ojin and Tazi," he moaned.

Sterrio hurried to the location of the helipad and watched as the chopper continued to gain altitude. She shot her weapon, but they were too far away. All she could do was watch as they soared over a nearby mountaintop.

Running back inside, she knelt next to Fresco and helped wrap a towel around his left arm to stop the bleeding. "We'll take care of you, love," she whispered. "Hang in there."

Just then, Chief Ganti and several of his deputies appeared behind them. Sterrio turned to the chief as he reported his status. "We took out the guards, but they got one of ours, damn it. How's Officer Fresco?"

"Very sorry about your man, Chief," Sterrio replied, shaking her head. "Fresco's been hit, but he'll live. I'm afraid our targets got away in a chopper. Our pursuit continues."

CHAPTER 18

After escaping the police raid, the helicopter piloted by Fon Tazi veered south toward Verona, Italy. She and Karsen Ojin landed at its airport and booked a flight to Munich International Airport. Once in Germany, Ojin thought he'd consider reaching his relative in Berlin. Ojin had access to plenty of money, so that wouldn't be an issue. His cousin, Ivy Ning, had connections with Chinese organizations that he hoped could help gain new identities and weapons for Tazi and himself.

As they sat in the Verona Airport bar waiting for their flight, Ojin asked with disgust, "How in the hell did they know where to find us?"

"Don't know, K. Possibly the phone calls I've made to the U.S. were not as secure as I'd hoped. As far as I can tell, my man Yao Min is still free. Even though the police arrested Cho En Dai and Din Shu Pu, I don't think they'd talk."

"The Consortium pharmas and my investments in them depend on those FDA docs testifying that the forged clinical trial data is real. It's our only hope of keeping RGB101 out of our markets."

"Yao will continue to remind the docs with the threatening phone calls. They'll either comply...or die." Tazi reiterated with a smile.

"I can only hope you're right, Fon," Ojin responded, as he took a sip of a cognac. Fon shook her head, as they both peered out at the tarmac.

It wasn't long before their flight was ready to board. They made it on the plane easily without any questions from the authorities. When they arrived in Munich, they boarded another flight to Berlin Brandenburg Airport. Upon their arrival, they took a taxi to a hotel and welcomed some much-needed sleep.

* * *

CHIEF SAMUEL ARITAN received the news that Interpol Officers Fresco and Sterrio attacked the castle owned by Karsen Ojin. While they were battling his armed guards, Ojin and Fon Tazi escaped. Sterrio drove Fresco to the Trento Medical Center to have his bullet wound patched up. He was lucky, Kara told him. He would heal quickly. They planned to help the local police investigate the castle property in search of evidence regarding the crimes that were committed in the United States.

Interpol's computer hacker, Sarah Graff, had uncovered the details of the financial portfolios of four European phar-

FORMULA FOR A FELONY

maceutical companies and two in the United States. In each of these, Karsen Ojin had sizeable investments. He wasn't a majority owner in any of them, but his stake made him extremely influential. The CEOs and company boards had to bow to Ojin's requests.

Chief Aritan set up a conference call with his teams. Officers Melvin Loewe and Phillip Wright in Innsbruck, Cameron Payne and Darren Deeds plus Jeanette Poole and Barron Kaide in Bruges, and Bella Gamba and Enzo Ferno in Rome.

"I've emailed the information that Sarah Graff uncovered about the four pharmaceutical outfits in Europe," Aritan began. "Based on her intel, Karsen Ojin is a major investor and has considerable control over the CEOs at each of them. As you can see from the background, there's reason to believe that Ojin and his sidekick, Fon Tazi, orchestrated the murders of an FDA Commissioner and possibly a U.S. Senator. These men were in favor of Jack McCabe's product being approved for the heart disease and diabetes markets. Because of their favored positions, they were taken out, literally. Then, men kidnapped and tortured NuPharma's Dr. Lennium. Fortunately, those responsible were arrested and are being held in prison. The police set Lennium free.

A couple of other items you should know. Jack McCabe's homes in Indianapolis and at Lake Maxinkuckee were also invaded by people who attempted to plant listening devices. Security people shot or arrested them before any harm was done. We've also learned that the senate committee presented falsified clinical study results.

Jack and his people don't have a clue how someone switched the results."

"Do you suspect the CEOs actually supported the murders?" inquired Officer Cameron Payne from the Bruges station.

"We don't have any proof that they did, but they may be complicit because each of them has a stake in either the heart disease or diabetes fields. None of them has a medication with the healing power of RGB101, so its approval would marginalize their products. There's an enormous risk for all of them."

"What would you like us to do, Chief?" Jeanette Poole inquired as she paused taking notes. "If we don't have any proof of their culpability, we can't charge them with anything."

"You're right, Poole," Aritan answered. "Sarah Graff is trying to find out where all the money came from for a specific pharmaceutical lobby. In exchange for millions of dollars donated to a few U.S. senators, the lobby expects them to bow to their demands. I'm hoping she can determine that the two senators who've been antagonistic toward McCabe's company were beneficiaries of this lobby money. If we can tie the cash back to the pharmas in question, we'll have a motive."

"So we know Ojin is a major investor in the four European pharmas," Phillip Wright added. "And we know that they have products that compete with McCabe's. Just to confirm, if Sarah can tie the lobby money to the pharmas, we've got a reasonable link to the crimes."

"Bingo, Wright!" Chief responded. "It would put them in a very suspicious position."

"Here's what I'd like to do. Gamba and Ferno, see what you can find out about Imelda Broglio of Drogari in Rome. Payne and Deeds, you've got Kahn Cordant of Curatif in Paris. Loewe and Wright, take Byrn Zaer of Medika in Vienna. And Poole and Kaide, check out Regis Volt of Genez in Brussels. I'm hoping we'll have more ammunition for you to work with in the next few days. Until then, each of you may have to come up with a way to disguise yourselves to get inside your assigned company. Learn everything you can to expose the CEO's association with Karsen Ojin and Fon Tazi."

STATIONED at the Rome Interpol office, Bella Gamba and Enzo Ferno didn't have far to travel to investigate Imelda Broglio. They studied her lifestyle and discovered where she spent time outside of the luxurious Drogari headquarters. An only child, Imelda inherited her position and wealth from the Broglio family. Her grandfather started the business as a pharmacist. When her father took over, he bought the rights to new medications that were successfully marketed under the Drogari brand. Now one of the leading pharmas in Italy, the company provided diabetes medication to help patients reduce their blood sugar and A1C.

Imelda Broglio married young but later divorced. Her two grown children were now employed by the company. In her late forties, the stylish and still lovely Imelda was an active participant in Rome's nightlife. If she and one of her wealthy girlfriends weren't seen at the opera in the Palazzo

Santa Chiara, the CEO frequently visited several night-clubs. Her favorites included the Marmo in the San Lorenzo neighborhood, the non-touristy Vinile with retro jazz and dancing, and the Sheket between Piazza Venezia and the spot where Caesar met his bloody death.

As a former boxer, the muscular Enzo Ferno decided he would go undercover and attempt to meet Imelda where she played. The officer thought he'd attempt to become friends and learn some of her secrets.

Bella Gamba, whose name meant "beautiful leg" in Italian, decided she'd masquerade as a cleaning person. After gaining a warrant, she signed on with a temp service. An opportunity developed quickly. She paid off the normal cleaning lady to cover the Drogari CEO's office. On the first evening after most people had left for the day, Gamba pushed her cleaning cart inside Broglio's office and closed the door. Quickly locating her equipment, she placed audio bugs in the land-line phone and several lights. Bella hid another inside the light in her private restroom. After checking through drawers and cabinets, then emptying the wastebaskets and looking for anything suspicious, she left. The next day she told the temp company she'd come down with a serious illness and wouldn't be returning.

Following her brief stint in the cleaning business, Gamba monitored the feed from the audio bugs. Broglio's activities during the day and evening were soon readily available to the Interpol officer. Imelda arranged to attend the opera with one of her girlfriends. As a result, Officer Ferno rented a tux and bought a ticket near her. During the intermission, he arrived at the bar and ordered a champagne. Mixing among the other well-dressed attendees, he nodded to Imelda, smiled, and raised his glass. She returned his flirtation, but they didn't speak to one another.

As the weekend approached, Bella learned that Imelda planned to go to the Vinile nightclub, where she hoped to listen to the music and enjoy a little dancing. Enzo upgraded his wardrobe and also showed up. During his time as a boxer, he found that learning various dance steps was a great way to improve his footwork. As a result, he was more than acceptable on the dance floor.

When the opportunity presented itself, Enzo sidled up to the bar next to Imelda. Getting her attention, he offered to buy her a cocktail. She agreed. "Didn't we see one another at the opera earlier this week?" he asked innocently. "My name is Enzo Ferno."

"Why, yes. I believe we did," she smiled. "I'm Imelda. Thank you for the drink. What brings you to Vinile tonight?"

"Love the music and always enjoy dancing," he began. After making small talk for a few minutes, Ferno asked if she'd care to join him on the dance floor. Imelda was delighted.

Most of the couples were swing dancing, so Ferno gave that a whirl. Broglio loved it. He had all the moves, and she appeared to be thrilled to have a partner who knew the steps. They continued for several songs. Afterward, she thanked him, kissed him on the cheek, and rejoined her girlfriend. When Enzo returned to the bar, he looked over at her table occasionally and caught her glancing his way.

Before leaving, Broglio joined Ferno at the bar and slid a piece of paper to him with her mobile number. "Give me a call, Enzo. I'd love to go dancing again." With a smile, she and her friend left the nightclub. Officer Ferno was probably ten years younger than his new conquest, but he had to admit that his target was quite attractive. *My dance moves may have paid off after all these years,* he chuckled to himself.

CHAPTER 19

C hief Aritan assigned Officers Jeanette Poole and Barron Kaide to learn all they could about Regis Volt, the CEO of Genez. Based in Brussels, the capital of Belgium, the two Interpol partners didn't have far to go from their base in Bruges. Only 100 kilometers away, they drove to their destination and checked into a hotel in the center of the city. As lovers, Poole and Kaide welcomed the opportunity for some intimacy.

Poole was multi-lingual and could converse with people in Flemish, German, English and French. In her late thirties, Jeanette was a stunning brunette who was a former martial arts competitor and race car driver. After competing in the junior Belgium Grand Prix, she was skilled in more ways than one. Barron was a former baseball pitcher with tattooed arms who was now known to fire fastball hand grenades and other objects as weapons.

Their target, Genez Pharmaceuticals, was near the center of Brussels, where energy from commerce, government, and the arts emanated. The Interpol team was interested to learn that Genez was also close to the Belgium Royal Palace, which they hoped to visit if time permitted.

During their research of Volt, Poole and Kaide discovered the CEO enjoyed rubbing shoulders with the leaders of government and the arts. In his early sixties, Regis was overweight, wore large, black-framed glasses, and shaved his head. Despite his appearance, his status as the wealthy owner of Genez enabled him to hobnob with Brussel's elite.

Volt gained his position at Genez through somewhat devious means. Over time, he purchased shares of stock in the company when his wealth from other sources allowed it. It wasn't long before he forced a hostile takeover of the ownership. His prized drug helped patients battle their heart disease with a cholesterol-lowering therapy. The product was the company's principal revenue producer. The thought of RGB101 entering the market sent shock waves through the board-of-directors and key shareholders like Karsen Ojin.

Thanks to Rome's Sarah Graff, Interpol had the mobile phone numbers of Regis Volt and the other CEOs. When they arrived, Poole got a wiretap order to capture any relevant conversations. They also learned that Volt frequently used a limousine service. Kaide bribed the limo company to handle Volt's requests. Barron needed to use a GPS to find his way around Brussels, but he didn't expect it to be a problem. Jeanette planned to attend an event where Volt might make an appearance. She would use her charms to get his attention and engage in a conversation when the opportunity presented itself.

The two Interpol officers monitored Volt's calls. Much of what they heard was of little use. Some of it was disturbing, especially his treatment of women. They learned that he was planning to attend a fundraising affair at the famous Atomium. This atom-shaped landmark rose above the city landscape. Barron Kaide would serve as his limo driver. Jeanette would dress appropriately and work her way into the event.

When Kaide arrived to pick up Volt at his stately home, he walked to the front entrance, knocked, and announced himself. A few minutes later, the CEO brought his young, beautiful trophy wife, Diana. Kaide opened the door for them when they reached the limo. The drive to the Atomium was uneventful other than a mobile call Volt took. The Interpol officer overheard him telling someone that there was little chance that the upstart from the U.S. would steal any of his prize products' share of the heart-disease market. Barron made a mental note of this comment.

Inside the reception, Jeanette was dressed to kill. Her sensual look caught the eyes of many of the men in attendance. As the evening wore on, several of them attempted to make an introduction with her, but she brushed them off. When Regis Volt's wife left to visit the powder room, Poole moved in. "Say, excuse me, but aren't you Regis Volt, the CEO of Genez?" she inquired innocently with a smile on her lips.

"Why yes, how did you know?" Regis responded, grinning and feeling flattered.

"I believe I've seen your photo in the newspaper. You're famous!" she added. "It must be exciting to own one of the largest pharmaceutical companies in the world!"

"Well, it's...and who might you be?" the rotund CEO asked with a smile.

"My name's Jeanette. I've been with the Belgium Grand Prix but travel to Brussels regularly to meet sponsors. I'm always interested in meeting successful men like you."

He laughed. "Are you seeking more sponsors for your race car, Jeanette?"

Chuckling along, she answered, "Our team is in good shape financially, but I'm always interested in meeting an important person who may be looking for a sports marketing opportunity."

After chatting for another five minutes, Volt's wife Diana returned and grabbed her husband's arm. "Who's your new friend, Regis?" she asked with a bit of a frown toward Poole.

"This is Jeanette, dear," Volt explained. "She's part of an auto racing team that may be interested in sponsors."

"Oh, I see!" Diana beamed. "How fascinating!"

"Well, I won't bother you any longer. My pleasure to meet you both," Poole stated, and turned to leave.

Before she departed, Volt reached into his suit coat and grabbed a business card, handing it to Poole. "Pleasure was all mine, Jeanette. Feel free to contact me about that marketing opportunity." She took his card and smiled at both of them as she walked away.

Returning to the bar, the Interpol officer sipped on another drink and listened to the string quartet playing nearby. Several men offered to buy her drinks again, but she told them she was waiting for her date to meet her. Not long after, she grabbed her coat and left to catch a taxi to her hotel.

Kaide met the Volt couple later and drove them back to their estate. During the ride, Regis excitedly phoned someone from his company to tell him about the race car driver he met. After returning his limo to the garage, Barron traveled back to the hotel and met up with his partner. She was listening to the mobile calls Volt made through the evening.

"How was the event, love?" Kaide asked, as he threw off his driver's uniform. Poole had already taken a shower and had a towel loosely wrapped around her.

"Not bad at all," she responded. "I got the guy's business card if I decide to reach out to him again. The sponsorship idea got him and his wife quite excited."

"Well, Jeanette, you're making me *quite excited*," Barron laughed, as he began kissing her neck and shoulders. She clicked off the audio feed, smiled, reached up, and gently stroked his cheek. Their evening's thrills were just beginning.

OFFICERS LOEWE and Wright arrived in Vienna and had similar success gaining information about Byrn Zaer of Medika. Likewise, Payne and Deeds flew to Paris and quickly became acquainted with Kahn Cordant of Curatif.

While the Interpol teams continued studying their targets, computer hacker Sarah Graff was getting closer to uncovering the group responsible for the money that had been donated to the U.S. Senators. She was particularly interested in finding out about the enormous funds provided to Emon Barras and Stuart Pitts. Whoever managed the money had moved it through an offshore account to make it nearly impossible to track. She wasn't giving up.

* * *

BACK IN THE UNITED STATES, NuPharma attorney Christopher Masse's office phone rang. After his assistant answered, she transferred it to his desk, telling him it was the senate committee calling.

"Yes, this is Masse. How may I help?" he answered.

"Mr. Masse, I'm calling from the senate committee requesting your attendance at a follow-up meeting," an aide announced. "This will be your opportunity to observe the testimony of the medical professionals who supervised your clinical trials." Then he gave Chris the date and time at the Capitol Building in D.C.

"Yes, thank you. I'll be there," Masse acknowledged, and the call ended. *Finally, we'll get some justice for NuPharma,* he thought to himself. He set up a three-way call to Jack McCabe and Milton Lennium. "I just received an invitation to attend a follow-up meeting at the senate chamber."

"Great! Now we can hopefully settle this once and for all." Jack smiled as he looked over at his wife and son sitting nearby. They had moved to a secret condominium location after the threats on his life intensified. Sara was in the middle of helping Amos with a math problem, as part of his home-schooling curriculum.

"I'd love to go, Chris, but I'm still not comfortable traveling," Dr. Lennium explained, regarding the terror of his recent kidnapping. "Believe me, I'm eager to get this thing behind us."

"I understand. My assistant and I will attend and represent the company," Chris confirmed. "We've got all the *correct* data. I hope whoever's behind the criminal activity hasn't gotten to the docs. Surely they wouldn't put up with any blackmail threats."

"We can only hope," Jack interjected. "I'll be eager to hear how it went."

* * *

AFTER FLYING to the nation's capital, Chris and his assistant entered the senate meeting room. An aide ushered the attorneys inside and directed them to their seats. The four physicians who'd managed the FDA clinical trials for the heart and diabetes studies of RGB101 sat across from them.

Sen. Barras called the meeting to order, swore everyone in, and introduced Masse and the four doctors. "I want to thank the attorney for NuPharma, Mr. Christopher Masse, and you four physicians for attending today's hearing to testify about your experience at the clinical trials. Drs. Morgan Talliti and Conrad Verm supervised the patients in the heart disease studies. Drs. Axel Mattick and Hamas Zaird handled the diabetes patients. I'd like for each of you to provide this panel with a report on your findings. Dr. Talliti, please begin."

Acting somewhat sheepish and reading from a script, Talliti gave her summary. "Thank you, Senator. I'm afraid that the benefits of RGB101 on the patients did not live up to anyone's expectations. We studied several thousand people with this disease in our third trial. Unfortunately, less than 25 percent received a positive experience. This result is not adequate for me to provide a recommendation for approval."

Chris sat open-mouthed in disbelief, and then blurted, "What? That's impossible!"

"Mr. Masse, I've warned you before to watch your comments in this chamber," Barras thundered. "Thank you, Dr. Talliti."

CHAPTER 20

The statements from the other physicians at the hearing were similarly shocking. Attorney Masse was dumbfounded. Sens. Barras and Pitts tried to hide their grins as they glanced back and forth from the four doctors and Masse.

"Well, this seems to be pretty cut and dried, Mr. Masse," Sen. Barras remarked with a subtle sneer.

Christopher Masse didn't immediately know how to respond to the apparent deception he'd just witnessed. He glared at the four physicians for several moments. They were staring off in space or down at their notes with glum expressions. Finally, Chris rose to make a statement. "Dr. Talliti, the staff at NuPharma monitored the trials and recorded the results of the patients. Nearly all of them who suffered from heart disease showed significant improvements from taking RGB101. I'm at a complete loss to explain your summary today. How do you and Dr. Verm, in all good consciousness, expect us to accept your statements?"

"Mr. Masse!" Barras bellowed. "Once again, you're treading on very thin ice. I warn you to avoid impugning the integrity of these upstanding FDA physicians."

"I'm sure you were expecting a more positive outcome, Mr. Masse, but the data from the study was conclusive," Talliti responded without looking directly at her questioner.

"Hmmm...Dr. Mattick," Chris continued, as he squinted at the doctors, "you and Dr. Zaird covered the diabetes patients. As you know, the NuPharma medical team monitored these people and confirmed their improved health after taking RGB101. At what point did you see their conditions decline?"

"Indeed, there was a modest health gain, but it was short-lived," Mattick testified, as he looked at his notes.

"I see," Masse replied, shaking his head in disgust. After thinking for a moment, he proposed a different tack. "Senators, I would like to produce a video of the patients from the trials being examined by independent physicians. When we have completed it, I'd like to present the results to this committee."

"This sounds to me like little more than a weak attempt to stall and take up more of our time, Mr. Masse," Barras barked. "I will confer with this committee and let you know if we accept your proposal. Until then, this meeting is recessed." The senator loudly pounded his gavel, and the participants rose to leave.

As an assistant ushered the physicians from the senate meeting room through a different exit than the attorneys, Chris tried to stop them to talk, but they didn't look back.

Once again, he noticed the smirking senators at the rostrum.

After venting with his assistant for several moments, attorney Masse set up a three-way call to Jack and Milt. "You won't believe this, but someone got to the FDA docs. They stated that our drug's benefit was too short-lived to be effective. I could have screamed!" Chris shook his head.

"What the hell?" Jack yelled. "Somebody must have threatened their lives. That's the only explanation. We've got to find these criminals and throw them in jail!"

"I-I just can't believe this is happening," Milt stammered. "Hopefully, the FBI or the Interpol people will catch these crooks."

"I proposed we develop a video of independent docs examining the patients from the trials and recording their testimonies," Masse said. "Surely that'll be conclusive. The senators will let me know if they approve that option. If not, they'll tell me to pound sand."

The three mumbled obscenities in disgust.

AFTER ESCAPING FROM THEIR CASTLE, Karsen Ojin and Fon Tazi arrived in Berlin and settled into their hotel. The next day, Ojin decided he'd reach out to his relative, Ivy Ning. "Hello, Ivy. It's your cousin, Karsen. I just arrived in Berlin. I hope you're doing well."

"My word! Karsen Ojin?" Ning replied with surprise as two hairless Sphinx cats hovered around her. "It's been a while. I'm doing okay. What brings you to this part of the world?"

"I was presented with a bogus tax issue in Italy, so I left," he explained. "What are you doing these days? Do you still have connections in the Chinese underworld?"

"Actually, I've had no reason to contact anyone in the past few years. My employer has maintained my position as the caretaker of his estate. As a result, I have no serious financial needs. What is it you want from my connections?"

"My associate and I would like to get a few weapons and new identities," Ojin replied. "We're also interested in finding a comfortable place to stay for a while. Are there any areas in Berlin you can recommend?"

Ivy instantly thought of a place that would work for her cousin. "There's a very nice condo you could consider staying in. It's owned by my employer, but he's currently in prison and won't be needing it soon."

"I see. Your offer is certainly appealing and very generous, Ivy," Ojin commented. "Sorry to hear about the owner. If I might ask, what trouble did he get himself into?"

"The less you know, the better, cousin," she responded. "I believe I still have contacts who can help you with the weapons and new identities." After sifting through her notes, she gave Karsen the address to the condo and asked him to meet her there tomorrow at 10 a.m. "I have another appointment at 11:30, so I won't be able to stay long."

He agreed.

* * *

OJIN AND TAZI drove to the upscale condo in Berlin, met Ivy Ning outside, and introduced Tazi. "This looks quite nice, Ivy. Please give us a tour of the inside," Ojin beamed.

After an initial view of the condo, he and Tazi said the residence was beyond their expectations. It had most of the creature comforts they'd hoped to find in a temporary residence. "What'd you say the owner's name was?"

"I didn't mention it, but it's one of the homes owned by Hayden Zeik," Ning answered. "He enjoyed staying in different places in Berlin."

"Interesting. Sounds like a good way of staying ahead of the law – when needed," Ojin commented, and smiled. Ning nodded. She then gave them the name of a person who could assist them with their requirements.

"One of our cousins, Rico Ning, should be able to get you what you need," Ivy offered. "You'll find his resources to be quite valuable if you have other requirements." She gave them his mobile number and said she'd reach out to let him know they'd be in touch. After giving her guests the key to the condo, she told them to make themselves at home and to call if they needed anything. "We should get together for dinner sometime soon," she said before leaving.

Prior to returning home, Ivy drove to meet the caretaker of a crypt behind a small, ancient church. Hayden Zeik had directed her to pay the man regularly to make sure the items stored there would be well-maintained. The secluded cavern included new security and an upgraded HVAC system. Zeik had given her the digital code to the door of the crypt, but never told her what was inside.

After meeting with the caretaker and handing him a large, thick envelope filled with cash, Ivy's curiosity got the better of her. Peering around, she walked to the crypt's entrance. Staring at the lock, she punched in the numbers.

The door slowly opened on creaky hinges. When the woman flipped on a light switch inside, she viewed a flight of worn-down stone steps. Ivy carefully made her way to the bottom, found another light switch, and flipped it on. At first, she couldn't see anything other than some sort of tarps covering items leaning against the walls.

What could be so precious that it needs to be stored in this secret crypt, Ivy wondered. Stepping toward one of the objects near her, she pulled the tarp back and saw there was another wrapping covering some sort of artwork. Turning it around, she gently pulled the cloth away and eyed it closely. *Oh, my! What's this?* She wasn't an art connoisseur, but thought it appeared to be important. Pulling out her phone, she snapped a picture, then covered the art back up, and returned it to its previous position. Ivy did the same with the remaining seven pieces. Before leaving, she viewed the photos and looked forward to researching them at home.

THE NEXT DAY, Ojin and Tazi checked out of the hotel and drove to their new residence. They appreciated the underground parking and an elevator that took them to their third-floor condo. After hauling their limited belongings inside, they started making a list of everything they'd need. Since they had to escape from the castle in haste, shopping for clothing, food, and other necessities was on the top of their list. Ojin also wanted to purchase necessary computer equipment. If he could locate a secure system to communicate with the Consortium, that would be another essential.

They went on a buying spree at a nearby mall, finding nearly everything on their list. During the afternoon, he set up his computer and video system, then reached out to the members to schedule a time to meet at 11 a.m. ET.

"Forgive me for the short notice. I've just arrived at a new location and wanted to learn how the latest senate hearing went," Ojin remarked. "Sen. Barras, what can you tell us?"

"Yes, K," Barras began. "Sorry you had to relocate."

"I'm afraid so. For now, I'll keep my location confidential."

"Well, Sen. Pitts and I were quite pleased with the testimony of the FDA doctors. They pulled it off convincingly, I'd say. Each of them reported that the NuPharma drug didn't have any lasting benefit, so they couldn't approve it. The attorney was fuming, but before he left, he proposed that the company videotape interviews with a large number of the patients and independent physicians in order to show that the latest findings were incorrect. I told them the committee would confer and let them know our decision." The members of the Consortium shook their heads and mumbled their discontent with the attorney's offer. "I commented that his request was simply a waste of time for the senate panel."

"Hmmm. So far, so good," Ojin remarked. "It appears the FDA physicians took our threats seriously."

"Indeed, none of them wavered from our demands," Pitts interjected.

"It occurs to me we could have a lawsuit on our hands if we deny them an opportunity," Regis Volt suggested. "If we allow them to proceed, which will take time, we may need to figure out another way to sabotage their findings. Possibly we can influence those *independent* docs like we did with the FDA physicians."

"Yes, I have to agree," Ojin responded. "Let's give that a try. It will offer more time to find alternative solutions to keep RGB101 out of our markets."

CHAPTER 21

When she arrived at her desk early in the morning at the Rome Interpol office, Sarah Graff was dragging. She'd been up late the night before trying to crack the source of the pharmaceutical lobby's funds, and its payments to U.S. senators. After searching several offshore and Swiss banks, she hit on one that sent stimulating chills up her spine. She popped the top of an ice-cold energy drink, took several gulps, and got a rush of inspiration and adrenaline.

Staring at her large computer screen, she peered at a photo of a tiny island in the Caribbean called Nevis. Nestled on the northern end of the Lesser Antilles, it was a dormant volcano surrounded by sandy beaches. With a population of just 11,000, Nevis had become well-known as a favorite of the wealthy for several reasons. It was an excellent place to incorporate a limited liability company or LLC due to zero taxes involved. The bank was a holdover for secrecy, avoiding pressure from the United States and other countries to open its client portfolios for investigation. Moreover, it had no taxation treaties with any of them.

Graff's hacking expertise suddenly opened the door to one such LLC called *OPC* that desperately intended to remain hidden. The young woman discovered that the account housed deposits from the six pharmaceutical companies she'd been investigating. ReMedin of New York, Pharmax of Tampa Bay, Drogari of Rome, Medika of Vienna, Curatif of Paris, and Genez of Brussels. Withdrawals from the secret account were being distributed to government leaders in the United States, specifically to Sens. Barras and Pitts. Another senator, Ronald Amock, also received benefits until his suspicious death when he fell down the steep *Exorcist* stairway.

Sarah attempted to determine who pulled the strings on this off-shore account but was struggling to identify a name. Thinking of names for the company listed as OPC, she finally hit upon Ojin Pharma Corp. *Could that be it?* she asked herself.

Excited with her revelation, she phoned Officer Bella Gamba who soon visited Graff's office. "Look at this!" Sarah exclaimed. "We might have our targets in the crosshairs."

Bella stared at the names of the companies that the Interpol teams were investigating. They were all there. It was their money that was being used to pay the senators. "This is terrific, Sarah!" the officer shouted. "The Chief will be thrilled to get the news. Great work!"

"I know this doesn't tie the pharmas directly to the murders, kidnapping, and other crimes, but it's a start,"

FORMULA FOR A FELONY

Sarah responded gleefully. She paused and took another gulp of her drink. "Let's look a little further."

After typing in more computer code, the screen instantly revealed two more beneficiaries. "Hey! This shows payments to names I don't recognize. Several have gone to someone named YM in three states: Boston, Massachusetts; Providence, Rhode Island; and New London, Connecticut. What in the world could they have in common, I wonder?"

Studying her screen a moment longer, she stated, "There are also payments to CED with an address in Chesterfield, New Jersey. Hmmm."

"Wait!" Gamba replied. "YM? Wasn't the person who had phone conversations with Fon Tazi named Yao Min?"

"Oh, My God! You're right!" Graff agreed. "And what were the names of the kidnappers the FBI captured in Boston?"

"CED? It must be Cho En Dai! You nailed it!" Gamba shouted and laughed. "Did anyone ever call you the digital Sherlock Holmes? Awesome, Sarah!"

With a chuckle, Graff beamed, "I'm calling Chief Aritan. He's going to love this. He'll be eager to let his FBI contact know what we've uncovered. His agents can get busy tying up loose ends in the U.S."

"Hey, Chief, It's Sarah Graff," she began when her call connected. "Did I catch you at a good time? I've got you on speaker with Gamba."

"Hello, Graff and Gamba!" Aritan responded as he blew out a plume of cigar smoke. "What's the latest?"

"Bella and I were going over something you'll be very interested in hearing. It appears the pharmaceutical lobby we've been tracking holds its money in a bank in Nevis in the Caribbean. I've located an account there with the initials OPC. Could that be Ojin Pharma Company or Corporation? Maybe the C stands for something else."

"By God, Graff! You've done it!" the chief barked. "What else?"

"Here's the kicker. Funds have been deposited by the six pharmaceutical companies we've been after. The four in Europe and two in the States."

"I'll be a son of a bitch...oh, excuse my French," chief exclaimed.

"There's more," Graff continued. "I found payments to two different people in the U.S. There's a YM at three addresses on the East Coast. Money has also been sent to a CED in New Jersey. Can you guess what those initials stand for?"

"Wait a second," chief replied as he thought and relit his Nicaraguan cigar. "YM, YM. Could it be...Yao Min?"

"You got it, sir!" Graff cheered.

"Okay, let's see. You said CED. Hmmm. CED...It must be Cho En Dai, the kidnapper of the NuPharma director!"

"Right again, Chief!"

"Amazing! This is the best news I've heard in a long time. Please email the details. I'll be setting up a conference call with the teams and informing FBI Agent DeLong in the U.S. Thanks for you hard work, Graff! You're the best!"

A few minutes later, Chief Aritan's email dinged, and he opened it to find a PDF. After a quick review, he read all the incriminating evidence against Ojin and his associates in the pharma companies. His initial question was whether they could legally use the information against them. Aritan thought for a few moments, then knew what he had to do.

The chief put a call into his old Army buddy, Myles DeLong. Seconds later, the FBI agent answered. "Hey, Myles, I've got some good news but need your help in order to legitimize it."

"Sam! What's happening in Innsbruck?" the agent asked.

"We believe we have strong evidence showing the six pharmaceutical companies and Ojin are behind the payments to the U.S. senators and the people who committed the crimes against the FDA and NuPharma."

"Wow! That's great to hear!" DeLong applauded. "Let's go get 'em, right?"

"One of our people discovered a bank account on the island of Nevis in the Caribbean that has deposits from the pharmas. We didn't have a search warrant and want to see if you can get one signed by a judge on the island. The company uses the initials OPC. We believe it stands for Ojin Pharma Corp. or something like that. There are deposits from the six companies we have on our radar. Plus, there are payments to the senators and people we think are Yao Min and Cho En Dai!"

"Holy Toledo, Sam!" Myles shouted after making notes. "You're right. We'll need a valid search warrant to use the information as evidence. I'm not familiar with Nevis but I know there are tight privacy restrictions in some of the Caribbean island banks."

"That's what I'm thinking. See what your team can come up with regarding the warrant. I'll send you the details and start prepping our team over here."

"You got it, Sam," DeLong replied with gusto. "I'll let you know when we've got it covered. And thanks to you and your people. This is wonderful news!"

THE NEXT DAY, Chief Aritan scheduled a conference call with his teams. Most of the officers were out in the field so he reached them on their mobile phones. Bella Gamba and Enzo Ferno were in Rome after their experience with Imelda Broglio of Drogari. Melvin Loewe and Phillip Wright were still in Vienna where they'd been investigating Byrn Zaer of Medika. Cameron Payne and Darren Deeds had uncovered some interesting details about Kahn Cordant of Curatif in Paris. Jeanette Poole and Barron Kaide were continuing to learn more about Regis Volt of Genez in Brussels. And Kara Sterrio and Alberto Fresco were completing the search of Karsen Ojin's castle in the Italian Alps.

"We got a breakthrough with the case thanks to Sarah Graff," he began. "She's uncovered a hidden bank account in the Caribbean that shows deposits from each of the pharmas you've been investigating. Plus, there are payments to the senators and the criminals. I've been in touch with FBI Agent Myles DeLong, who's going to get a search warrant. This will allow him to legally access the information Sarah discovered."

"That's amazing, Chief!" Sterrio said. "How long do you think it will take DeLong to get the warrant completed?"

"He's going to start immediately. If he has to, he'll pull

some strings to get it done quickly. This is an enormous case for him and his agents, so he's eager to get it solved."

* * *

AFTER ENDING the phone call with Chief Aritan, Agent DeLong initiated the search warrant process with a Nevis judge, which took much longer than he hoped. Finally, he prevailed. The FBI learned, however, that the bank was not going to be easy to deal with. The FBI was forced to secure a $100,000 bond to prove that their investigation was legitimate. Once again they waited longer than DeLong had hoped. Eventually, the team prevailed against the difficult bank president, Augusto Tofwin.

"Very well, Agent," Tofwin grimaced. "I reluctantly grant the FBI access to the account of OPC. This will damage my bank's reputation, but your evidence of the company's wrongdoing has been persuasive."

DeLong was able to gain the information he and his people were seeking. "Your confidentiality regarding our investigation is critical. Do not, under any circumstances, alert the people involved in this account. Is that understood?"

"I agree to maintain confidentiality, sir," Tofwin agreed with a look of disgust.

DeLong and his team left the bank and took a flight from the small island of Nevis back to D.C. with the evidence in hand.

CHAPTER 22

When the FBI team returned to its offices, Agent Myles DeLong assigned Andrew Friese and Barbara Dwyer to work together to bring the CEOs of the two U.S. pharmas to justice. They would initially visit Rubin Bisch at PharMax in Tampa Bay. After his arrest, the agents were to bring him to D.C. to stand trial. Afterward, they'd pursue Barron Lidst of ReMedin in New York. Following their visits to the two pharmas, they needed to locate Yao Min. Since the agents had three addresses for the criminal, they knew that capturing him could be a challenge. Cho En Dai and his partner were already arrested for the kidnapping of Dr. Milt Lennium.

DeLong soon contacted Interpol Chief Aritan with the report. "The bank president created some roadblocks for our access to the OPC account, but we prevailed. I've got the tangible evidence in hand and will send you a copy showing their deposits, withdrawals, payments, and the people involved."

"Excellent, Myles!" Aritan roared. "As soon as it arrives and I've distributed it to the teams, I'll have them move forward here in Europe."

That evening, Agents Friese and Dwyer took a flight to the Tampa Airport. Upon their arrival, they reached the hotel where the FBI had booked two rooms in advance. The next morning, they met for breakfast. Barb and Andy had evidence that the company joined Ojin's lobby to preserve its diabetes medication's competitive position. The possibility of NuPharma's drug being approved by the FDA sent chills through the board of directors and key shareholders including Karsen Ojin.

After taking a few sips from a mug of steaming black coffee, Andy Friese commented on their duties, "Okay, Barb, we've got the warrant for the search of PharMax's financial records."

"Right. And we've got all the evidence we need to take him back to D.C. to stand trial," she replied as she stabbed her fork into a piece of sausage that remained on her plate. "Are we missing anything?"

"We'll hold him in his office until we've got a copy of the company's financial data," Friese confirmed. "Then we should be ready to go."

After checking out of their hotel, they drove to the PharMax headquarters, parked, and went to the reception desk. Agent Dwyer pulled out her FBI badge and announced that they needed to see Rubin Bisch.

"Oh, my! I'm sorry, but I've been told that Mr. Bisch is in a meeting, and he doesn't want to be disturbed," the receptionist responded with obvious concern.

"Ma'am, if he's in, we need to see him," Dwyer pressed the young woman. "What floor's he on?"

"You can find him in his office on the fifth floor. Shall I notify him you're here to see him?"

"No, thank you. We'll introduce ourselves at his office," Dwyer answered as they left to take the elevator.

As soon as the two agents moved away from her desk, the young receptionist phoned her friend, the CEO's secretary, and whispered, "Hey, there's two FBI agents coming up to visit Mr. Bisch. They didn't want me to let him know but thought I should tell you."

"Oh, my! What in the world do they want?" the woman answered as her skin began feeling clammy.

"They didn't say."

The secretary buzzed her boss and told him. "You've got FBI people coming to see you, sir."

"What the hell?" Bisch snapped and hung up. "Excuse me, you have to leave," he told two people who were in his office. When they departed, he opened a desk drawer and looked at his pistol. Thinking further, he closed it. Just then, there was a knock at his office. A man and a woman came in and closed the door behind them. Bisch, mid-fifties with thinning gray hair and wire-rimmed glasses, shrank down in his expensive leather chair. "Uh, w-what's the idea of barging in on me like this?" he stammered, slowly raising his hand to grasp the drawer handle.

Agent Friese pulled out his badge and stated his purpose, "Mr. Rubin Bisch?"

"Yes. What do you want?" Bisch sheepishly responded.

"We're here because you're a person of interest in a murder and kidnapping case involving NuPharma Corporation," Agent Friese began. "We have a warrant for the last five years of your financial records. Please call the person from your accounting department who can assist us.

"I-I'm not sure if she's here today," Bisch stalled.

"We need to speak to someone who can get us what we want. Call her now," Dwyer demanded.

Slowly, Bisch lifted the receiver from his desk phone and punched in three buttons. "Come to my office immediately." After he hung up, he brought his right hand down, and slid it next to the desk drawer handle. He glanced back and forth from the drawer to the agents as they waited.

A few minutes later, a knock came at the door. Bisch shouted for the visitor to enter. He introduced the woman as Misty Teycker, head of accounting. As Dwyer pulled a document from her briefcase, she explained they had a search warrant to access the past five years of the company's P&L statements.

"Well, uh, okay," Misty mumbled as she glanced at Bisch for his approval and then at the agents. "It might take some time. Will a CD with the information be satisfactory?"

"That will work," Dwyer responded. "Please do what you can to expedite the process." Looking at Friese, she advised that she'd follow Teycker while she burned the CD. He nodded.

"Also, Mr. Bisch, you're being charged for your part in the payment of money to the criminals in the murder and kidnapping case I described," Andy explained. "You're coming with us." As soon as Friese made the assertion, he was momentarily distracted by posters on the walls showing the company as a sponsor of the Bucs and the

Rays. During the few seconds Friese looked away, Bisch slowly opened the desk drawer and grabbed the pistol. He cocked it and pointed it at the FBI agent.

"You won't be taking me anywhere today," Bisch barked defiantly. Friese spun his head around to see the CEO holding a loaded firearm, pointed directly at him. Seconds later, Bisch raised the pistol just below his chin.

Friese screamed, "No, Bisch! No!"

It was too late. The man pulled the trigger. Half of his skull and brains exploded against the mahogany credenza behind him. The gun dropped from his hand. What remained of his head slumped to the side. "What the hell, Bisch!" Friese yelled, stunned by the shocking horror.

Barb Dwyer stormed into the office and shrieked. "Oh my God, Andy! What the hell happened?"

"I-I don't know. Before I ordered him to stand to be cuffed, I glanced at the posters on the wall. All of a sudden, he announced he wasn't coming with us. I turned. He had a gun pointed at me. Then he pointed at himself."

With the sound of gunfire, panicked staffers quickly flocked outside the CEO's office. His secretary poked her head inside and wailed.

"Call an ambulance and the local police," Friese ordered loudly, as he shook his head in disbelief. The secretary turned and ran sobbing to her desk to make the calls.

The blast of sirens was soon heard outside the PharMax headquarters. Agent Dwyer hurried to the elevator and met the local police and the EMTs, as they rushed inside. She showed her FBI badge and quickly described the hideous scene in the CEO's office on the fifth floor. The police officers and med techs gasped at the news, then followed

Dwyer upstairs. When they arrived, they waded through the crowd of staffers who'd gathered, many of whom were sobbing hysterically.

Agent Friese displayed his badge and the search warrant. He then repeated the details of the suicide. The EMTs inspected the body. The police officer was busy making notes of the grisly spectacle before them. Friese explained the crimes behind their visit. Dwyer returned to the accounting office, as Misty was finishing burning the CD. Tears streamed down her cheeks. Several minutes later, she completed her task and handed Dwyer the disk in a plastic case. The agent thanked her and returned to the crime scene. As the locals continued to inspect the office, the two agents moved further away for privacy.

"Sure didn't expect something like this when I was eating my eggs this morning, Barb," Andy commented. "How long do you suppose we'll need to stick around?"

"I'm going to phone DeLong." She pulled out her cell and made the call. He picked up fairly quickly when he saw it was her.

"What's the latest, Dwyer?" he asked with interest. She detailed the horrific events that just took place and informed him they had the financial statements on a CD.

"I'll be a damned, Dwyer. Let me speak to Friese." She passed the phone to her partner. "Sorry to hear about the shitstorm you just witnessed, Andy," DeLong groaned. "How you holding up?"

"Yes, sir. I was stunned, but after the initial shock, I'm doing okay," Friese lamented. "How long do you think we'll need to stick around?"

"See what the local PD wants to do. It sounds like an

obvious case of suicide. Happened pretty damn fast, it sounds like."

"It did, indeed, sir," Andy agreed. "Okay, I'll see if they need me to confirm a report, then we should be good to fly back."

After ending the call with DeLong, Friese spoke with the officer on the scene who had the documents with him. Andy quickly described his memory of the events. When the policeman completed the paperwork, the FBI agent signed his statement. Soon thereafter, he and Dwyer left to catch the flight back to D.C.

Upon their return to D.C., Dwyer and Friese met with DeLong in his office. "You never know how someone will react when the pressure's on," Myles commented. "Doesn't sound like there was much you could do to stop the guy. You were lucky. He could have pulled the trigger, and they'd have been taking you out in a body bag."

"Uh, yeah. Have to say I'm obviously relieved it didn't go that way." Andy frowned. "There wasn't anything I could do to stop the man. I should have cuffed him immediately. Just didn't imagine him to be that desperate and unhinged."

"Hindsight is twenty-twenty as they say. Next time you'll make the right decision," DeLong replied. "Guess you'll be heading to New York City to visit with Barron Lidst of ReMedin?"

"Yes sir," Dwyer responded. "Got a flight in the morning."

CHAPTER 23

Interpol partners Kara Sterrio and Alberto Fresco had spent the past week searching Karsen Ojin's castle. There wasn't much evidence to tie the man to the pharmaceutical lobby or the secret off-shore bank account on the island of Nevis. They saw that Ojin had removed his computer hard drives and taken any other devices that might have incriminating information.

Carefully inspecting all the nooks and crannies in his study, Fresco noticed a wooden panel behind his desk that looked suspicious. It appeared to extend farther out than the others near it. Pushing on the various edges of the molding, one piece of polished wood popped out. "A-ha!" Alberto shouted. "Kara, check this out!" When he opened the door panel, he discovered an electronic device or receiver inside. Reaching in, he lifted it out with wires attached behind it.

"What the hell's that?" Sterrio wondered as she joined him. Inspecting the buttons on its face, it looked like a video transmitter. "Could he have wirelessly connected this to his computer for conducting remote video conferences? Let's take this back to Rome. Maybe Sarah can identify the links to the transmissions."

"Right!" Alberto agreed. "Hopefully it will connect the people involved with the off-shore account."

Before leaving, they thanked Chief of Police Gino Ganti and his men for their help. They also expressed their condolences again for the officer who was killed during their attack. After packing up at the hotel in Trento, they drove back to Rome carrying the video transmitter they suspected would provide more answers. During their ride, they phoned Chief Aritan to provide an update.

Aritan was happy when the documentation from the Nevis bank account arrived earlier from Agent DeLong. He had it copied and emailed to his people in the field. The chief reminded them to get search warrants and go after the pharma CEOs in question. They were all implicated.

* * *

In Rome, Bella Gamba and Enzo Ferno had become acquainted with Imelda Broglio, the CEO of Drogari. Ferno had previously introduced himself at a bar and invited her to dance. She adored the attention and asked him to contact her later for a dinner date. Gamba had also disguised herself as a cleaning lady at the Drogari offices and planted audio devices to capture any conversations. Unfortunately, Broglio was careful not to divulge her relationship with Ojin.

"Okay, Enzo," Gamba began with a grin, "we've got our

evidence, warrant, and orders to arrest Broglio. How would you like to play this? You're her dancing sweetheart, so that's one way to get her alone."

Ferno chuckled. He thought for a moment. "I'll feel a little slimy using my flirtation to trap her. But it would make things easier to meet at a restaurant or bar to arrest her. I can't imagine there would be any guards nearby. After her arrest, we can return to her office, search for more evidence, and request the company's financial statements. There should be clues to the funds that were sent to the Caribbean bank account."

"She'll never trust another man again after you set her up for an arrest." Gamba smiled. "Hey, she's a criminal and part of the conspiracy. You're the undercover guy doing your job, even if it's not the *undercover* she had in mind."

After collecting his thoughts, Ferno pulled out Broglio's phone number and stared at it for a few moments. He thought of the places she liked to go to dance and decided on the Sheket night club, located between Piazza Venezia and the spot where Caesar fell to his bloody death. *Maybe this will be the most appropriate,* he thought to himself. It was for an older crowd, quite exclusive, and played the type of music she loved.

Ferno punched in Broglio's phone number. She picked up after the second ring. "Hello, Imelda! It's Enzo. I hope you remember me. We met a week ago at the Vinile and enjoyed dancing."

"Oh, yes, Enzo!" she answered. "I've been hoping you'd call. How are you?"

"Doing fine, thank you. I trust all is well with you," he continued. "We had such a lovely time dancing that I was wondering if you'd care to meet me at another spot in town, the Sheket?"

"I'd really love to, Enzo. I'm very familiar with it. This weekend looks to be rather busy, but let's try the following Saturday if it works for your schedule."

"Perfect, say nine o'clock?" he responded.

"I'll look forward to it. Thank you so much for reaching out to me. I had so much fun the last time."

After the call, Ferno joined Gamba and described the conversation he had with Broglio. "We're set for a week from Saturday. She'd already accepted an invitation for this weekend."

"You didn't have any problem reeling her in, you charmer!" Gamba retorted. "What can we do to nab her before then? We could simply go to her house and pick her up."

"Check your audio surveillance and see if there's any clue to what she's doing this Saturday," Ferno advised.

"Good idea. I'll let you know if I learn anything." Bella soon logged into her computer monitoring application that recorded Broglio's conversations. The officer had kept up with them but hadn't listened to any in the past few days. Clicking on the last missed date, she put on her headphones and listened to the tracks. Most of it was mundane business. Imelda was soon heard taking a phone call that intrigued Gamba. It was apparently her banker, asking if she'd attend the opening of a new play at the renowned Teatro Olimpico. The offer instantly thrilled Broglio and she agreed. He would pick her up in his limo at seven Saturday. Gamba replayed it, then called Ferno in to listen.

When he heard the track, he thought for a moment, looking at his partner.

"I like it," he responded, then smiled, "but I'm a little jealous. Okay. Where do we pick her up? At her home or the theatre?"

"It'll certainly be less chaotic at her house," Bella answered. "It's hard to imagine the banker will feel like impeding her arrest."

"I agree," Ferno confirmed. "Should we bring some backup just in case?"

"Sure. I'll ask a couple of our people to follow us."

* * *

THE INTERPOL OFFICERS realized they didn't have to wait until Saturday to pick up Broglio. But they assumed she'd have security in her home and didn't want to attract a police response. The woman would be leaving home attended by her banker friend on Saturday evening. They'd nab her then.

Ferno and Gamba arrived near the CEO's home in an unmarked vehicle, followed by a pair of their fellow Interpol officers. At 7 p.m., a sleek Mercedes limo pulled up in front of Broglio's place. A driver got out and opened the door for the banker, who walked to the door, knocked, and waited. Moments later, the man entered. In the meantime, Ferno and Gamba had left their car and hid behind shrubbery.

Shortly thereafter, Imelda and her friend walked from the home toward the limo. Enzo and Bella nodded to each other and began moving briskly toward the couple.

"Excuse us, Ms. Broglio," Bella announced as she flashed her badge. "We're with Interpol and have orders to arrest you for your role in crimes committed in the United States regarding an FDA clinical trial. Come with us, please."

"What's the meaning of this!" the banker shouted and tried to shield Imelda, who shrieked.

Broglio glanced at Enzo and recognized him. "Oh no, Enzo! What in the world?"

Without notice, the limo driver pulled a pistol from a shoulder holster and barked, "Hold it right there! Put your hands in the air." He nodded for the banker and Imelda to get into the vehicle, opening the door with his free hand.

Stunned by the driver's actions, Ferno and Gamba glanced at each other and didn't argue. They raised their arms and watched as the couple hurried inside the limo. The driver rushed to jump behind the wheel and start the engine. Before he could accelerate, the other Interpol car raced to block the limo's exit. The driver quickly reversed the Mercedes, spun around the Interpol car, and sped down the street.

"Mama mia, Bella!" Ferno yelled. "I didn't see that coming. Let's go." They ran to their car, jumped in, and followed the other Interpol vehicle as it chased the limo. Both police cars punched on their sirens and flashers, pursuing the banker's driver who ran stop signs and fishtailed around turns.

"Is that guy insane or what?" Bella shouted, shaking her head. The pursuit continued for several minutes. Suddenly, during another reckless turn, the limo lost control and spun before hitting a light pole. The man tried to restart

FORMULA FOR A FELONY

the engine, but it wouldn't turn over. Both Interpol vehicles arrived and stopped in front of and behind the lunatic driver. Ferno, Gamba and their partners jumped out and drew their weapons at those inside the limo.

"All right, out!" Ferno yelled. "Keep your hands where we can see them. As the three slowly opened their doors and exited, the defeated driver no longer held his revolver. One of the Interpol cops found it laying on the front seat. Broglio was helped out by the banker, who had cut his head during the crash.

"Enzo, you're a damn fraud!" Imelda shouted, as she wept, holding the arm of the banker.

One of the Interpol cops called the Rome police to assist. They handcuffed and searched the driver, banker and Broglio. Gamba escorted Imelda to their car and directed her inside. Ferno drove them back to their station, where Gamba fingerprinted, booked, and locked the woman in a cell. The Drogari CEO remained quiet during their drive as she whimpered. Occasionally, Broglio hissed Italian curse words at the pair.

The other Interpol officers brought the banker and his driver to the station for their part in an effort to resist arrest. Rome police took care of the wrecked Mercedes.

"Hope you don't beat yourself up too much over Broglio, Enzo," Gamba told her partner with a smile. "Sometimes love can be unkind."

"Call of duty, Bella. Call of duty," he laughed.

CHAPTER 24

The next assignment for FBI Agents Friese and Dwyer was a visit to Barron Lidst, the CEO of ReMedin, based in New York City. The agents flew to LaGuardia Airport, rented a vehicle, and drove to their hotel with a search warrant in hand. From the background they'd studied about Lidst, they knew his family had started the business decades ago. Barron was now the majority shareholder. A man from Europe name Karsen Ojin owned the next highest number of shares. The company's premier product was used to treat heart disease.

As Friese and Dwyer motored through Manhattan, they complained about the traffic. The agents would have preferred taking a taxi, but they needed a vehicle to take Lidst to the airport with them. Finally locating a parking space, the partners entered the tower that housed ReMedin's headquarters. At the initial guard station in the lobby, they presented their badges and had to pass through a security checkpoint. Friese showed another guard his badge and the search warrant. The guard quickly allowed the agents to proceed to the tenth floor. After they arrived and left the elevator, signs directed Andy and Barb to the company's receptionist.

"Looks like a hell of a lot of security in this place, Barb," Andy commented as they noticed several well-built men in suits who appeared to be packing shoulder holsters with weapons.

"Yeah, I saw that too," Barb replied, as they approached a woman behind a fashionable desk. A large sign behind her announced the pharma's name and logo.

"Welcome to ReMedin!" the attractive young woman intoned. "How may I help you?"

"Yes, we're here to see Mr. Lidst," Andy began. "We're with the FBI and have some questions we'd like to ask him."

"Oh, I see," she replied and scanned her computer to check the CEO's schedule. "I'm very sorry, but it appears Mr. Lidst will be a bit late today. He had an appointment outside of the office. If you'd care to have a seat, he's expected to arrive soon. Please help yourself to some refreshments."

The agents glanced at each other, thanked the receptionist, then ambled to the coffee service that also offered a selection of pastries. "These look tasty," Andy said, as he picked out a blueberry muffin to go with his coffee.

The FBI partners soon spotted Lidst walking briskly from the elevator toward a hallway that led to his office. Two more beefy security guards accompanied the CEO. Andy and Barb rose to get his attention, but he didn't look their way. They followed behind the three men.

"Excuse us, Mr. Lidst," Andy shouted to get their attention. As the trio turned, the FBI agents pulled out their badges and introduced themselves. "Mr. Lidst, may we have a word with you?"

"What's this all about?" Lidst demanded, as he and his guards stopped. "I've got a busy schedule."

"Would you prefer to discuss our inquiry here in the hallway or in your office?" Barb shot back.

"If you must. Follow me," Lidst snapped, as he led the others to his inner sanctum.

When they reached his office, Lidst turned to face the agents with a scowl. "Let's hear it," he barked.

Friese pulled the search warrant from his briefcase and presented it to the CEO. "Mr. Lidst, we have overwhelming evidence that you're associated with a group that's behind the murder of an FDA commissioner and the kidnapping of an executive at NuPharma Corporation. You will need to come with us to D.C. to stand trial." Lidst was dumbfounded.

The CEO's two goons reached for their weapons, but Barb grabbed her sidearm before they could get to theirs. "That wouldn't be a wise move unless you want to spend time behind bars!" she thundered. The guards stood their ground.

"This search warrant entitles us to access your financial records. Please contact someone who can provide us with a CD showing the past five years of your statements," Andy ordered.

"This is outlandish!" Lidst shouted back. "What sort of damn evidence do you have that shows we're involved in any such thing?"

Andy reached inside his briefcase again, sifting through folders. He took out a few papers and handed them to the CEO. "These documents from the Nevis bank clearly identify your organization as a contributor to a pharmaceutical lobby that's behind these crimes." As Lidst read the evidence, the man seemed to grow weak, needing to take a seat in a chair near his desk.

"I-I don't know where this came from...or how you got it," Lidst stammered as perspiration beaded on his balding head. "It must be a mistake." The guards took a step back and didn't intervene.

"We followed the money, Mr. Lidst," Barb smirked. "Now, about your financial records. Please call someone who can provide the CD."

The CEO rose from the chair and moved to his desk. Picking up the receiver on his phone, he punched a number and requested the person to come to his office. Moments later, a middle-aged man knocked and entered. "Gus, these people are with the FBI and have a warrant to get a copy of the past five years of our financials. Can you make a CD?"

"Uh...yes, sir," Gus mumbled as he glanced at the scene in his boss's office.

"My name's Agent Dwyer, Gus. I'll accompany you. Let's go." The two left as Andy remained with the others.

"You guards are excused. Please go," Andy demanded.

Lidst nodded for his guards to leave.

Andy then ordered Lidst to stand and turn around. "Place your hands on your head, sir," he insisted, then grabbed them to cuff the CEO.

"This is a mistake. A set-up. You won't get away with this!" Lidst scowled.

When Barb and Gus reached the accounting office, he reluctantly sat at a desk, logged into his computer, then tapped on the keyboard. In a flash, a list of statements by years displayed on the monitor. Reaching into his desk, he grabbed a CD and inserted it into his computer. He selected the past five years of the financial data and loaded them on a CD. Moments later when it was finished, he ejected the CD, wrote on its surface, stuck it in a jewel case, and handed it to Barb. "Will that be all, agent?" Gus asked with a frown.

"Thank you. I think this should do it," she shot back, then left to rejoin her partner. "Okay, Andy, I've got what we need. Ready to go?"

"We're leaving now, Mr. Lidst," Agent Friese ordered, then escorted him from his office with Agent Dwyer leading the way. As the three of them made their way to the elevator, the CEO looked down at the floor. A crowd of people observed in horror.

Suddenly, the overweight Lidst screamed, bent over, and slumped down to the floor. He exhibited anguish on his scrunched-up face, rolling back and forth. Andy undid his cuffs. The man grabbed his left arm. "H-heart a-attack!" Lidst groaned. Several of those in the area shrieked.

"Is there a doctor here?" Andy yelled, as he looked up at the crowd gathering close by. A woman edged through the group and announced that she was the staff physician.

"Let me examine him!" she replied anxiously, kneeling on the floor, probing his neck, then pulling out her stethoscope to check his heart. "He's definitely having an attack. Call for an ambulance! Did you take your pills today, Mr. Lidst?" she asked calmly.

"No!" Lidst sputtered as he squirmed in pain. "I got interrupted."

"Where are they?" the doc inquired, as she continued checking the man's vitals.

"In my pocket!" Lidst slowly growled. The physician patted his coat pocket and located the vial, reached in, and opened it.

"Get me a cup of water," the woman yelled.

The receptionist rushed to provide the water. The doctor put two pills on Lidst's tongue and lifted his head to take a few sips. Moments later, the CEO seemed to relax.

Just then, two EMTs appeared at the elevator with a gurney. They quickly began giving Lidst oxygen and gently eased him onto the stretcher. The doctor hurriedly gave them a description of his medical condition. As the paramedics began to leave, Barb asked which hospital they were taking him. She gently advised them of the situation and asked if she could ride along. They agreed. Andy said that he'd meet her there.

After the ambulance arrived at the hospital, medical staff rushed Lidst to the ER, where he was treated for his heart attack. He was soon moved to a private room. Barb stayed close and watched from the hallway as nurses cared for him. Out of breath, Andy arrived and rushed to his partner, eager to hear how their new prisoner was doing.

"He seems to be okay. Not sure how long he'll need to be out of commission," Barb explained.

"We can wait a few days for his recovery. If necessary, the agency will airlift him to D.C. for further treatment to wait for his trial. We'll see what the attending physician tells us," Andy commented.

The FBI agents hoped to get an update from the hospital doctor. Finally, a young man stepped toward them to provide a status report. "Mr. Lidst is resting comfortably and should be fine to discharge from the hospital tomorrow."

"Thank you, Doctor," Barb began. "You may have heard that he needs to be taken to D.C. for a trial. Is he okay to fly?"

"Shouldn't be a problem as long as he maintains his medication regimen."

As soon as the hospital released the CEO, the agents drove him to the airport and boarded their flight. Throughout the journey, Lidst maintained his medication protocol along with a dour disposition.

CHAPTER 25

After stocking up with supplies for the Berlin condo provided by Ivy Ning, Karsen Ojin and his paramour, Fon Tazi, were getting restless. Ning had provided Ojin with the name of an underworld Chinese contact who could provide them with weapons and new identities. Ojin phoned Rico Ning and described his requirements. Ning asked the man to meet him the next day in Berlin's Little Asia.

Ojin and Tazi parked and found their way to an address above a Chinese restaurant. When they took the stairs to the second floor, a small man greeted the couple and invited them to be seated at a table.

"Yes, Ivy told me what you wanted. I'll do my best to provide the items you need," Rico announced. "By the way, I understand we may be related." Ojin acted surprised. "Let's see, I have three sidearms you may like." The man turned to lift three separate handguns from a shelf and returned to place them on the table in front of the visitors.

"I have German Walther P-38, a Luger 08, and a Mauser C96. Also plenty of ammunition." Rico stood back as Ojin and Tazi inspected the firearms. After several minutes, they nodded and said they'd take all three.

"Do you have another Walther P-38?" Tazi asked.

"Um, yes, I believe so," Rico turned again and searched his shelves. After locating the weapon, he placed it on the table with the others.

Tazi and Ojin nodded to each other and told Ning these would suit their needs. "And we would like to get new identities. We understand you can set those up for us," Ojin requested.

"Yes, yes," Rico responded with a smile. "What names, please?"

"I'll be Justin Elias. She'll be Kamela Kazi."

"Fine, fine. Please step over here, so I take your photos for new passports and licenses," Rico offered. The two guests followed him and went through the process as Ning stood behind a camera and snapped their images. When they'd completed their requirements and Ojin paid the fees, Rico suggested they have a meal at the restaurant below. "Excellent food! Please enjoy!"

Noon was approaching, so they thanked Rico and had lunch as their host recommended. After the meal, they discussed their next challenging steps with the Consortium. One of Drogari's executives sent Ojin an encrypted message alerting him Interpol had arrested Imelda Broglio. Later, he received similar information from people at PharMax and ReMedin in the U.S. Their own CEOs had experienced tragic events. Rubin Bisch committed suicide and Barron Lidst suffered a heart attack before being taken to D.C. for trial. FBI agents led both of the raids.

"It's not looking good, Fon," Karsen moaned, as he sipped his hot tea. "What the hell can we do to keep my investments from tanking? And who will be the next CEO to be hauled in? Maybe Interpol has identified all of them."

"These are certainly setbacks, K," Tazi agreed, as she played with her fortune cookie. She cracked it open, pulled out the message on the small piece of paper, and read it out loud. *"You don't have to be faster than the bear, you just have to be faster than the slowest guy running from it."* Fon looked up at K and grinned. "What the hell, K, we're faster than the slowest damn guy, aren't we?"

Ojin smiled and shook his head. "We've got to get pressure on the docs NuPharma's hiring for the video evidence to be shown at the next senate hearing. Do you think your man can find out who they are and put the fear of God in them?"

"I'll reach out to him and see if he's game," Tazi replied, as she took a bite of her cookie. "This could be more difficult than intimidating those FDA docs."

When they returned to their Berlin condo, Tazi phoned Yao Min. Both used new burner phones to avoid being monitored by a wiretap. She explained the recent complicated circumstances and asked her man if he could get to the docs who'd be giving videotaped testimony. What could be done to stop them from testifying that the heart and diabetes patients had maintained their newfound health from RGB101?

"This could present a challenge, Ms. Tazi. I'm not sure how to locate these people since they will be spread out across the U.S. Let me consider your request before I agree," Yao responded, as he scratched his small goatee.

"Understand, Yao. Time is critical, as always," Tazi said in closing.

* * *

NUPHARMA HAD a list of all the patients in the third phase of its clinical trials for both the heart and diabetes tests. The people in the studies were in a variety of cities. As a result, the video documentation of the doctors with their patients was going to be a logistical nightmare. "This is what I recommend," Dr. Milton Lennium offered to NuPharma's CEO and its attorney. "I've assigned four project managers for each study. We'll train them to take the videos to complement their medical knowledge. Each will have a corresponding project coordinator here in Boston to schedule their visits. We'll need to get authorization to videotape the patients with their physicians. This will be a tedious process, but it will verify the health of those who've taken our medication."

"You've certainly given this a lot of thought, Milt," CEO Jack McCabe replied from his hidden location in Indianapolis. "It'll be expensive, but it's the only way we'll get enough legitimate testimonials from the physicians and their patients. We have to refute the lies leveled against our product in the senate hearings."

"I like it, Milt," Christopher Masse added. "When can you get started?"

"We're lining up dates with the docs and their patients," Lennium explained. "There'll be lots of airfares, hotel rooms, and meals to expense. As the project managers complete their assigned visits, we'll take all the videos to a studio and edit them together. There'll also be a narrator who'll describe the statistical summary of the results. I'm hoping we can get the visits finished in three weeks. The editing will take another week after that."

"I'm all for it, Milt," Jack beamed. "I'll be eager to see the results."

"With all the dirty business we've encountered, I'm hoping the people behind the pharmaceutical lobby won't figure out a way to obstruct our efforts," Chris chimed in. "I don't think they have our patient lists and can't imagine they'll know when these visits will take place.

"I've been meaning to tell you about the progress the FBI and Interpol have made," the attorney continued. "FBI agent DeLong gave me this information. The Interpol's computer hacker extraordinaire discovered a secret bank account in the Caribbean with deposits from the six pharmaceutical companies we've heard about. There've been significant payments to Senators Emon Barras and Stuart Pitts. As you know, they're the guys who've been supportive of the false information we've witnessed at the hearings.

"There've also been payments to the criminals who we suspect committed the FDA commissioner's murder and Milt's kidnapping. Since these deposits and distributions were discovered, the FBI has arrested the CEOs of the two U.S. pharmas. In fact, one man committed suicide. The other had a heart attack as he was being arrested."

"Oh, my God!" Jack responded with sudden surprise. "It

sounds like the walls are caving in on these people. What do you hear about those in Europe?"

"As I recall, Interpol is in the process of arresting the four CEOs in Europe. They also think they have Karsen Ojin and Fon Tazi on the run," Chris commented.

"Do you believe it's safe for me to return to my normal routine?" Jack asked. "I'd love to move back to my house and visit my Lake Maxinkuckee cottage."

"I'll feel better if you give it a few more weeks to see if they capture Ojin and Tazi – they're the ones who've been giving the orders to the criminals," Chris said. "I also understand that Interpol is looking into more evidence that will prove the two senators are guilty of more than we suspect."

"Won't that be a sweet turn of events?" Jack grinned. "Milt, keep us posted on the teams out in the field."

"Will do, Jack," Lennium replied. "Thanks for the update, Chris."

* * *

IN THE WEEKS THAT FOLLOWED, the eight project managers hopscotched across the country. The video testimonials came off beautifully. They showed the primary care physicians confirming that the clinical trial patients were doing better than expected after taking RGB101. The doctors were so enthusiastic in their endorsements, they were eager to access the drug for their other patients. The few problems that existed were the result of a doctor or patient having a last-minute, unexpected conflict.

Most of the scenes had the physician in the foreground

after the patient examination and went something like this. The doc would turn to the camera and describe how well the person was feeling. "Without question, this drug has done wonders for him. I didn't expect he'd being doing so well after such a short time on it, but the results speak for themselves. Bravo NuPharma."

Despite the challenges of completing the assignments in the time allotted, the product managers returned with all their segments in hand. Milt arranged for the video company to organize all the components and begin editing. Even though they weren't able to see every patient, the project managers met with a majority of them. The only ones who hadn't been successfully treated were the few suffering from comorbidities. Milt was surprised his drug didn't cure those medical problems as well.

When the video company completed its assignment, Milt and some of the project managers visited the studio to view the DVD. The NuPharma people were ecstatic as they viewed the entire presentation. When it was over, they cheered their appreciation for all the hard work. Before leaving, they requested multiple copies. They planned to ship some to Jack and Chris that day. Milt knew they'd be thrilled with the finished product.

CHAPTER 26

Interpol Officers Kara Sterrio and Alberto Fresco returned to their Rome headquarters. They brought the video equipment they discovered hidden inside a wooden panel behind Karsen Ojin's desk. Alberto walked into Sarah Graff's office and asked if she could do her magic. "You probably heard about this device we found at the castle near Trento."

"Yes! Kara told me you wanted to find out if there were signals in its memory that would correspond to the locations of our suspects in the pharmaceutical lobby," she answered. "I'm not sure this is something I can do, but I'll explore."

"Thanks, Graff. I'm sure you'll figure it out," Fresco smiled.

After he left her office, Sarah studied the system to determine what remnants of previous video communications might still exist. Searching online, she found the schematic for the product. Sitting back, the young woman took a long sip from her energy drink and read through the details. *If I can break the password, I'll be able to see what's there,* Sarah determined. It didn't take her long to do it.

The brilliant hacker discovered that the system had a built-in analytics tool that provided information about the people who'd connected with Ojin. Among other details, she could see the location of the viewers. There was also information about the time each participant watched or was online with the video signal. From what she could tell, the episodes were like Zoom meetings, with eight participants. *Isn't this interesting,* Sarah exclaimed to herself. *Let's see where these dogs are from.*

Using an algorithm from the analytics tool, she was able to identify each person's location. *Okay, we've got people in the U.S. and Europe.* She found two in D.C., one in Tampa Bay, and one in New York City. *Hmmm.* There were four in Europe including Rome, Vienna, Paris and Brussels. *How about that! Locations of all the people we've been investigating.*

Excited to nail the geographic part of the puzzle, she contacted Fresco. "You'll be interested to see what I've found!" Sarah reported on the phone.

When he hurried in to join her, she described the process she went through to discover the analytics. Once she had that, the locations came easily.

"Wow! That's incredible, Sarah! You're the best!" Fresco shouted. "Remind me to give you a big raise."

"I won't argue with that, Alberto!" she chuckled.

Fresco buzzed Sterrio who quickly came to Graff's office. Upon her arrival, Sarah described what she uncovered, especially the locations of the Zoom-type meetings that took place periodically.

"This is terrific, Sarah!" Kara beamed. "We probably know who everyone is except the two in D.C. Could they be the unfriendly senators the NuPharma people encountered at the FDA hearings?"

"I'd put money on it," Fresco said. "Is there any way of getting more information about these participants? Can you identify phone numbers, email addresses...anything like that?"

"Let me work on it a little longer and I'll know for sure. Initially, I could only find the locations of the people."

"Well, this is great. If there's more we can use as evidence, especially about the senators, it could put nails in their coffins," Kara said. Moments later, the two officers let the cyber detective get back to work.

Each of these people had to use their computers for a link to the video. That means there must have been a virtual private network address for each of them. Sarah plugged in the algorithm again to backtrack to the sources for the viewers. The two in D.C. used *.gov* for their top-level domain or the right part of an address. Most of the others were using *.com* or a country designation.

"I got a little closer, especially to the D.C. addresses. They were both *.gov*. Has to be the senators," she told Fresco on the phone.

"Excellent!" Alberto shouted. "I knew you could do it. I'll let Chief Aritan know so he can reach out to the FBI." When he finished meeting with Graff, he phoned Aritan and gave him the details of what Sarah discovered.

"Holy smokes, Fresco!" the chief barked. "I don't think there's anything Sarah can't do. The FBI will be interested to know this important bit of information. I'm not sure if it will hold up in court, but it would certainly give them enough ammunition to bring the two senators in for questioning." As he relit a Columbian cigar, he dialed his friend, Myles DeLong.

"Hello, Sam!" DeLong replied when he recognized Aritan's voice. "What's the good word from Innsbruck?"

"I may have told you that my people discovered a hidden video device in Ojin's castle. They took it with them to Rome and our computer expert ran a diagnostics analysis of it. She uncovered information related to the people who joined in Zoom-type meetings. In each case, there were eight people. The locations matched the six pharmaceutical companies. There were two more from D.C. who used a website address ending in *.gov*. Do you suppose those could be the senators who've antagonized the NuPharma people?"

"Well, I'll be, Sam!" DeLong exclaimed. "It has to be. Can't say that'd hold up in court, but it should make them nervous. Might be enough for us to question them."

"That's exactly what I thought," Aritan responded. "Good luck putting pressure on them. The chief sat back in his chair and relit his cigar. *The walls are closing in on them,* he said to himself.

* * *

IN BRUSSELS, Jeanette Poole and Barron Kaide were informed that Regis Volt and Genez were connected to the secret bank account on Nevis Island in the Caribbean. Even though Karsen Ojin had set up the account, the six pharmaceutical companies made deposits to it. Payments to criminals in the United States using the account funds were evidence of their involvement. Moreover, the video device showed the locations of the participants in meetings with Ojin. Now the Interpol officers had to determine the best way to arrest the CEO of Genez.

"Should we simply go to his house and arrest him, Barron?" Jeanette asked her partner. "Or I could use the ruse of the auto racing sponsorship to meet him somewhere to capture him?"

"Your second idea sounds intriguing," Kaide offered. "It's hard to imagine he'd have a security team around him at a bar or restaurant. Whatever you'd like to do works for me."

"Okay, let's try that," she agreed. "I've been checking out upscale restaurants. Volt prefers seafood, and Le Pecheur is one of the best. If I can arrange a meeting with him there, you could get a table not far away and be ready to assist me when I break the news to him. He probably won't recognize you since you were wearing the chauffeur cap when you drove him."

After thinking through her pitch, Poole gave her target a phone call on his mobile. "Hello, Mr. Volt! It's Jeanette. We met at the fundraising gala held at the Atomium."

"Yes, yes!" he replied as his interest piqued. "I've thought a lot about you since then. How are you doing, my dear?"

"Very well, thank you. I was hoping we could continue our discussion of the auto-racing sponsorship," she purred. "I'm representing Belgium's own driver, Stoffel Vandourne. He's making a comeback and will compete in the Formula One Grand Prix at the end of August. There's one more brand sponsorship available. I thought it would be wonderful for Genez."

With endorphins flooding through his brain, Regis was beside himself with interest. "Oh, my yes, Jeanette! I'd love to talk to you about this opportunity. Where can we meet?"

"So happy to hear you're interested, Mr. Volt. May I call you Regis?"

"Certainly, my dear," the CEO responded with his eyes wide.

"Wonderful, Regis. If you like seafood, why don't we schedule a time to dine outdoors at Le Pecheur. When would be the best evening to meet?"

"I love seafood! And Le Pecheur is one of my favorites. Let me check my schedule for a moment, please." Volt tapped onto his computer to pull up his date book. "How does this Thursday at seven sound, Jeanette?"

"Let me see if I can get a reservation and I'll confirm. Will it be you and your wife?"

"Yes, Diana would be thrilled to hear your offer, Jeanette," Regis cooed.

"For three then. I'll let you know as soon as I find out their availability."

"Excellent! I'll be eager to hear from you."

After the call, Poole contacted the restaurant and requested an outdoor table for three for Thursday at seven. The receptionist told her they'd see her party at that time. Kaide also called and made a reservation for one. He told the reservationist he'd like to be seated near the Poole party of three. Poole then called Volt to confirm their dinner plans. As expected, he was exuberant with his response.

The night of their reservations, Poole came early and waited for her guests to arrive. Kaide had a small table for one not far away. They both pretended to be focused on the menu. Shortly after seven, a robust Volt and his lovely wife strolled into the outdoor eating area, spotted Poole and moved to her table.

"Greetings, Jeanette!" Volt expressed. "You remember Diana?"

"Yes, but I'm afraid I won't ask you to be seated," Poole stated. "I apologize for the false pretenses, but I'm actually with Interpol. You're being charged for your part in crimes committed in the U.S., specifically murder and kidnapping."

With Volt's jaw dropping and his eyes narrowing at Poole, he barked, "This is utter nonsense! You can't prove anything! What the hell are you talking about?"

"Actually, I have evidence that you're associated with a man named Karsen Ojin along with five other pharmaceutical companies," she calmly stated as she pulled a few documents from a slim portfolio and handed them to the CEO.

As he read about his charges, he looked around at two men seated nearby and nodded with a scowl on his face. Suddenly, one man jumped from a nearby table and gave Poole a jolt to the head with an empty wine bottle. Other diners in the area screamed. Another unknown guard seated with others began ushering Volt and a sobbing Diana from the restaurant.

Chapter 27

Even though the guards surprised him momentarily, Barron Kaide responded. When he saw his lover receive a shot to the head, he grabbed a water carafe and flung it at her attacker's skull, knocking him to the ground. Before Volt could leave, Barron plucked an empty wine bottle from another table and threw it at the man escorting the CEO from the restaurant. It hit him square on the noggin, dropping him instantly. More diners shrieked at the violence and ducked down.

Kaide reached into his belt and pulled out his revolver and flashed his badge, shouting, "We're with Interpol. That's far enough, Volt!" The stunned big man turned with rage in his eyes. "Raise your hands!" The CEO reluctantly did as he was ordered. "As my partner said, you're coming with us."

Poole reached up to grasp the edge of the table next to her and pulled herself up. Rubbing the back of her head, she looked down at the man who'd clocked her and rolled him to his stomach. Reaching for his hands, she bound them with flexi-cuffs. She then darted to the other guard and did the same.

"Good work, Barron!" she said, then spun the big CEO around and cuffed him. "Where'd you get all the help, Volt?"

"I don't go anywhere without security, but they weren't too damn good," he fumed.

Diana sobbed and covered her face as the two Interpol officers led Volt to their vehicle. She meekly cried, "Oh, Reg! What will become of me?"

Before pushing Volt inside their vehicle, Poole phoned the local police to request that they arrest the men hand-cuffed at Le Pecheur. The Interpol pair then drove to the local police station and booked Volt for his offenses. She explained the situation to the officer in charge and asked if they'd hold him without bail until she could transfer him to their headquarters in Bruges. They were happy to accom-modate her requests.

Later, Poole asked her lover if he actually knocked out the two guards with the bottles.

"Well, sure!" the former baseball pitcher responded with a smile. "Got to keep my arm in shape, don't I?"

Before heading back to Bruges, they returned to Le Pecheur and enjoyed a peaceful, romantic dinner. They also apologized to the owner about the chaos from the previous day. The man told them he was happy the local police arrived quickly to arrest Volt's groggy guards.

* * *

OFFICER POOLE CONTACTED Chief Aritan about their arrest of Volt and the arrangements to transfer him to Bruges for trial. The other Interpol teams also confirmed that they'd captured the European pharmaceutical CEOs for their part in the crimes. With this information in hand, Aritan still needed to locate the masterminds, Karsen Ojin and Fon Tazi. Local police continued to search for their helicopter.

The chief phoned his FBI contact, Agent Myles DeLong to give him an update. "Hey, Myles, hope all is well!" Aritan announced after he took a sip of hot coffee.

"What do you know, Sam?" DeLong responded, eager to hear about Interpol's progress.

"Our people have rounded up the four CEOs, but we're still searching for Ojin and Tazi."

"I see. After we took care of the two CEOs here in the States, I've given Agents Dwyer and Friese the order to question the senators who are involved. From your discovery of the potential evidence from the video device, Senators Barras and Pitts are the only ones who make any sense."

"I know that won't hold up in court, but it may be enough to at least rattle their chains," Aritan concurred. "They were the primary beneficiaries of the large donations shelled out by Ojin's lobby."

"That's how we're looking at it," DeLong replied. "We'll also be looking for Yao Min, but so far he's eluded us. The only thing we have are his three addresses. Eventually, our agents will track him down."

* * *

Since they were both free, Sens. Barras and Pitts met for coffee at a small café inside the U.S. Capitol Building. They selected a secluded table to avoid anyone eavesdropping. "It's not looking good, Stu," Barras said glumly, as he poured creamer into his mug, shaking his head.

Pitts looked around, then responded, "I know what you mean. The Consortium has hit the skids. That message from Ojin was ominous. He and his assistant are the only ones left. The authorities have hauled in all the CEOs. And Bisch took his own life. I can't believe it! The poor bastard."

"Ojin wasn't able to stop the progress of NuPharma's series of video testimonies confirming their patients have actually done well." Barras growled, as he stirred the coffee. "We may not have any alternative except to endorse their damn FDA approval. I'm going to hate seeing those cocky S.O.B.s back in the senate meeting room."

After finishing their discussion, the two senators paid their bill and left the café. Waiting for them outside were a man and woman flashing their FBI badges. "Excuse us, Senators," Friese demanded. "I'm Agent Friese and this is Agent Dwyer. We'd like a word with you separately. Sen. Barras, let's go to your office. Sen. Pitts, Agent Dwyer will accompany you to yours. There's evidence that you are both connected to a pharmaceutical lobby that has committed crimes in the U.S."

"This is total rubbish!" snapped Pitts with a stern look on his face.

"Indeed! How dare you suggest that we've had anything to do with any crimes," Barras bellowed, as he looked around to make sure they weren't being heard.

"If you'd rather not make a scene, I suggest we accompany you to the privacy of your offices," Agent Dwyer ordered, nodding her head in that direction.

"H-how the hell did you know where to find us?" Pitts asked defensively as he turned to walk to his office.

"Your secretaries were most accommodating, sir," Barb answered. "Let's go." The two senators acted as if there was nothing unusual happening when various people greeted them along the way. As they reached Barras's office, he told his secretary he didn't want to be disturbed. They went inside the mahogany paneled room. He closed the door before moving behind his desk.

"Okay, let's have it, Agent. My time is valuable," the senator sneered, folded his hands, and cocked his head to one side.

Friese reached inside his briefcase and grabbed a folder. He took a few pages out, scanned through them momentarily, then handed them to Barras. The senator took out his reading glasses and studied the contents.

"Yes, of course. Pharmaceutical lobbies have been quite generous with me over the years. What does that have to do with the crimes described here?"

"We have evidence you may have participated in video Zoom-type meetings with the head of the lobby that's poured so much into your senate coffers. As you can see from this brief, they're the same people who paid known criminals for murder and kidnapping. From what the attorney for NuPharma has reported to us, you and Sen. Pitts have displayed an obvious distaste for their product in the FDA hearings from the beginning."

"Well, Agent, you can't believe everything you hear

from disgruntled legal representatives. We've attempted to present a fair review of the facts to determine if their product is safe and worthy of mass distribution to patients with serious illnesses."

"How is it, then, that patients from the clinical trials have been represented unfairly in your hearings?" Friese asked sternly.

"We can only go by what the physicians have testified, and what the data has shown, Agent Friese," Barras said, as he gently tossed the evidence back toward Andy.

"What can you tell me about your relationship with Karsen Ojin?"

"You've got me there, Agent. I don't know the name."

"Then tell me why you're connected to the video meetings the man conducted?"

"You're beating a dead horse, Agent. You have nothing that implicates me. If this is all you've got to discuss, I'd say our meeting is over." Barrass stood and waved his hand, indicating the FBI agent should leave. Friese stared at the senator for a few seconds then departed.

In Sen. Pitts' office not far away, Agent Dwyer presented him with the same evidence Friese showed to Barrass. Pitts read through the document and laid it on his desk. "This certainly doesn't indict me, Agent. Yes, I've received generous campaign donations, like many others in Congress. Last time I looked, this isn't a crime."

"That alone is not, but we've identified you circumstantially as a participant in video meetings with the leader of the lobby. The others were CEOs of pharmaceutical companies who had much to lose if RGB101 got FDA approval. It appears you've shown your bias against NuPharma's product in the hearings. We can only assume that the lobby paid you to protect the competing pharmas' interests."

"Ha! That's a stretch," Pitts rebuffed, but Dwyer noticed a twitching in the man's eye. The senator reached up to rub his lid. "You have no evidence that we're involved with this lobby other than as beneficiaries of their generosity."

"You may be right," Dwyer agreed, "but we're still hunting for evidence. You and your pal aren't out of the woods yet." She packed up her briefcase, rose, and left the office.

Friese waited for her in the hallway.

"Barras didn't flinch. How about Pitts?" Friese whispered to his partner.

"He didn't bite either, but I sensed a tinge of guilt from the guy," Dwyer replied with a smile. "I'd like to wiretap their phones. Who knows, we might get lucky."

When they returned to their office, Barb asked Agent DeLong about the wiretap. He said he'd speak to a judge and describe the evidence they had so far.

Later in the day, the agent buzzed Dwyer to tell her the judge agreed. With a reference to the old saying, *Where there's smoke, there's fire*, he approved the wiretap on both senators' phones. "This could be the only way we'll prove these two are dirty."

CHAPTER 28

FBI Agent Myles DeLong contacted NuPharma's Christopher Masse to report on the latest arrests. "That's good news, Agent. I'm sure Jack and Milt will be relieved to hear," Masse replied as he jotted notes at his desk in Indianapolis. "What do you know about Interpol's efforts to capture Fon Tazi, Yao Min, and the kingpin, Karsen Ojin?"

"So far, they've eluded us, but we haven't stopped searching," DeLong said. "We've got addresses for Yao along the east coast and our agents are tracking him. As for Ojin and Tazi, Interpol is looking for the helicopter they used to avoid capture in Trento, Italy."

"How about the two senators we've butted heads with at the FDA hearings?" Chris asked as he scanned through the case file.

"Our people have interviewed them, but we don't have enough evidence to charge them."

"I'm expecting a follow-up senate hearing where we'll

be able to present our video showing the positive testimony of the patients and their physicians. It will be interesting to see the look on their faces when they're forced to give our product the green light." The attorney grinned.

After his conversation with DeLong, Masse phoned Jack McCabe and Dr. Milton Lennium on a three-way call. "I wanted to provide you with the latest from the FBI," Chris began. "The lobby's CEOs have been arrested, but Karsen Ojin and Fon Tazi haven't been located yet. Interpol is hoping to track them once they've found their chopper."

"This sound encouraging," Jack replied from his secret condo. "I'm ready to move back to my home and we'd like to visit our Lake Maxinkuckee cottage before the cold weather sets in. I have to hope the criminals are on the run at this point."

"I'll leave that up to you, Jack," Chris replied. "We can only hope they've stopped their criminal activities."

"We've completed our video, and I'll get you copies," Milt said. "Shall I send them to you, Chris? Then you can provide one to Jack?"

"That works for me, thanks," Jack agreed. "Who's going to the next FDA senate hearing? I think I'll continue to stay out of the public for a while longer."

"I'm feeling more comfortable about getting around. I can meet you in D.C. when the time comes, Chris," Milt offered.

After their phone conference, Jack informed Sara and Amos that he felt safe enough to return to their home in Indianapolis. "How would you like to visit the lake next week?"

"Wow, that would be great, Dad!" Amos shouted. "I miss that place so much. Will it be warm enough to ski?"

"It's possible. I'll contact Hans to see how everything is looking."

"I hope we're making the right choice about leaving our secure hiding place, Jack," Sara cautioned. "I'd prefer to continue home schooling Amos until we hear the FBI and Interpol have arrested the criminals."

"That makes sense, honey," Jack replied as Amos jumped on the couch to join him. "I know you miss your friends, Amos. Hopefully, it won't be long before we feel safe sending you back to your regular school."

While they were packing to move back to their Meridian-Kessler home, Jack called Hans Kriechbaum. The young man was not only his caretaker but also his security guard whenever they visited their lake house. "Hello, Hans!" he began enthusiastically. "It looks like we've got the bad guys on the run, so we're going to visit for a few days at the cottage. I hope all is well there."

"Yes, Mr. McCabe, things are fine!" Hans responded. "I've done some painting touchups this past week. The lake side of the cottage was showing signs of wear. I think you'll like it. I also ran the speedboat to make sure it was running nicely. The water's still warm if you decide to take Amos skiing."

"Sounds wonderful! Thanks for looking out for everything – as always," Jack acknowledged. "By the way, I've still got my pistol and would appreciate some target practice while we're there. I'd like to sharpen my shooting skills."

"I'll be happy to help, Mr. McCabe. Any time."

"By the way, Hans, from now on, why don't you call me by my first name. I feel like we're almost family."

"Well, sure...Jack! I feel the same about you too," Hans responded, feeling the emotion of the moment. "I'll be eager to see you three, especially Amos. He just gets bigger all the time."

"I haven't spoken to Detective Tenant lately. I think I'll call and fill him in on all the FBI activities we've learned. I'll give you all the details when I see you, Hans."

After their phone call, Jack rang his bearded friend, Lewis Tenant. When the detective picked up, Jack greeted him warmly and described everything that had occurred in the last month. "That's incredible, Jack!" Tenant replied. "Sounds like Interpol has been as busy as the FBI finding the criminals."

"Yes, but they haven't located the source of all the trouble. Karsen Ojin and his assistant escaped when Interpol attacked his stronghold in Italy. Since then, they've disappeared. We're also trying to locate one of their people in the U.S. who's ordered the murders and kidnapping. The FBI has clues of his whereabouts but hasn't found him yet. By the way, I'm bringing the family to the lake this week and wanted to say hello."

"Happy you did, Jack. If there's ever a problem, you or Hans can always find us."

After he hung up, the McCabes packed their belongings for the move across town to their home. The project took most of the day before they were ready to check out of the condo.

Sara smiled as she unpacked items when they returned

to their home. "I hope we don't have to do this again, Jack."

"How soon can we go to the lake, Dad?" Amos asked, as he paused from playing his hand-held video game.

"Let's go in a few days after we get organized here, if it's okay with your Mom," he replied as he restocked the refrigerator.

"Sounds good to me," Sara agreed. "We've got a big pitch coming up with our ad agency, but they seem to have everything well in hand."

The time to leave for Lake Maxinkuckee couldn't come fast enough for young Amos. He was excited for another opportunity to slalom ski.

* * *

AFTER LOADING UP THE AUDI, the McCabes set off for their favorite place. When they neared the cottage, they played the game of *who can see the lake first*. Driving along the hilly country road, they neared Maxinkuckee. The three of them focused on the trees ahead to get a glimpse of the glistening sun bouncing off the water. As Jack drove near the last turn, Amos shouted, "I see it! I see it!" His parents chuckled. They always let him be the first to make the announcement.

They soon veered onto East Shore Drive, then turned into their driveway. Hans spotted them from the pier, waved, and hurried to meet them. He greeted the McCabes as soon as they got out of the car. "You made it! So happy to see you!" the blond-haired young man shouted.

"Hi, Hans!" Amos yelled and ran to give him a high five.

"How's the old Chris-Craft doing? Hope it's ready for a spin around the lake!"

"She's running great, Amos!" Hans replied. "Can I help you bring your luggage inside?" he asked Jack and Sara.

"Sure, thanks much, Hans! Great to see you. The cottage looks wonderful," Jack greeted warmly.

"Are you still dating that cute girl from Culver, Hans?" Sara asked as they carried things inside.

"Yes, we're seeing each other a lot. Hanna and I get along great!"

"How about that!" Jack cheered. "Hans and Hanna! Sounds like a match made in heaven." They all laughed.

"Yep, the names are a coincidence, I'll admit." Hans gushed.

"We brought enough food to feed an army if you and Hanna would like to join us for dinner," he offered.

"Well, let me ask her. Thanks so much...Jack."

That night, Hans brought Hanna, and they all enjoyed an excellent meal the McCabes prepared on the grill. Jack opened a bottle of wine that they quickly consumed. Hanna brought a delicious apple pie she baked herself.

"Please tell us about you and your family, Hanna!" Sara asked as they finished their meal.

"Let's see. I graduated last spring from Valparaiso with a degree in computer science," Hanna began while Hans beamed. "They offered me a scholarship, so I couldn't say no. Currently, I'm working at Culver Military Academy in their administration department. I'm learning a lot."

"That's fantastic, Hanna! Congratulations! So are you from Culver?" Jack asked.

"Yes, I grew up here. My mother's a nurse and my

father works in construction," the attractive brunette explained. "You might have met him. His name's Cal Kulis. He was the construction supervisor of DeMann Suites."

"No kidding?" Jack exclaimed with surprise. "I think I met him one time. Detective Tenant introduced us. Well, it's a small world, but it is Culver, after all." Everyone laughed. "Actually, as you probably know, DeMann Suites was named for Hugo DeMann. He was one of the best friends I had here on the lake."

"Yes, it is a small world," Hanna smiled as Hans reached over to grab her hand.

The next morning, Amos got his wish. The family rose early and sped via the speedboat to a calm spot on the lake. Sara floated both skis in the water, as the young man jumped in then surfaced to grab them. Once they were on, he gave his dad the thumbs-up sign. Jack revved the engine. The boat soon reached its speed, and Amos was skiing gracefully. Moments later, he dropped one ski and slipped his left foot in the sleeve behind his right. He didn't miss a beat, continuing to slalom for several minutes. The young McCabe even ventured outside the wake and back. Finally, he let go of the ski rope, smiling ear to ear.

"You did it, honey! You're the best!" Sara shouted, as she helped him get back into the boat.

"Wonderful, Amos!" Jack yelled. "So happy you got on the skis again...I mean *ski*! It's been too long."

CHAPTER 29

Karsen Ojin and Fon Tazi didn't know what their next steps were going to be. Deep down, Ojin realized that unforeseen circumstances had destroyed his plans. As he sat stewing in his borrowed condo in Berlin, he kept thinking Jack McCabe was the reason he'd failed. It was also apparent that once the FDA approved NuPharma's drug, Ojin's investments in the competing pharmas would lose hundreds of millions of dollars. As he wrote notes on a pad, he squeezed the pencil until it broke in half. Anger swelled in his thoughts. Revenge bubbled to the surface.

"Fon, our situation is dire," Ojin hissed. "I can't think of anything we can do to get back on course."

"Yes, K, it appears bleak," Tazi responded, trying to be positive. "As someone said, 'every dark cloud has a silver lining.'"

Ojin smiled weakly and muttered, "I keep thinking if it weren't for that damn McCabe and his company, we wouldn't be in this mess. I'd like to put him out of commission, permanently."

"Hmmm. We know where the man lives in Indianapolis. He also has a home on that lake. I can contact Yao Min to see if he knows a contractor who can take care of the problem. If that's what you want to do."

Ojin considered the possibility of an assassination. "It could turn their miserable little company into turmoil if its owner was out of the picture. It might give us more time to find an alternative." He considered his options further. It made sense. "Okay, see what you can do."

Tazi soon phoned her resource in the U.S. "Hello, Ms. Tazi. It's been a while," Yao answered. "How may I be of service?"

"We're running out of options, Yao. I'd like to see if you know someone with the skills to take out Jack McCabe. As you recall, he has a place in Indianapolis and one on that lake."

Yao thought for a moment, then announced, "Yes, I see. There's one person who's never failed to accomplish my missions. Her name's Erma Geddin. She's ruthless, effective, and won't leave a trace. Stasi, the German secret police, trained this woman as a killer. I'll see if she is available."

"Very well, Yao. Let me know when it's done."

He quickly found Geddin's number. On the first call, he had to leave a message. Later that day, she called back. "Yes?"

"Erma, I have an assignment, if you're free," Yao announced.

"I've just completed one that's taken longer than I'd

planned, but I'll be available in a few days. What do you have in mind?" Geddin asked, as she stopped cleaning a Luger pistol and silencer.

Yao gave her the two addresses in Indiana and described the target. "I don't know where he'll be, but you'll find him. It shouldn't be a problem."

After discussing her fee, she hung up.

Erma was resting up in a St. Louis hotel. Her previous job was eliminating a major drug cartel dealer. Her client was the dealer's U.S. adversary who used Geddin to avoid being implicated. Erma enjoyed being mobile. Even though her permanent residence was in New York, she didn't get home often. The woman went by several aliases to remain unknown to the authorities. Few people knew how to reach her. Yao Min was one of them. Erma figured it'd be a quick trip to Indianapolis. She'd stake out McCabe's address to determine when and how to take him out.

GEDDIN CHECKED out of her hotel a day later and drove a rented BMW into Indiana, soon arriving in the state capital. Locating McCabe's address was simple. She bought something to eat at a fast-food restaurant and sat in her car near his house, watching for any activity. Later, she left to get a hotel room for the night, then returned to the residence. There were no signs of activity, but she'd give it more time. Experiencing the same the following day, the assassin lost her patience. She was ready to investigate his Lake Maxinkuckee cottage near Culver.

Cruising to McCabe's location, she slowly drove by and

saw an Audi parked in the driveway. Inching along East Shore Drive, she saw a man in the backyard cooking on a grill. From the photo Yao Min gave her, she knew he was the target. She drove into Culver and tried to get a room at the Culver Cove, but they'd booked everything. *Screw it,* she said to herself. *I'll sleep in the damn car if I have to. I won't be here long anyway.*

As the sun descended below the lake horizon, Geddin drove past the East Shore Drive address, did a U-turn, and went by it again. She pulled off the road a few houses down. Exiting her BMW, Erma walked onto the golf course and spotted a high hill. When she arrived at the top, she could see it was one of the greens. In her backpack, she carried a sniper rifle with a silencer and tripod. The assassin quickly assembled her weapon. Throwing a small blanket on the dewy ground, she laid down with the rifle in front of her. Viewing through the scope, she could easily spot several people in a back room through a series of windows. There were two men, two women, and a boy. She only needed to take care of McCabe.

Inside the family's kitchen, Jack, Sara, Hans and Hanna were having a nightcap. This was the second dinner the McCabes hosted for Hans and his new friend. Amos left to watch TV in the other room. They'd been enjoying each other's company around the large table. Sara brought a baked snack to the table for them to enjoy. As she began to place the plate of treats on the table, one accidentally fell to the floor. Jack bent over to reach for it. Suddenly, with a loud *CRACK*, a bullet pierced the window, exploded into the room, and barely missed hitting Jack.

Hans yelled, "Get down! Shooter!" Everyone screamed

and dropped to the floor. Sara yelled for Amos to get down and stay in the room. Hanna shrieked and stayed low.

Across the road on the number-five green, Erma cursed that she'd obviously missed. *Son of a bitch! How could that happen? Lucky bastard,* she thundered to herself. Quickly, Geddin broke down her rifle, tossed it in the backpack, and hustled back to her car twenty-five yards away.

Sprawled on the floor, Jack phoned Detective Tenant. Hans darted to the front door. He kept a revolver holstered under a chair, out of sight. Checking to make sure it was loaded, he ran outside, scurrying toward the backyard. It wasn't completely dark. The moon was bright. He'd be able to spot something out of the ordinary. Hans crouched low, hurrying across the street to the golf course. He knew the shot came from that direction. All at once, he spotted someone moving swiftly toward the road. Hans rushed closer. Approaching the person fleeing the scene, he could see she had a backpack. A BMW was parked on the edge of the road. Hans crept nearer, then yelled, "Stop, that's far enough!"

Geddin spun around to look. The man's voice alarmed her. *What the hell,* she thought, running to the driver's side of the car to jump in. Tossing her backpack onto the passenger seat, she revved the engine, stomped on the accelerator, and spit dirt and gravel behind her wheels as the car gained traction.

Hans raced to the road and took aim at her tires. Holding the revolver with two hands, he squared his feet beneath him. He took a quick breath and fired. *POW!* The left rear exploded. *POW!* Then the right rear. Immediately, the BMW went into a spin then rolled over several times before it slammed loudly into a light pole. "Holy crap!" he yelled, then rushed to the crashed vehicle. Smoke was rising from the front. In the distance, he heard the siren of a police car. Hans arrived at the vehicle and looked inside. It was a woman. Her head had broken through the front windshield. Blood poured down the front of the BMW's hood. On the floor next to her was a backpack. Poking out of it was part of a weapon.

The squad car screeched to a stop, with its siren blaring and lights flashing. The bearded Detective Lewis Tenant turned off the siren and popped out. His deputy, Jerry Atrich, slowly got out of the passenger side. "Oh, my God! Hans?" Tenant shouted. "What the hell happened? Jack called to tell me someone took a shot at them." The Culver police officer then peered at the car to inspect the gruesome sight of the woman.

Out of breath and jolted by the horrific event, Hans described the shocking sequence to the police.

Deputy Atrich tried opening the door to the passenger side. At first, it wouldn't budge. Finally, he yanked it open. Grabbing a small flashlight, he pointed it inside. First at the woman, then to the backpack on the floor. Peering inside it, he could see a disassembled rifle, silencer, and tripod. "Well, I'll be a monkey's uncle," he barked. "Hans, looks like you captured the gunman...or gunwoman."

"We'll be examining her weapon for a match to the bullet that thankfully missed the McCabes," Tenant announced, shaking his head. He then phoned an ambulance and gave them their location. "Jerry, wait here for the ambulance. Hans, let's head to Jack's and find that bullet."

The two hurried down the road and turned into the

driveway. Jack saw them and opened the back door. Sara and Hanna were in tears. Amos was hugging his mother. "What happened on the road?" Jack eagerly asked the arrivals after hearing the gunfire. Hans described the events again as the McCabes welcomed them into the house.

"Hans, you saved the day – at least that's what it appears," Jack marveled. Hanna rushed to embrace Hans.

"Okay, I see where the bullet pierced the window," Tenant noticed as he still wore blue gloves. "From the golf course, the trajectory would put the bullet somewhere on a lower wall." The lanky detective carefully examined areas in the room that he suspected would take the hit. Seconds later, he mumbled. "A-ha, this looks suspicious." Kneeling on the floor, he spied a cabinet door with a hole in it. Slowly opening it, he peeked inside to see several metal water canteens. A bullet had penetrated one of them. "Yep, this poor canteen took the hit." Tenant grabbed the container and held it up for the others to see.

"That's amazing, Detective!" Jack gasped, shaking his head. "That was too close for comfort. If I hadn't bent down on the floor...Sara, you saved me when you dropped that macaroon!"

She smiled and pulled her husband and Amos together in a warm embrace.

The ambulance soon arrived at the crash scene. The EMTs carefully dislodged the woman's head from the car window and carried her to their gurney and body bag. "We'll need to fingerprint her for our records, boys," Deputy Atrich ordered. A tow truck drove up as they were completing their analysis. Several neighbors appeared in their yards, talking anxiously about the frightening sounds of the night. Atrich grabbed the backpack and its contents and placed it all in an oversized evidence bag. Detective Tenant soon rejoined his partner. The police officers discussed the next steps to identify the woman and match the bullet with her rifle. Together, they searched through the vehicle to discover her purse with an ID, phone, and other belongings.

A day later, forensics confirmed the bullet and rifle were a match. The woman's fingerprints were everywhere. They identified her as Erma Geddin. She appeared to be a German citizen living in New York City. They'd examine her recent phone records to discover who ordered the assassination attempt.

CHAPTER 30

Interpol computer hacker, Sarah Graff, was still digging through the video equipment Kara Sterrio and Alberto Fresco brought back with them from Ojin's castle. Sarah was confident there was more evidence to identify but hadn't uncovered it yet. So far, she tracked the pharmaceutical lobby's money to the secret, off-shore bank account managed by Ojin. Several pieces of information came to light after the FBI forced the bank to release documents showing deposits, withdrawals, and payments.

Two U.S. senators suspected of being part of the organization received the lion's share of the lobby's contributions. Even though the FBI obtained authorization to wiretap the cell phones belonging to Sens. Barras and Pitts, they hadn't recorded any incriminating conversations.

Another piece of information gleaned from the bank account were the payments made to Yao Min. He was the U.S. connection for Fon Tazi, Ojin's enforcer. There were three addresses for Yao Min. FBI agents Barb Dwyer and

Andy Friese gathered with their boss, Myles DeLong, to discuss how to go after the elusive Yao.

Looking at a map, they contacted the local police in each city, including Boston, Massachusetts; Providence, Rhode Island; and New London, Connecticut. They ordered a stakeout at each residence that matched the payment addresses. Since they provided a photo of Yao, the officers would spot him coming or going.

As they continued to study the map, the three agents brainstormed connections among the cities. "Maybe he's got family in those cities," Myles suggested.

"He obviously wants to stay off the radar and avoid being in one place any longer than necessary," Barb said.

"What else connects those cities?" Andy asked. "Hey, doesn't a train run from one to the other?" He immediately conducted an online search. "Sure enough, Amtrack has scheduled routes between them. That would make it easy for him to move from place to place."

"Good call, Andy!" Myles exclaimed. "I'll contact the local police stations and request they monitor the surveillance cameras at the stations in addition to his residences. They should be able to identify him."

WITHOUT ONE OF HIS DISGUISES, Yao was husky, bald and had a small goatee. People who knew him said he reminded them of Oddjob from the movie *Goldfinger*. When in Boston, Yao went by the name Morris Sari and dressed in a black wig and black-framed glasses. For Providence, he used the identity of Noah Ting and wore a gray wig with a large, matching mustache. During his time in New London, people knew him as Hoyle Paloi where Yao donned a longish beard and bucket hat. When he received payments from the Consortium and others, they would address them to his alias *in care of Yao Min*.

Yao hadn't heard anything from his hired assassin, Erma Geddin. It was becoming clear the plans had gone awry. Realizing the FBI may be tracking him, he remained on high alert. After leaving the train station in Boston, the criminal drove an older VW Beetle to his small, rented home. Arriving on the street, he scrutinized all the vehicles parked nearby. Inside one unmarked black sedan, two men sat idly watching the houses. Without stopping, Yao was concerned and returned to the train station. Before leaving his car, he changed from his black wig and glasses of Morris Sari to the gray wig and mustache of Noah Ting.

Using his train pass, he boarded and found a familiar seat for the trip to Providence. Yao didn't seem concerned that surveillance caught him getting on board. Upon his arrival at his destination, he exited the train and went to his older Dodge Dart in the parking lot. Once again, the surveillance video captured him leaving.

When Yao drove to his unassuming rental in Providence, he was disturbed at seeing another unmarked vehicle with men sitting inside. Without hesitation, Min returned to the train station. Before leaving his car, he changed into his disguise as Hoyle Paloi with the long beard and bucket hat. When the train destined for New London arrived, he got on and located a seat. Again, the camera recorded him at the station. Upon the arrival in Connecticut, Yao left to find his Ford Escape parked in the lot. Surveillance video spotted the man again. At this point, he was getting even more anxious to find men staking out his rental home there as well. He didn't stop.

The local police had seen no one coming or going from the addresses they had for Yao. FBI Agent Andy Friese requested a search for the names tied to the properties. The police soon found that in Boston, Morris Sari was the renter. In Providence, it was Noah Ting. And in New London, Hoyle Paloi. The officers from each city regretted to inform him that there was no listing for the name of Yao Min.

Andy wasn't giving up. He and Agent Barb Dwyer visited the train station. They had a photo of Yao Min from his time in prison. They hoped it would help them identify the man. When they arrived at the Boston station, the FBI partners went to the security office and requested access to the surveillance tapes. "We need to look at video from inside the stations, and people getting on and off the trains that connect with Providence. I'll also need views of the parking lots," Andy requested. After studying the video for hours with the help of a technician, and fast-forwarding through much of it, they hadn't spotted their target.

Suddenly, "Andy, look at this guy," Barb shouted as she leaned forward in her chair, focusing on a freeze frame. "Can you zoom in on this?" she asked the technician. He did as she requested. "Also, can you print an image of this character?" Soon, a still photo tumbled from the printer. After comparing it to the photo they had of Yao, she handed both to Andy. "What do you think?"

"Hmmm," Andy responded, as he squinted at the images. "Without the dark hair and glasses, it could be," her partner agreed. "Okay, I'm sold. Let's look at the parking lot." The tech re-racked his digital tape and sped through it until they spotted the same guy leaving in a VW Bug to enter the station. "Can you zoom in on the license plate?" he asked. The tech quickly pulled in tight on the vehicle.

"You want a print?" he asked.

"That would be great," Andy replied. In an instant, the printer spit out the still image with a close-up of the license plate.

Barb called the police department again and asked for the owner of the plate. Minutes later, the officer came back on the line with the name Morris Sari. "Okay, so Morris Sari has this VW and rents the house. Could this be an alias Yao uses here in Boston? Do you have a DMV photo of Morris Sari on file?"

"We should, ma'am. If you can hold for minute, I'll check," the officer replied. When he came back on, he had the image on his computer. "Yeah, here he is in living color."

"Great, please email that photo to me ASAP," Barb requested. It wasn't long before her email dinged, and she opened the photo. "Check this out!" she beamed, handing the phone to her partner.

Andy held the prison photo up to the DMV photo of the man with the black hair and dark glasses. "Bingo!" he responded.

"Okay, we need to get these two photos to our facial-recognition unit for a positive ID." After contacting the Bureau, she informed the agent she needed a comparison of the two photos she would send. The woman told Barb it would take a few minutes, so she and Andy went to the cafeteria for lunch. As they were finishing their meals, her phone rang. The agent informed her it was definitely the same person. "Great, thanks for your help!" she replied. "Ready to head south to the Providence train station? Hopefully, we'll find Yao disguised as Noah Ting."

An hour later, they arrived at their destination. Once again, they visited the security department and requested a review of the surveillance tapes. It took a while, but, as expected, there was a person who resembled Yao, but he had gray hair and a bushy gray mustache. They scanned the parking lot and located the same man leaving a Dodge Dart. Zooming in on the image, they were able to read the license plate and get a print. The local police promptly confirmed the name of the person who rented the house was the same as the owner of the Dart – Noah Ting. After receiving the DMV photo, she sent it to her contact at the Bureau. Before long, the agent verified that the prison photo was a match. "Strike two!" Barb yelled with a grin.

"What do you suppose our target will look like in New London?" Andy asked his partner. Barb shrugged her shoulders. They nodded to each other to head for the New London, Connecticut train station.

After another hour in the car, they reached the station, parked, and visited the security department. Following the same painstaking process, they identified a man with a similar build as Yao's wearing a long beard and bucket hat. Fortunately, there also was an image of him leaving a Ford Escape in the parking lot. With help from the local police, they confirmed Hoyle Paloi owned the car. The two agents weren't surprised that the prison photo matched his DMV photo.

Agents Friese and Dwyer got word from the police officers in Boston, Providence, and New London that their target still had not arrived at his residences. "Yao was obviously alert to the possibility of stakeouts at his houses and didn't stop," Andy said. "Based on the time-stamps of the videos, New London was his last train trip. If he didn't stop at his home, where would he go?"

"Unless he changes vehicles, we know he's driving a Ford Escape with the license plate we've ID'd. I'm going to contact the local and state police to BOLO Yao's vehicle."

"That's about all we can do, Barb," Andy agreed as they sat at the New London coffee shop with their notes in front of them, sipping from their hot mugs.

After moving on from his rental home in New London, Yao drove through the city, finally stopping at a small Japanese restaurant called Sushi Hiro to grab a bite to eat. When his order came up, he grabbed his chopsticks and began enjoying the sashimi. As he ate, he tried to determine where he should relocate to avoid capture. *Maybe it's time to return to New York City. I know it well and it'll be easy to disappear.*

CHAPTER 31

The New London Police Department received the notice to *be on the lookout* for an older Ford Escape with a certain license plate. Riding in their squad car, two average-looking, middle-aged officers named Bill, cruised their route looking for any signs of trouble. Since they had the same first name, they called each other by their last names, Bourd and Lowney. When the BOLO came through, they stayed alert to spot the vehicle. As they passed the Sushi Hiro restaurant, Bourd shouted, "Hey, isn't that the Escape we're looking for? Slow down!" Lowney pulled into the small parking lot behind the vehicle in question.

"Looks like our perp could be downing some dinner, Bourd." They exited their vehicle with the lights flashing. As they entered, they instantly recognized the bearded man with the bucket hat at the bar. Bourd shouted, "Mr. Paloi? We're Officers Bourd and Lowney. Slowly put down the chopsticks, stand up, and place your hands on your head." Two cooks dropped behind the counter.

Before the officers could pull out their weapons, Yao deftly flicked a chopstick into the face of each of them. Yao jumped over the bar and ran past the cooks toward the kitchen entrance. Lowney ripped out his sidearm, aimed and fired. The bullet pierced the doorway frame. As Yao ran through the entrance, he knocked over a stunned server carrying a tray of volcano rolls. Everything flew into the air, as the young man squealed.

The owner of the restaurant, Hiro Ito, heard the police tell their suspect to surrender. He instantly screamed for Yao to stop. The criminal continued to flee, running behind a large metal preparation table stacked with porcelain dishes. Above Yao hung a series of butcher knives.

Lowney pursued his target but hid safely behind the door. Yao side-armed porcelain dinner plates at Lowney like Frisbees, hoping to hit the officer. They crashed on impact against a wall.

Ito yelled again for Yao to give up, "You wrecking my place! Stop! Stop!"

The hunted man ignored the owner and scanned the area behind him for a back exit, but the route would put him in the cop's line of sight. Yao reached up, grabbed several knives, and expertly whipped them at Lowney, who fired his weapon between Yao's throws. Both missed their targets. Yao whizzed more plates and knives at his pursuer.

"I'm warning you!" Ito shouted.

Yao turned and threw one of the knives at Ito. The owner ducked, and the blade stuck in the wall behind him. Ito then reached down and pulled out a samurai sword below a counter. "You wrecking everything!" Pulling the sword from its scabbard, the owner leapt forward and thrust the long blade into Yao's neck. Blood sprayed out, covering Hiro's apron. Seconds later, he pulled the weapon from its victim. Yao dropped to his knees, then slumped to the linoleum floor. A red puddle spread quickly.

"Oh, my God!" Lowney bellowed, as he watched the owner plunge his sword into the criminal.

Bourd hurried to join his partner. "Holy hell? You okay Lowney?"

"Yep, this man saved the day," Lowney gasped. "Who are you, sir?"

"I'm Hiro Ito, owner of Sushi Hiro. This man was wrecking everything. He would not stop. So I stopped him."

"Uh, you sure did, Mr. Ito," Bourd grunted. "I'd say you were defending your property."

After Bourd called it in, additional police and an ambulance arrived. Lowney explained to the EMT that their suspect was in disguise. The gowned technician approached the slain man. Following an initial examination, he gently pulled the fake beard from the dead man's face. Before the police wrapped up their duties, the police station alerted FBI Agents Friese and Dwyer.

"Well, I didn't expect his capture to happen so soon, Barb," Andy said to his partner, as they sat at their FBI office. "I've asked the police to send Yao's phone to us for inspection. From the report, our suspect's life came to a brutal ending."

"Sounds like it! We got lucky finding Yao's vehicle on the surveillance videos. He must have thought he was off the radar." Barb grinned. "I just wish we'd been able to question him.

* * *

SOON THEREAFTER, Christopher Masse, the attorney for NuPharma, received word that the Senate had agreed to review additional evidence in the FDA hearing. The pharmaceutical company had conducted extensive video testimonials of clinical trial patients with their physicians. In all the interviews, RGB101 clearly benefitted people who'd suffered from either heart disease or diabetes problems.

Masse quickly got the company owner, Jack McCabe, and its director, Dr. Milton Lennium, on a three-way call. "The Senate is ready for us to present the video evidence you've prepared, Milt."

"Great news, Chris!" Jack exclaimed from his home in Indianapolis.

"Yes! It'll be rewarding to contradict the false evidence that was presented earlier," Milt echoed. "I hope we'll be able to find out who forced the FDA docs to lie under oath."

"Maybe the FBI can get to the bottom of it," Chris responded. "I received a call from Agent DeLong informing me the local police caught Yao Min, the man behind the various crimes. Certainly he was responsible for your murder attempt, Jack."

"More good news!" McCabe nearly shouted. "I feel like things are moving closer to a resolution. I'd like to join you at the hearing in D.C. How about you, Milt?"

"Yes, I'll see you both at the hotel near the Capitol Building."

* * *

THE NEXT WEEK, the three men from NuPharma arrived at the D.C. hotel. They agreed to have an early breakfast at the café. "I've got the DVD and extra copies for the senators," Milt confirmed to his associates as Jack poured coffee from a carafe. "It's a long video, so they may not want to watch all of it. I'm betting they'll be ready to concede before the first half hour."

After checking out of the hotel, they took a taxi together to the senate meeting room. As expected, Sens. Barras and Pitts scowled when they entered. "Our time is short, so please inform the committee what you've prepared as rebuttal evidence," Barras announced after he brought the meeting to order.

"We've produced a series of video testimonials of patients and their physicians attesting to improved health after being on RGB101," Milt stated confidently, then handed several copies of the DVD to an aide. "If you would, please put this on the TV screen for everyone to see." Moments later, the presentation began with titles introducing the patients and physicians along with their locations. As the program continued, the NuPharma men noticed most of the senators nodding and sharing positive comments with one another. Only Barras and Pitts sat glumly, shaking their heads in disdain.

As Milt proposed, Barras didn't want to see the video past the first twenty minutes. "Okay, okay," the senator barked. "You've made your point. We'll take this evidence into consideration, as we attempt to reconcile it with the other testimony by the FDA physicians. Your video appears believable, but we must determine why the physicians' statements and the data we received contradict your presentation."

"Senator, with all due respect, we submit that someone threatened the FDA physicians to testify as they did or face dire consequences. And a hacker certainly changed the data presented previously. I'm sure the senators are aware of the crimes committed in connection with our FDA proposal. Just think of it. An assassin murdered the former FDA commissioner. Police and the FBI captured the men who kidnapped and tortured our own Dr. Lennium to reveal our product's formula. One of your senators *accidentally* fell to his death. And Jack McCabe was recently the target of a murder attempt. Moreover, security and police stopped criminals from planting surveillance bugs in his two homes. With these vicious felonies in mind, it's easy to understand that a person threatened the FDA physicians to testify as they did." Jack and Milt nodded in agreement. Several of the senators covered their mouths in shock.

"Of course, that's *your* opinion, Mr. Masse," Barras rebutted. "We'll keep your suppositions in mind, as we determine a resolution." Moments later, he slammed his gavel and recessed the meeting. The three NuPharma men tried to object, but the senators rose to leave.

As soon as Jack, Chris, and Milt were outside the meeting room, Jack said, "They won't give up, will they? Now that police have taken care of Yao Min, could the FBI interview the FDA physicians to determine what or who coerced them into their false testimonies?"

"Good call, Jack," Chris agreed. "I'll reach out to Agent DeLong to see if his team will do that. Surely Yao's death has reduced the threat to the doctors."

Before leaving D.C., Chris contacted the FBI agent and described the situation with the FDA physicians and the erroneous data. DeLong agreed it was worth investigating.

* * *

AGENTS DWYER and Friese received a briefing on the threats the FDA physicians may have experienced prior to their senate testimonies. The agents invited the four doctors to attend a private meeting at a secure location in Silver Spring, Maryland. When the doctors arrived, Agent Friese offered them a refreshment and then described the situation, as he activated his recording device. "We appreciate your time today. Agent Dwyer and I wanted to inform you of the circumstances surrounding the FDA trials for RGB101. You may know that there've been murders, attempted murders, kidnapping, torture, and attempts at unlawful surveillance at the homes of the NuPharma CEO. We know there've been threats to others in this case. In fact, we listened to the deep voice that warned the former FDA commissioner to alter the results of the clinical trials or face death."

The four doctors were obviously on edge but tried to remain unmoved by this information. Dr. Morgan Talliti finally broke down. In the middle of sobs, she sputtered, "I-I can't remain silent any longer. Yes! Yes! We all received the same warnings. We were told that someone would murder our families if we didn't do as the voice demanded."

Friese and Dwyer glanced at each other and back at the physicians. "We wanted you to know that the man who we believe sent those threats is dead. Someone killed him during his recent capture," Dwyer explained calmly.

Each of the doctors looked stunned but relieved to hear the news. "Oh, thank heavens!" Dr. Axel Mattick shouted, as tears welled in his eyes.

The other doctors expressed their relief and commented quietly to each other.

Dr. Talliti described how an unseen attacker shot her husband with tranquilizer darts while he jogged near their home. Afterward, the deep voice called again to tell her it demonstrated how the assassin could have easily killed him.

"Very interesting, Doctor," Dwyer replied as she made notes. "We also believe that the people behind the crimes manipulated the clinical data to make RGB101 look like a failure. It's hard to imagine a hacker breaking through the FDA's cybersecurity and data encryption, but someone must have accomplished it.

"How can we be sure that we're safe now?" Dr. Hamas Zaird asked as he wiped perspiration and tears from his face.

"From everything we know, a person in Europe was giving orders to two people," Friese explained. "As mentioned, one is now dead, and the other is behind bars. You should also know that the person who ordered the crimes is on the run. Interpol believes it's closing in on her."

"Will we face legal charges for our false testimony?" Dr. Conrad Verm sheepishly asked the agents.

"There are certainly extenuating circumstances with the threatening calls you received," Dwyer answered. "The court will realize that your family's lives were at risk. You and your attorneys will have an opportunity to state your defense. In the meantime, we'd like to copy the phone messages you received from the deep voice as evidence."

Immediately, each of the FDA physicians grabbed their cell phones and began searching for the voice messages that led them to give false testimony at the senate hearing. Agent Friese used a device to download them. Dr. Talliti also provided the one she received after the assassin tranquilized her husband. As the four physicians left the meeting with the FBI, they appeared relieved to hopefully have their lives back.

CHAPTER 32

After Agent Myles DeLong learned of the meeting with the four FDA physicians, he telephoned the NuPharma attorney, Christopher Masse. "I've got good news for you! Our agents met with the four docs. When they learned that someone killed Yao, it became clear that the threat no longer existed. Eventually, they admitted to the false statements they gave at the hearing. The deep-voiced demands were like the ones sent to Jack McCabe and the FDA commissioner."

"Good to know, Agent! I'm sure Jack and Milt will be pleased to hear," Chris replied. "I'll get word to the senate committee that the physicians have come clean."

"Yes, and we've got their revised comments on tape,"

"I'm sure the committee will be willing to listen to them."

After his conversation with DeLong, Masse phoned his clients. "The FBI got the FDA physicians to admit they were threatened by the deep voice to lie under oath," he explained.

"It's no excuse, but I certainly understand they were under a lot of pressure from the death threats," Jack agreed. "I hope the interviews are enough to sway the senators."

"I wish we could determine how someone changed the data," Milt added.

"Too bad we don't have Interpol's top-notch hacker. I'll bet she'd figure it out," Chris responded.

* * *

AFTER RECEIVING and listening to the physicians' audio files with disdain, Sen. Emon Barras knew someone who'd be furious. In the privacy of his office, the senator phoned Karsen Ojin with the terrible news. "Very sorry to tell you, K, but the FDA docs admitted they lied under oath at the hearings."

"What? Don't they realize their lives are at risk?" Ojin barked in a sudden fury. Fon Tazi sat nearby in their Berlin condominium with a look of dread on her face.

"FBI agents informed them that your U.S. handler, Yao Min, is out of commission. The threat they feared no longer exists."

"Son of a bitch. I'll get back to you." he yelled, before punching his phone to end the call.

"What the hell?" Tazi responded to her partner's rage.

"The FDA docs screwed us," Ojin fumed. "Have to think this through before I lose millions. Your man Yao is dead." Tazi covered her mouth in stunned silence.

* * *

"HEY, ALBERTO," Sterrio shouted, as she rushed to the next office to speak to her partner. "The Verona Airport located a helicopter that's been abandoned. Ready to go on a field trip?"

"Sure, I'm finishing up a report. Let's head out in the morning," Fresco acknowledged with a smile.

* * *

THE NEXT DAY, the two Interpol agents took a flight from Rome to the Verona Airport. When they arrived, they visited the security department to inquire about the chopper. A heavyset man met them and introduced himself as Umberto. "Yes, Officers, we were expecting you. I assume you'd like to examine the helicopter?"

"Thank you, yes," Fresco responded, then followed his host out to the tarmac.

"Let's take a golf cart. It'll be faster," Umberto offered.

"After we examine the helicopter, we'd like to review your surveillance tapes from two weeks ago," Sterrio said.

"Of course," Umberto responded. He then radioed his security office for the technician to prepare the video the Interpol officers wished to see. "Here we are." As Umberto pulled to a stop, Fresco and Sterrio approached the aircraft and opened the door.

"This is the one I remember, Alberto," Sterrio advised.

"Definitely. Let's see if they've left any evidence behind," Fresco proposed. Using tools from his bag, he dusted for fingerprints, then inspected all the compartments. A serial number was the only identification they located. "Let's conduct a search to see who purchased this craft."

When they finished examining the helicopter, Sterrio asked Umberto to take them to see the surveillance videos. The supervisor sped back to the main terminal in the cart, then led them to his office.

"This is my associate, Lorenzo. He'll be happy to help you spot the people you're seeking," Umberto offered graciously, then stepped away.

"Hello, Lorenzo. We're Officers Sterrio and Fresco from the Rome Interpol," Kara began. "There's a German man named Karsen Ojin and a Japanese woman known as Fon Tazi. They would have arrived here by helicopter two weeks ago. We want to determine if they took a flight to another city."

"Of course, I'm happy to be of service," Lorenzo offered as he made notes of the information Sterrio provided. He then called another office to request a search using their names. "We'll see if we have a record of them taking a flight." The young technician then began zooming through his surveillance feeds, keeping the two Interpol officers glued to the monitors.

After twenty minutes, Fresco shouted, "Stop! I think I saw them. Back it up." Lorenzo moved his joystick to reverse the video. "There they are!"

Sterrio narrowed her eyes and shook her head. "Good catch, Alberto! What concourse is that? Can you tell what flight they're going to board?"

"I'll check with my associate in the next office," he responded. When he got the person back on the phone, he reiterated the details he requested earlier. "Okay, thanks. Yes, your people were taking a flight to Munich under the names you gave me."

"Wonderful, Lorenzo!" Sterrio beamed. "Let's fast-forward to watch them board." Switching to another camera feed, the tech caught Ojin and Tazi moving onto the jetway. "Yep, sure looks like they were on their way to Munich." Moments later, she asked if she and her partner could borrow an office to phone Munich's security department.

Rising from his chair in front of the controls, Lorenzo led them to another office and told them to make themselves at home. "Thanks! You've been very helpful," Fresco replied with a smile.

The Interpol officer searched for the number, then called the airport security department in Munich. When the representative answered, Alberto told her he was with Interpol and needed to verify the travel plans of the two suspects.

She scanned the passenger manifest for the names and date Fresco described. "Yes, Officer, I see that Karsen Ojin and Fon Tazi transferred from their Verona flight to one going to Berlin."

"Excellent!" he replied. "Thank you for your help." Turning to his partner, he explained, "They flew to Berlin. We'll see if there's any record of them continuing on from there." After finding the number for the security department at the Berlin Airport, he called and reached an official. Explaining the details, Fresco eventually learned that there was no record of Ojin and Tazi leaving on another flight. "Unless they took another form of transportation, they didn't fly out of Berlin. Maybe they've got a reason to stay there."

"Okay. We should contact Chief Aritan. Sounds like an assignment for Poole and Kaide."

Fresco phoned the chief and filled him in on what he and Sterrio learned from their trip to Verona. "That's great!" Aritan boomed with a Columbian cigar tucked in the corner of his mouth. "As you know, Poole and Kaide spent time in Berlin hunting the leaders of that sex-trafficking operation. They know their way around the city. After hauling the CEO of the Brussels pharma to jail, they should be available. Thanks."

When he concluded his conversation with Fresco, the chief punched in the number to the Bruges office. "Hello, Poole? Aritan here. What are you and Kaide doing since you finished your last assignment?"

"Hello, Chief! All's well in Bruges," Officer Jeanette Poole answered warmly. "Barron and I've been busy with a local crime spree, but we can hand it over to another team if you've got something you'd like us to tackle."

"Turns out Karsen Ojin and his sidekick, Fon Tazi, may have flown from Verona to Berlin after they fled from their castle in Trento. I'd like you and Kaide to head over there to see if you can locate them."

"Very interesting, Chief. Sure, we'll pack up and be there soon. We've got a good relationship with the local police. Your contact, Detective Alex Blaine, was a great resource during our last case."

* * *

FBI AGENTS HAD WIRETAPPED the phone of Sen. Barras. His call to Karsen Ojin was the conversation they'd been hoping to capture. "Andy, this is Agent Horton. We finally recorded a call between Barras and Ojin. We've tracked the location of Ojin to Berlin. I'm sure you'd like to get his number to our friends at Interpol."

Agent Friese eagerly reported the news to DeLong, who then phoned his Interpol contact, Chief Aritan. "Hey, Sam, glad I caught you. Our people recorded a wiretapped conversation between Senator Emon Barras and Karsen Ojin. It turns out Ojin is now in Berlin. I'll send you his phone number."

"Ha!" the chief bellowed. "We beat you this time, Myles, but I'll be happy to have his phone number. The helicopter that Ojin and his partner escaped in was at the airport in Verona. After an investigation, we learned they flew to Berlin. Two of our people will arrive there soon to track them down."

"Good news either way," DeLong replied. "We'll be paying a visit to Sen. Barras. He's got a lot of explaining to do."

CHAPTER 33

The four FDA physicians agreed to provide their testimony again at the senate hearing. Much to the humiliation of Sens. Barras and Pitts, the doctors' return to the witness stand would not be a pleasant experience. Jack McCabe and Dr. Milton Lennium joined attorney Christopher Masse to view their interrogation.

After they filed in, the FDA medical experts took the oath to provide honest answers to the senators' questions. The NuPharma team eagerly waited to hear their revised statements. Sen. Barras led off. "Thank you for returning to this committee as we continue to deliberate the status of RGB101. It is critical that we determine if it's a legitimate and safe medication for patients with heart disease and diabetes. I have to say that I'm puzzled why you're ready to change your story about the product's performance at the clinical trials. Previously, there didn't seem to be any doubt about your position that the drug wasn't safe or effective. What's changed?"

Dr. Axel Mattick was first to offer his explanation. "The four of us were threatened to testify that NuPharma's product was not a qualified medication. If we didn't, we were told we'd face death. To demonstrate the warning was real, an assassin fired tranquilizer darts at Dr. Talliti's husband while he was jogging near their home. He survived, but the person phoned later to tell Dr. Talliti that it would have been easy to kill him. We were petrified to think that our lives and those of our families were at risk. We all agreed to fabricate the findings."

"I see," Barras replied. "Why didn't you go to the authorities with this threat?"

"We were told that a killer would murder us if we went to the police," Mattick answered. "Believe me, it tormented us not knowing what to do. As soon as the person attacked Dr. Talliti's husband, that settled it."

"Hmmm. With this in mind, why would you suddenly change your position?" Sen. Pitts asked, as he cocked his head and tapped a pen on a tablet in front of him.

"The FBI told us that someone killed the person who was believed to be behind the threats. The agents also explained how Jack McCabe and the former FDA Commissioner received the exact same threats."

"Okay. So, are you now prepared to tell us that the drug is safe and effective? You believe we should approve this product for distribution in both the heart disease and diabetes markets?" Pitts inquired.

"Yes, that's what we're ready to testify," Mattick responded confidently.

"Do the rest of you feel the same about this product?" Pitts continued.

The other three physicians acknowledged that they also believed the drug was excellent and had outstanding curative value in the pharmaceutical markets.

"The only question I have is why the data did not corroborate your findings," Barras rebuffed. "I know the NuPharma people think someone hacked the data, but we don't have any proof of that. Until we can get that detail clarified, I will need to delay the approval of this product." He then banged his gavel and rose to leave.

Jack, Milt and Chris tried to stop him from departing, but the senators were already rising and walking away from the rostrum. "You've got to be kidding me?" Jack blurted. The FDA physicians shook their heads in disbelief as they also began leaving.

"Somehow, we've got to find out who manipulated the data," Milt demanded.

"This is ridiculous," Jack fumed.

In the hallway outside the senate meeting room, an FBI man and woman stepped in front of Barras. Holding up his badge, Agent Andy Friese stated, "Sen. Emon Barras, we have a warrant for your arrest. You're being charged with collusion in a plot to defraud the Food and Drug Administration. We also need to question you about felonies committed in relation to the clinical trials for RGB101."

"What? This is absurd!" Barras snorted, as he started to walk around them.

"Not so fast, Barras!" Friese snapped, grabbing the senator's arm. Agent Barb Dwyer seized his other arm and pulled it behind him. Friese slapped a pair of handcuffs on his wrists, then led him to the exit.

"How dare you! You're gravely mistaken. I'll have your

badge for this outrage!" Barras shouted, as onlookers and other senators in the hallway gasped at the sight of the respected politician being escorted from the building. Sen. Pitts appeared shocked, and quickly scurried away in the opposite direction.

Standing in the hallway, the three NuPharma men watched from a distance as the agents escorted their nemesis from the building. They couldn't help themselves and grinned at such an unexpected scene. Barras caught sight of them, looked down, and cursed under his breath.

"Well, I wonder what they got him on?" Chris asked his associates as they shook their heads in disgust. "We had our suspicions, didn't we?"

"Now that's something I didn't expect to see today," Jack added with a smile. Moments later, when the agents and their suspect left the building, he asked, "How can we make our case with the FDA about the hacked data. Surely they have resources who can determine if someone tampered with their files. An expert broke through their firewall and changed everything connected to our clinical trials."

"I think the new FDA Commissioner's name is Samuel Mirch," Chris recalled. "I'll ask Agent DeLong if he has any ideas."

While he was at the airport waiting for his flight back to Indianapolis, Chris phoned Agent Myles DeLong. "Hello, it's Christopher Masse, the attorney for NuPharma."

"Yes, Chris. I hope all is well," Myles responded. "You may have witnessed quite a shocker at the Capitol Building today."

"As a matter of fact, we were stunned," Masse agreed. "I

didn't think I'd ever see Sen. Barras so humbled. You must have caught him in a very incriminating act for your people to haul him away like that."

"Yep, red-handed as they say," DeLong smiled. "He's got a lot to answer for."

"As you may know, the FDA physicians came clean after learning that the person behind the threating voice is dead. They provided a clear and honest testimony today. We're thrilled that things are moving in the right direction. One thing remains unsolved, however. Someone hacked into the FDA database to change the results of the clinical trials. We would like to know if the new commissioner can look into how that happened. The organization's website security was certainly jeopardized."

"I have to agree that with all the crimes someone carried out against NuPharma, hacking the FDA data would not be beyond them. I'll contact the commissioner to inquire about the integrity of their web-based security."

"Much appreciated, Agent DeLong," Chris acknowledged. "We'll be very interested to hear what you find out."

The next day, DeLong contacted the FDA and soon met with the new commissioner, Samuel Mirch. He invited his head of data security, Xavier Cache, to attend the meeting. After the FBI agent described the unexplained change to the clinical trial data, Cache was astounded.

"I'll look into this matter right away! I'm not aware of any network attacks. We use encrypted data protocols, but we know there are hackers who find new ways to invade systems. There are ransomware, backdoor entries, and types of malicious trojans that allow them to access data in organizational cloud storage. I'll run a full-scale analysis to determine if and how someone got past our cybersecurity." DeLong asked if he could wait to see if Cache would spot something quickly. He'd make some calls and enjoy a coffee.

After their meeting, Xavier excused himself and logged into the back-end of the FDA's website. When he'd completed several iterations of testing, he discovered what happened. Forty-five minutes later, he reported to Mirch and DeLong. "I'm very sorry to say that a hacker deactivated our built-in detection system. It's surprising our entire system didn't crash. It appears the person employed an exotic reverse encryption logic to change the database from the NuPharma clinical trials. When the person left, he put everything back as it was. As a result, I never noticed the break in our firewall. It was ingenious. I'll have to beef up our pipeline defense protocols."

"I'm glad you figured this out so quickly," the commissioner replied. "Of course, we need to do whatever possible to avoid this type of thing happening again."

"Yes, sir, I'll begin immediately," Xavier agreed.

"I have a question," DeLong interrupted. "Does the original data still exist? Or has it been totally eliminated?"

"It appears the hacker changed everything, sir. I'm sorry," Xavier admitted. "However, we do have the paper logs from the trials, so we can recreate the data from that. It will take a while, but it's doable."

"Good to know," the FBI agent responded. "How long will this take?"

"If I put my entire team on it, we should have the correct data restored within a week."

"Okay, do what needs to be done," Mirch ordered. He

then chuckled. "Thankfully, we have the old paper trail to rely on."

"The people from NuPharma will be pleased to know there's a reason the data was completely different than their records," DeLong acknowledged.

After his meeting, he phoned Christopher Masse.

"You'll be happy to know that the FDA discovered someone did hack the records," Myles told him. "Of course, you and your associates suspected that was the case. Now the FDA has confirmed it. They say the corrected database will be back online within a week."

"I know two people who will be thrilled to get this report. Thanks again for investigating it."

When Chris informed Jack and Milt on a three-way call, they were overjoyed. "This is great news! Finally, we can get our product to all the people who desperately need a cure for their diseases," Milt exclaimed as he sat in the R&D facility at the NuPharma headquarters.

"This will hopefully put the finishing touches on our clinical trials – and the senate approval. Hopefully nothing else will go wrong?" Jack grinned, but thought to himself, *After all the setbacks and foul plays against me and my company, I can only pray that the worst is behind us.*

CHAPTER 34

Not long after the discovery that someone hacked the FDA website, news reports heralded the new drug that would reshape the heart and diabetes healthcare markets. In the weeks that followed, the senate committee and the FDA approved the drug for distribution. Reading online, the stories sickened Karsen Ojin as he thought of the millions of dollars he'd lose. He was a major stockholder in six pharmaceutical companies that directly competed with the amazing remedy from NuPharma. As he tracked the share prices of his investments, it was immediately evident that his once-coveted position in these businesses was now a fraction of its original value.

"Good heavens, Fon!" Ojin fumed to his partner and lover. "I'm in deep, deep trouble!"

"Sell your stake in those pharmas before it's too late, K!" she shot back, as they sat in their borrowed Berlin condo drinking tea.

Ojin quickly contacted his broker and gave a sell order

for his shares in Genez of Brussels, Curatif of Paris, Medika of Vienna, Drogari of Rome, PharMax of Tampa Bay, and ReMedin of New York. The broker informed him that the stock prices had fallen steeply in the last few days. He'd take a tremendous loss.

"I don't give a damn!" Ojin shouted. "Just sell what's there!"

After he ended the call, Fon asked him, "K, don't you have money tied up in the castle in Italy?"

"It was a borrowed asset, I'm afraid. Now that the police are after me, they'll certainly take possession of it." He slumped back in his oversized chair and clenched his fists. "I'm ruined."

"Does your cousin, Ivy Ning, have any resources? Maybe you can borrow from her? I recall her saying she was comfortable financially."

Little did Ivy Ning or Ojin know just how well off she was or was going to be. Life in prison for Ning's benefactor, Hayden Zeik, had become very dangerous. The court sent Zeik to jail for his role in the sex-trafficking business he launched with money he raised selling fine-art master-pieces. Zeik's father was a German Nazi officer who hid famous paintings stolen mostly from Jews during World War II. The Allies found many of them after the war, but Hayden came into possession of a dozen that had remained a secret. He sold two to a Greek shipping tycoon to raise initial funds for his business. Later, when Interpol closed in on him, Zeik lost considerable resources, so he sold two more.

As his property manager and lover, Zeik had ordered Ning to maintain payments to the caretaker of an ancient church crypt. During a recent visit to make a payment, Ivy visited the crypt and discovered that it was the storage facility of her employer's mysterious works of art. In the weeks that followed, she returned to the catacomb and photographed them. She wasn't familiar with their value and didn't know how Zeik came into possession of them, but knew they had to be worth a lot. Later, online research confirmed that they were indeed priceless treasures.

* * *

AS FOR HAYDEN ZEIK, fellow inmates eventually learned that the court imprisoned him for sex-trafficking crimes. Infuriated at this offense, several overly aggressive convicts routinely ambushed him in the shadows and sodomized him. Unable to fight back, Hayden had to accept their vicious attacks. After each event, the tormenters left him bruised, battered, and bleeding on a cold cement floor. As the months went by, the defilements continued. Eventually, Zeik was forced to go to the prison infirmary to heal. He could barely walk.

An inmate named Oscar who worked in the prison hospital was sympathetic to Zeik's plight. He told him there may be a way to buy his freedom. Claiming to have connections with the warden, the inmate told Hayden he'd find out what the price would be. Of course, Oscar would receive a cut. The paperwork would have a forged signature from an authority granting his release. Fearing for his life, Zeik was open to the proposal.

Several days passed before Oscar came to Zeik's bedside with an offer. The fee was exorbitant, but he thought he could raise the money if Ning would sell one of his paintings. Prisoner visiting day was approaching and Hayden made a phone call inviting her to come at an appointed time. His assistant drove to the Berlin facility, parked, and made her way to the visitor center through clanging doors and loud buzzing sounds. Ivy waited at a table. She was shocked to see Zeik rolling himself through a door in a wheelchair. A bandage was wrapped around his head and his left arm was in a sling. As he drew nearer, Ning hardly recognized him. When he reached the table, she remembered him from the gleam in his eyes.

"Oh my, Hayden! What have they done to you?" Ivy muttered. Stunned at the sight of this once-proud man, she put one hand on his and the other to her mouth. Tears welled in her eyes.

"I know. I know," he managed to say between lips that were partially swollen from the beatings. "I'm sorry I look so horrible, love. People here hate me for what I did. They've subjected me to repeated brutalities. I recently ended up in the hospital." He looked down at himself and shook his head slowly.

"Goodness, is there anything I can do to help?"

"That's one reason I wanted to see you. I met a man who said he can arrange for me to be released from prison for a certain fee."

"Is he someone you can trust, Hayden?"

"He says he has connections with the warden. I'm desperate. I'm afraid the bastards will kill me if I'm here much longer."

"You have money in your bank account. How much do you need?"

"The fee is $500,000 in U.S. currency. I have something you'll have to sell to raise that amount of money."

"Please, what is it?"

"You've paid the caretaker of the crypt?"

"Yes, of course."

"Inside there are eight masterpiece paintings. Do you recall the Greek shipping heir I sold to previously? His name's Apollo Diakos. You set up a meeting for me the last time I visited him. Do you remember?"

"Yes, of course. Do you think he'll be willing to buy another one?"

"It's worth a try. He's fair, but you may need to negotiate," Zeik said. Slowly, he reached inside the sling on his arm and pulled out a slip of paper. On it were the names of the paintings, artists, and prices he estimated for each. His prices ranged from several hundred thousand dollars to more than a million. "Please go to the crypt and photograph each of the paintings. Then research them to find out what they'd sell for today."

"I see," Ning replied, but she didn't tell him she'd already done the research. "I can locate Diakos' phone number. What if he doesn't want to buy? Then what?"

"As I recall, you have relatives in the Chinese underworld. If the Greek refuses, you can carefully explore buyers through one of them. I don't know anyone else who'd be safe to contact."

"Okay, I'll do what I can. How do I reach you?"

"Phone the prison and ask for a meeting with me."

Ning squeezed his hand, offered a weak smile, and left. When she returned to the condo, she was immediately besieged by Zeik's two hairless Sphinx cats, Skull and

Bones, looking for food. Ivy shooed them away and went to Hayden's office. Since the police took his computer, she pulled out his hidden notebook. She bought a new laptop since then, but the notebook had what she needed. It didn't take her long to find Diakos' mobile number. Before phoning him, she got out her list of the paintings and their values. Taking a deep breath, she made the call.

"Yes, who's calling?" Diakos answered.

"Sir, you don't know me. I'm Hayden Zeik's personal assistant, Ivy Ning. He has not been well and asked that I reach you to ask if you may be interested in purchasing another masterpiece for your collection."

"Oh, goodness! I hope Hayden is not too ill. What's the problem with the old boy?"

"I'm afraid he's come down with a rare disease. Currently he's not able to get around very well."

"So sorry to hear. I hope he recovers quickly. As for the paintings, Ms. Ning, I may be interested, but the global pandemic has hurt my shipping operation. As a result, my cash supply is somewhat limited. Nevertheless, I'm intrigued. What pieces are available?"

"Currently he has eight, but he wants to see if there are any artists that would complement your private collection."

"Certainly. Let me think. Hmmm. I'd love to have something from Raphael. Or maybe a Degas."

"You may be in luck, sir," Ning responded with a smile. "There's the *Portrait of a Young Man* by Raphael. Plus, he has *Five Dancing Women* by Degas. Are you familiar with those?"

"Yes! Yes! I believe so, my dear. Let me do a little research and I'll call you back. Will that be okay?"

"Of course, sir. I look forward to hearing from you."

After they disconnected, Ivy sat back and grinned, thinking she may pull this off to help Hayden.

* * *

AS SOON AS Interpol Officers Jeanette Poole and Barron Kaide arrived in Berlin, the lovers settled into a hotel near the police station. After a passionate evening together, followed by a hearty breakfast in the hotel café, Poole phone their friend, Detective Alex Blaine. He'd been a constant companion during their investigation and ultimate arrest of Hayden Zeik and his Neo-Nazi comrades. "Hello, Detective! It's Jeanette Poole. Barron and I are back in your fair city on another assignment. We'd love to meet at your convenience to fill you in."

"Officer Poole!" Blaine answered. "What a delightful surprise. I wondered when I'd hear from you again. Sure, would you like to come by the station and have some coffee?"

"Excellent, Alex. We'll be there soon." After paying their café bill, the Interpol partners drove to their meeting. Blaine welcomed them with gusto. He was an older, slightly heavyset police detective with graying hair and a bushy mustache. His ready smile made him instantly likeable.

"So wonderful to see you both!" Blaine shouted as he gave them both a brief, but hearty embrace. "Please follow me. I'm eager to hear what's going on."

CHAPTER 35

After catching up on their past year's activities, Officer Poole described the team's current assignment. "This is another case that's a little outside our normal area. It revolves around a wonder drug from Boston's NuPharma Corp. called RGB101. The product has gone through clinical trials for approval in the heart and diabetes disease markets. Foul play started in the United States with the murder of the commissioner of the Food and Drug Administration, who was in favor of the drug's approval. Then there was the death of a U.S. senator, which the FBI believes was *not* accidental. Following that, two men kidnapped and tortured the director of NuPharma to learn the drug's formula. Fortunately, the authorities freed him and apprehended the criminals. The man's okay. As if that's not enough, there were attempted murders and the planting of listening devices at the homes of the NuPharma CEO."

"Wow, this *is* a complex case!" Blaine responded as he shook his head.

"There's more," Officer Kaide said. "Criminals threatened the physicians responsible for the FDA trials. They were told to change their senate hearing testimonies or lose their lives. Plus, someone hacked into the FDA website to change the results from the trials." A look of astonishment appeared on the detective's face.

"Our computer expert in Rome, Sarah Graff, broke it open when she discovered a secret bank account in the Caribbean that was set up by a man named Karsen Ojin," Poole stated. "Six pharmaceutical companies – four from Europe and two from the U.S. – deposited hefty sums of money into the account. Then there were withdrawals and payments to two senators and two criminals involved in the crimes. Since then, we were able to connect the CEOs of those six pharmas to the bank account."

"Unbelievable, Officers!" the detective barked between sips from his steaming coffee.

"Two of our Interpol people from Rome attacked Ojin at a castle in northern Italy. From there, he and his accomplice, a Japanese woman named Fon Tazi, escaped in a small Cicare 8 helicopter. Security eventually located the chopper in Verona, Italy. From there, we traced the two fugitives to Berlin," Poole caught her breath and smiled.

"So far, our role has involved the arrest of the CEO of a pharma in Brussels," Kaide explained. "It got a little messy, but we brought him in without too much trouble."

"I see!" the detective marveled. "The last time you were here, you took down those Neo-Nazis along with the sex trafficker Hayden Zeik. The last I've heard, he's serving time in a local prison."

"Yes. Did anyone ever discover the hiding place of those stolen masterpiece paintings?" Poole inquired.

"We're not aware of it," Blaine responded. "We haven't talked to Zeik's assistant since last year. If anyone else knows, it would be her. We had nothing on her at the time, so she's remained free."

"Hmmm. We'll keep that in mind," Poole replied with interest as she made a note to herself. "Okay, I'd imagine Karsen Ojin and his gal pal have purchased new burner phones since they escaped from Italy. That puts us at square one, right? If they needed help, who would they turn to?"

"There are many underworld characters they could buy weapons and other contraband from. What do you know about Ojin?" the detective inquired.

"From our research, his family is a mix of German and Chinese," Kaide offered. "Tazi was on the Japanese Olympic team as a champion martial arts competitor. She was also in the Japanese Air Force where she learned to fly a chopper."

"Talented woman who I'm sure is quite resourceful. She must be deadly with her hands and feet," Blaine suggested. The Interpol partners shook their heads in agreement.

"Do you have any confidential informants in the underworld who might know someone like Ojin making a weapons purchase?" Poole asked.

"I'll check with my team here in Berlin. We'd have to throw out a wide net since we'd be looking for German and possibly Chinese underworld characters."

"Great, thanks, Alex!" Poole beamed. "Let us know if anything of interest surfaces. In the meantime, Kaide and I'll search the Interpol portal for leads."

* * *

A FEW DAYS passed since Ivy spoke with the Greek shipping heir. He eventually returned her phone call. "Greetings, Ms. Ning!" Diakos began. "I've given your proposal some thought and looked at those two lovely works of art. I'd forgotten how captivating Raphael's *Portrait of a Young Man* is. I have to say that it would be a wonderful addition to my collection. From research, however, the price may be beyond my current resources."

"Possibly we can work something out, sir," Ning responded, getting nervous that she'd be low-balled on the price.

"Well, I know it could go for well over a million dollars – maybe as much as $1.5 million. Unfortunately, my current budget for such an investment is well below that."

"I see. From our understanding, it could go for even more. What did you have in mind?"

"Well...I might go as high as a million, but that would stretch me."

After pausing for a second, Ivy responded, "Would you consider a $1,250,000?"

"Ooh. Ooh. Let me think..." He paused momentarily and pretended to flip through pages of notes. "I might be able to go to a $1,150,000."

"We may be getting close, Mr. Diakos. Please let me

speak with Hayden and I'll get back to you. Will that be okay?"

"Yes, of course, dear. I'll look forward to hearing from you. And please give the old boy my best wishes."

"Surely! Thank you, kindly."

After she disconnected, the experience exhilarated her. *Did I actually negotiate for a piece of classical art?* Her next step was to reach out to Hayden to see if he approved of her attempt to make a deal. She phoned the prison and asked if she could meet with Hayden Zeik. The guard told her she would have to wait until next Saturday, but he would put her name on the list and inform the prisoner. That was only two days, she thought, so Diakos hopefully wouldn't lose patience.

When Saturday arrived, Ivy rose early and prepared for her trip to the prison. After feeding the cats, she went to the garage and slid into Zeik's Mercedes GLA 250 SUV, which she loved to drive. Arriving at the prison entrance, she eventually passed through the clanging and buzzing doorways past security. As she waited at the same table, the decrepit Zeik soon hobbled into the room using a cane. As he approached, Ivy thought he looked a little better.

"Hello, Ivy," Zeik sputtered with lips that weren't as swollen as the last time she saw him. "I hope you're here to tell me you've contacted Apollo."

"Yes, Mr. Z. You look better!" she smiled. "Diakos sends his greetings. We chatted. He's mostly interested in the Raphael. We discussed several prices, finally settling on $1,150,000. Does that interest you?"

"Well...beggars can't be too choosy, can they?" Zeik

managed a weak smile of his own. I'm desperate, Ivy. He's getting a steal, but I'll have his money. Let's go for it.

"Very good, sir. I've photographed them and am familiar with the one he wants. I noticed a carrying case that could be useful for the trip. Do you have any advice on finalizing the deal?"

"Be sure to examine the check he gives you. You need to be sure it's for the correct amount. I know you'll do fine. Apollo is a decent fellow."

After saying goodbye to Zeik, Ning returned home and took the phone from her purse. Punching in the number to Diakos, he answered on the third ring. "Hello, sir, it's Ivy. I've discussed the price of the painting with Hayden. He's agreeable."

"Excellent!" Apollo bellowed. "How soon can you make the trip to see me?"

"I need to make arrangements with a private jet. I'll confirm as soon as I have the date. We'll fly to your personal runway on the Greek island if that's acceptable."

"Of course," Apollo responded. "You're more than welcome to stay over if you wish."

"Thank you, sir. I'll need to return to Berlin after I've delivered the artwork."

As soon as Ivy scheduled the Charterjet, she phoned the Greek to alert him of her schedule. Her next step was to visit the storage space to pick up the masterpiece. She motored to the church and walked to unlock the crypt door. Slowly stepping down the worn stairs, she had to recall the location of the Raphael. Moments later, she located the painting, placed it inside the carrying case, locked the door, and drove back to her residence to make final preparations.

The next day, she sped to the airport and found the Charterjet counter. She completed her payment, met the pilot, and walked to the plane. The flight was fast and efficient, zooming high above the clouds on their way to the Greek island. When they landed, she saw a limo heading in her direction. Apollo bounded out of the vehicle and greeted Ning warmly.

"You must come to my villa for a quick bite to eat, Ivy!" he demanded. She agreed and carried the portfolio with the artwork into his limo for the short trip. They soon arrived in his luxurious chateau and relaxed on colorful silk-covered pillows. Ivy was relieved to be out of the oppressive heat. Apollo's staff began serving wines and various dishes. "I can't wait any longer, my dear!" he boomed. "Please let me savor this beautiful piece of art."

Ivy unzipped her case and lifted out the 22-inch by 28-inch canvas for him to hold in his hands. "Aah! Magnificent!" Apollo marveled as his eyes beheld the painting. He was instantly smitten and stared for several minutes. "Please, help yourself to some lunch, Ivy. How rude of me!"

"I'm so happy the Raphael meets you expectations, sir."

"Oh, more than that! I'm in love!" he beamed, then laughed at his emotion. He then reached inside his tunic and pulled out a check that was made out to Hayden Zeik. Ivy studied the amount carefully, then smiled as she looked up at the buyer. After they completed their pleasantries and had a bite to eat, she told him it was time for her to depart. Hayden was right. Apollo was a charmer.

CHAPTER 36

As soon as Ivy returned to Berlin, she drove to the bank and deposited the check from Diakos. Zeik had authorized her to conduct business in his name. Afterward, she took a deep breath to relax. It thrilled her to have completed Zeik's assignment. Her next step was to determine how to get the money transferred to Hayden's contact at the prison. When she phoned the prison, she learned the next visiting day wasn't until the following Saturday.

In the days that followed, Zeik tried walking more on his own, but he still used a cane. The infirmary attendant removed more of his bandages and provided pain pills that they would distribute daily. Once he returned to the general prison population, he fearfully searched for the goons who brutalized him. They were nowhere to be found. Even at night, when the call for *lights out* boomed over the loudspeakers, he remained anxious.

On the third day, the guards required Hayden to report to the laundry room for chores. His injuries limited him, but he pitched in folding shirts and pants for the guards. As his shift ended and evening drew near, he hobbled back to his cell. Unfortunately, he had to pass through a dark tunnel to the main prison.

Suddenly, the brutes appeared. One had a chain, another flashed a shiv – a knife fashioned from a spoon. Zeik turned to escape. Too late. One of their pals stood in the way. Before Hayden could scream, they pounced on him. The thugs were relentless. This time, they delivered chain whippings and repeated stabbings. The third man ripped down his pants and started sodomizing him. Little did they know their target was dead before the third man had his way. They soon realized Zeik was no longer moving...or breathing. They glanced at one another, then scurried away like rats from a sinking ship. Blood puddled from Zeik's wounds on the cold concrete floor.

Another prisoner discovered Zeik's body several minutes later. The horrified inmate shouted to a guard. A horn blew, announcing a lockdown.

"Someone will pay for this tragedy," the dour warden stated to the news media. Stories identified Zeik as the criminal responsible for sex-trafficking hundreds of young women in various parts of Europe and even America.

Ivy read the news on her laptop before the authorities contacted her. She was the only person listed in prison records that was close to a *next of kin*. Zeik's last will and testament identified her as the beneficiary of his estate. Tears ran down her cheeks as she tried to come to grips with the devastating details. Skull and Bones nuzzled close to her to provide comfort. The realization that he was gone left Ivy devastated.

* * *

OFFICER JEANETTE POOLE read the same news report on her phone as she and her partner finished breakfast and sipped coffee. "This is amazing, Barron. Zeik's body was found in the prison. His enemies apparently beat him to death."

"I didn't see that coming! Who's the next of kin?"

"His property manager, Ning. It listed her as his only survivor. Apparently they were in a relationship."

"It would be interesting to visit her in a few days to see if she knows anything about the hidden paintings," Barron proposed.

Later, when they returned to their hotel room, Officer Kaide logged on to his laptop to search the Interpol portal for Ivy Ning. She didn't come up, but another Ning did. "Well now," Barron exclaimed. "There's a Rico Ning who appears to be in the Chinese underworld. He should also be on our list of people to see. What are the chances they're related?"

"Good catch. Is there an address listed for Rico?" Jeanette asked.

"I'm not sure how current it is, but there's one we can visit."

"Are you up for checking it out? He may be worth pursuing. Who knows? Maybe he'll have some information." Jeanette proposed. "I'm going to phone Detective Blaine to see if he's aware of the man."

After the call went through, Blaine answered, "Berlin Police, Detective Blaine."

"Yes, Detective. Poole here. Did you see the news about Zeik's murder in prison?"

"Actually, we were just discussing it. Didn't sound like a good ending for the man."

"We noticed that his next of kin, or at least his beneficiary, is Ivy Ning. Barron searched and found a Rico Ning on the Interpol portal. Are you familiar with him?" she asked.

"The name sounds familiar, but he must have stayed under the radar. He's not on our list."

"Barron and I are going to visit an address that's listed for Rico. It's probably old, but it might lead to something. We'll be in touch if we need your help."

After the call, the Interpol partners packed their gear and left in the rented vehicle. Using the GPS device on their phone, it took a half hour to reach their destination. They slowed as they passed the residence, then parked down the street. Nodding to each other, they exited the car and ambled to the entrance. Barron knocked. No answer. He rang the doorbell.

Moments later, an elderly Chinese woman answered. "Yes, yes. What is it?" she asked in a broken German accent.

"Hello," Poole answered in German and presented her badge. "We're with Interpol. Does Rico Ning live here?"

"Rico? No, he moved. Not here."

"I see. Do you know where he lives now?"

"Wait. I get an address," the woman offered, and left. A minute later, she returned with a piece of paper with an address scrawled over it. "This is last I know."

"Thank you kindly. Are you related to Mr. Ning?" Poole inquired after taking the paper.

"Maybe."

"Do you know Ivy Ning?"

"Yes. Why do you ask?"

"I see," Poole beamed and put two and two together. "So that means Ivy and Rico are also cousins."

"Yes, yes. Why do you ask?"

"No problem, thank you. We'll look for Rico here," Poole stated as she held up the new address. The Interpol pair nodded, bowed, and returned to their car.

"Fill me in, Jeanette."

"Okay. The lady is connected to both Rico and Ivy. So Ivy knows people in the underworld."

"Hey, let's ask the lady what her relationship is to Karsen Ojin," Barron smiled. "Who knows?"

They turned and went back to the front door. Poole rang the doorbell and glanced at her partner with a smile.

Minutes later, the elderly woman answered and gruffly asked, "Okay, you were just here. Now, what is it?"

"We were also wondering if you may be related to Karsen Ojin?"

The woman looked surprised to hear the name and stepped back. "Maybe I am. The name is familiar. Not someone I know well. His mother is a cousin."

"Ah, I see! Thank you," Poole replied, glanced at Kaide, then they left.

"Holy cow, Barron. If she's connected to Ojin, they're all relatives."

"I'll be damned!" he grunted. "One big, happy family."

* * *

KARSEN OJIN and Fon Tazi were getting restless. Their financial resources had dwindled precipitously since the six pharmas tanked. With the news of RGB101 being approved by the FDA, Ojin's investments lost considerable market share almost overnight.

As they sat in their borrowed condo, Fon suddenly ran across the news story about Hayden Zeik's death on a tablet computer. "K, listen to this!" Tazi began as she read the report. "Your cousin, Ivy, may have come into a lot of money. Her employer was murdered in prison and she's his beneficiary. How much could she be worth?"

"That's incredible!" Ojin sat up straight in his chair. The wheels turned in his brain. "I'll have to reach out to her and extend my condolences."

"Of course, K."

"I wonder if she'd allow me to invest some of her newfound wealth," he sneered, as he glanced at his lover.

"What would you recommend?"

"I'll need to determine a plan to present to her. There are certainly a number of alternatives to consider. It could allow us to get back on track with a new enterprise."

"We may need to lie low, K. The authorities are certainly still looking for us."

"Hmmm. You may be right, but we can still discuss some options with my cousin."

"One thing I'd like is a more spacious accommodation. This condo is beautiful but there's little room to stretch out."

FORMULA FOR A FELONY

"I agree. I recall Ivy said her employer had several residences. Maybe we can see if there is another option."

"Let's give her a few days to mourn. Unless you'd like to extend your condolences sooner."

"Yes, I was thinking the same thing. I'll phone her tomorrow," Ojin agreed.

The next day, Ojin was eager to reach Ivy. Her phone rang, and she picked up. "Hello," she answered weakly.

"My dear, Ivy. We just saw the news of your employer's sad ending. Fon and I are so very sorry for your loss. Is there anything we can do to help you?" Ojin began as he stirred his tea.

"Oh, Karsen, thank you for your consideration. I'm still trying to come to grips with this horrible situation. I just saw him recently. He hoped to be freed from prison soon. Now he's gone."

"Yes, it's so terrible, dear. I can tell you're still very upset. Just know that you can count on us to help you in your time of need."

"Thank you. I will," Ivy responded, then clicked off.

"Well, damn. She short-circuited me," Ojin responded in a huff. "I'll call in a few days to ask if there's another place we might use."

CHAPTER 37

U sing the address of Rico Ning that his elderly relative provided, Officers Poole and Kaide drove through the Berlin traffic to their destination. He apparently lived in a loft apartment above a restaurant. After parking, they made their way to the entrance and rang the doorbell. There was no answer. They decided to ask the restaurant owner if they knew the man.

"Yes, he may be home. Just use the stairs to his place," the proprietor suggested.

Poole and Kaide left the restaurant and took the stairs as directed. When they arrived at his door, they were greeted by a smallish Chinese man. "Yes, what do you want?" Rico barked. "I usually meet with appointments only."

"I see," Poole replied. "We're looking for a man named Karsen Ojin. Do you happen to know him. We understand that you are cousins."

"Hmm, cousins?" Rico played dumb at the insinuation. "Don't have many relatives. Why do you ask?"

"We met an elderly woman who is your relative. She said you, Ivy Ning, and Ojin are cousins."

"Very strange to hear!" Rico answered. "News to me, I'm afraid."

While Poole tried to get the man to talk, Kaide scanned the interior of his apartment. In the distance, he could see cases of handguns. He nudged Poole to look and nodded toward the weapons. "Looks like you're a weapons dealer, Mr. Ning." She proposed.

"Oh, no. Just a hobby. I'm a collector, you might say." Rico deflected as he glanced at his array of guns.

"Okay, but you and Ivy Ning are cousins, correct?" she asked.

"Yes, yes. I'm related to Ivy." Rico admitted.

"I don't have any more questions at this time, Mr. Ning. Thank you," Poole stated as the two Interpol partners turned and walked down the stairs.

"He claims he doesn't know Ojin. I'd say we visit Ivy. She may still be in mourning, but we have questions."

* * *

BEFORE ATTEMPTING to visit Ivy Ning, Kaide asked his partner if they should get a search warrant and wiretap Ivy's phone. "Maybe we'll get her to open up about some of Zeik's properties or possessions. We might also catch her on the phone with Ojin. Blaine's team will monitor her calls."

"Good idea, I'll contact Detective Blaine to see if he'll expedite a warrant and the wiretap." After reaching their friend, the documents were soon produced and signed for them to pick up at the police station. Poole and Kaide had been to Ivy's house previously when they looked for clues to Zeik's criminal operation. At that time, they located a laptop that was hidden inside a grandfather clock. Kaide was fortunate to guess the password – Zeik's father's name, HEINRICH.

"I've got Ivy's phone number, so I'll try her," Poole advised. When the phone rang, Ning picked up after the second ring.

"Yes," Ivy responded in a quiet voice.

"Hello, Ms. Ning, you may remember me. I'm Officer Jeanette Poole from Interpol. We met a year ago during the investigation of your employer, Hayden Zeik. First of all, my condolences for your loss."

"Oh, yes. I remember you," Ivy replied as she quickly wondered why the police would be interested in reaching her. "Hayden's passing is a huge loss for me. Thank you."

"My partner and I would like to have a few words with you if you're going to be home," Poole stated.

"Well, I'm pretty busy taking care of Zeik's estate, but I can spare a little time."

"Thank you. We'll see you soon."

After the call, she looked at Kaide and shook her head. "She may not be involved with anything illegal. Hard to tell how she got involved with a man like Zeik."

The Interpol pair left their hotel, picked up the search warrant, and drove to meet with Ivy. When they arrived, she buzzed them in and they took the elevator to her floor. Opening the door to her condo, the two Sphinx cats stayed close to Ning as Poole and Kaide were welcomed in. She invited them to relax in the living room while she made tea.

"Once again, we're very sorry for your loss, Ms. Ning." Poole offered as she glanced at their host and the ghoulish pets that hovered nearby. "We've come into some information that we want to ask you about."

"Hmm, what would that be?" Ivy tried to act innocent as she looked back and forth at the officers.

"We're aware that you're related to several people who have dubious pasts. Specifically, you are the cousin of Rico Ning, who is a known underworld figure. More importantly, you're also related to Karsen Ojin, who is wanted for his part in multiple crimes, including murder, kidnapping, attempted murder, and other charges. Are you aware of this?"

Ivy's eyes widened and she began squirming noticeably as Poole listed her relative's offenses. "Goodness, how do you know that I'm related to the man?"

"We had an unexpected meeting with an elderly woman who gave us the information," Kaide added, and cocked his head as he stared at Ivy. "You should be aware that if you're harboring Ojin and his associate, you could be charged with a criminal offense."

"What does that mean? Harboring?" Ivy asked, with guilt written on her face.

"For example, you may have hooked up Ojin with a place to stay. You may have also referred him to Rico for weapons. You get the idea," Barron explained.

"Is Ojin in Berlin?" Ivy asked, but it was a feeble attempt to continue her deception.

"We believe you know exactly where he is. The clock is ticking, Ms. Ning. Tick tock, tick tock. You need to come clean with us."

Tears began welling up in Ivy's large eyes, then ran down her cheeks. "Okay, okay, what do I have to do?"

"Tell us where we can find your cousin for a start," Poole urged. She and her partner were stunned that the woman broke so easily.

Ivy stalled for a moment, then gave them the address to the condo. She broke down and sobbed. The cats were more fidgety than normal.

"One more question, Ms. Ning," Barron asked. "We are aware that Zeik has possession of stolen masterpiece paintings. You can do the right thing and tell us where we can find them."

"Ugh, paintings?" she deflected. "I heard Hayden speak of those at one time, but I can't say I know where they are."

"Tick tock, tick tock, Ms. Ning," Poole probed, as she glared at the woman.

"I'm sorry. I'll see what I find when I search through Hayden's notes."

"Hmmm. Okay. Please let us know if you run across anything." Poole paused a few seconds. "That will be all for now. Thank you for your candor." Poole and Kaide then rose to leave. Ivy showed them to the door.

As they walked back to their rental car, rain began to fall. Thunder erupted overhead. Kaide looked up at the dark sky, then to his partner. "I didn't see that coming. You really got to her. I wonder if she'll try to warn Ojin?"

Poole decided to phone Detective Blaine. "Hello, Alex. We just met with Ivy Ning. She cracked when we threatened her with harboring a fugitive. We suspect she'll try to phone Ojin. Ask your people to be on alert." Blaine said he'd get on it immediately. "Also, we got the address for Ojin. He's staying at one of Zeik's condos." She gave him the address and requested police backup.

Shortly after Interpol's visit to Ivy, she received a phone call. "Hello, Ivy, it's Karsen. I hope you're feeling better today."

"Oh, Karsen," Ning paused. "I was going to warn you that the police were here. They told me they were looking for you and that I'd be involved in a crime if I didn't tell them where you are. You must leave."

"What? No!" Ojin screamed, then disconnected his call. "Fon, we've been blown. Ivy was pressured into telling the cops where we are. Start packing. We've got to get out of here."

"How could she...?" Tazi shouted back, then scrambled to collect her things. She began wiping down everything they'd touched in the past weeks.

"Too late, we've got to leave," Ojin barked. Outside, the rain became a steady downpour.

Poole and Kaide drove to the condo and looked around. "I'm going to block the garage exit," she told her partner.

Just then, Detective Blaine called to alert Poole that Ning warned Ojin. "They know you're coming. I've got men on the way."

"I'll check the garage, you take the lobby," Poole advised her partner. As she ambled down the ramp to the underground parking space, the Interpol officer was surprised to see Ojin and Tazi come through the door from the elevator. Tazi jumped behind a vehicle not far from the doorway and grabbed her sidearm. Poole did the same at the other end of the underground lot and shouted into her comms to alert Kaide. Ojin turned and went back into the elevator.

Tazi fired her weapon repeatedly, but Poole was protected behind a large SUV. They exchanged fire for several minutes. Neither of them was close to hitting the other. As Tazi spent her clip, she reloaded, giving Poole a chance to get closer. The sound of gunfire echoed through the garage.

Upstairs in the condo lobby, Kaide spotted Ojin darting from the elevator to try to escape. When he saw the Interpol officer, Karsen dove behind a half wall, then pulled out his own handgun to begin an assault on his pursuer. Barron remained behind a large column and exchanged crossfire. The battle raged.

In the garage, both Poole and Tazi eventually depleted their ammunition. The Interpol officer quickly realized it would come down to a hand-to-hand clash between her and the Olympic champion. Slowly, each of them moved away from the bullet-riddled vehicles they'd used for cover. Tazi nodded, indicating she'd like to take her on. What she didn't know was that Poole had been a martial arts champion herself.

CHAPTER 38

Jeanette Poole and Fon Tazi stepped out into an opening in the garage. They could hear the thunder cracking outside. The two women circled each other. Suddenly, Tazi threw a kick. Poole evaded her thrust and tried to grab her leg but missed. Fon closed in and attempted a feigned kick combined with a punch. She caught Poole on the side of the head, knocking her back against a parked car. The officer regained her balance and moved toward Tazi. They circled near each other again. Fon faked a punch and threw a kick at Poole's gut, forcing the Interpol officer to lose her breath, double over, and clutch her midsection in pain. Tazi saw an opening. She kicked again with a thrust that landed squarely on Jeanette's jaw, knocking her to the ground. Quickly, Poole crab-legged backward to avoid another punch. As Fon tried a kick to the head, Jeanette grabbed her opponent's foot and flipped the woman back. The Interpol officer had a chance and jumped up. She was in pain but fought through it.

271

In the lobby, Kaide exchanged fire with Ojin. One of Karsen's bullets hit the column in front of Barron. A chunk of marble exploded off and ricocheted at the Interpol officer's forehead. Blood seeped from an instant gash, but it wasn't deep. Soon, they both spent their ammunition. Ojin thought he'd make a run for it. There was a side door behind the lobby counter not far from his position. Barron reacted quickly and rushed to grab two metal candle holders from a coffee table. He wound up and propelled the first one at his target. It caught Ojin on the side of the head in mid-stride. He staggered but kept moving. Ojin thought he could escape, but his mind was quickly going dark. The second metal object also hit its mark. Karsen flew in the air a moment, then skidded along the marble floor. Blood puddled below his head when he came to rest. Kaide ran to examine him. He'd live. *Only took two strikes,* he thought.

Fon continued to attack her opponent in the underground lot. Jeanette wanted to lure her to a place where her footing wouldn't be as secure. She jumped on the hood of a parked car and leapt to the next one. Fon followed, trying to make contact with another punch or kick. The Interpol officer stopped on top of a sedan, waiting for her adversary. Tazi moved closer. Poole jumped to another car's hood. Tazi tried to close the distance between the two of them. Jeanette stopped again on top of a vehicle roof. Fon jumped to the hood of the same vehicle and tried to reach for Poole's leg. She missed. As she reached forward, Poole used Tazi's momentum and kicked her in the head, stunning her. Fon lost her balance and flew into an open convertible. It was like watching Fon in slow motion as she fell headfirst into the front seat. Unable to catch herself, she smacked awkwardly on the gearshift. It pierced her eye. Blood squirted onto the leather seats and console. Tazi flailed for a moment, then stopped. Her arms dropped to the seat and floor. The sequence stunned Poole. She grabbed Tazi's wrist to feel for a pulse. There was none. She contacted her partner on the comms, telling him Tazi was down.

Outside, the rain continued to pelt the street. Sirens blared. Flashing lights reflected on the wet pavement. Two German police officers tore through the lobby door. Another pair ran into the garage. In the lobby, Kaide yelled to get their attention. He flashed his Interpol badge and explained the shootout. Debris from their firefight covered the floor. Bullet holes perforated the walls.

"Call for an ambulance," Kaide barked to the officers. "My partner's in the garage. She was in a fight with this guy's partner." The police looked down at Ojin. He was breathing, but probably concussed from the double trauma to his head.

Kaide hurried down to the garage to find his partner. She ran to him and they embraced. "Wow, you took her out, Jeanette! You're amazing!"

"I was lucky," Poole remarked with a grin. "What happened to your head?"

"Some marble dislodged from one of Ojin's bullets. It's nothing," he commented as he wiped blood from his forehead and cheek. "So tell me, how did you overtake Tazi?"

"She had the upper hand for a while. Got me good with a couple of punches and kicks. It turns out she couldn't handle a stick shift."

"What?" he replied. She nodded and they walked

toward the convertible as two police officers were examining the body. It was difficult for them to dislodge Tazi's
skull. The Interpol partners shook their heads, walked
away, and hugged again.

"How did you take out Ojin? What happened?"

"We exhausted our ammo, then he tried to escape. I
grabbed some heavy metal candlesticks and fired at his
skull before he could get away. He's alive, but he'll have a
wicked headache." Poole hugged and kissed her partner.

Later in the day they gave Chief Aritan a call. "Hello,
Chief, Poole here. Get ready to light up another fine cigar.
Kaide and I were able to track down Ojin and Tazi here in
Berlin."

"I'll be a son of a bitch! That's the best news I've heard
in quite a while! There are a bunch of people who'll be
happy to hear it. Give me all the gory details."

Poole described how Ojin was related to the two Ning
cousins. She explained how Ivy broke down under pressure
and told them that Ojin was staying at one of Hayden
Zeik's residences. Poole also described Zeik's brutal
murder in prison. Because of his death, Ning suddenly
became quite wealthy. Later, when they cornered Ojin and
Tazi at the condo, they had to fight it out. "Both of us
ended up with some minor injuries, but nothing serious."

"Thank goodness, you're both okay," Aritan bellowed as
he relit the Nicaraguan cigar tucked in the corner of his
mouth. "I'll contact my friend at the FBI and fill him in.
DeLong will be thrilled to learn that you've solved the
case."

"We're not done, Chief. Ivy Ning appears to be suspicious as hell, so we'll be watching her."

* * *

THE WIRETAP on Ivy Ning's phone was crucial. The Berlin police monitored a call from Ivy to Rico Ning. "I need some help! The police came here asking about stolen paintings that Hayden has stashed in a church crypt. They're masterpieces from World War II. They're very rare and worth millions. Do you know anyone who might buy them? I just sold one to a Greek friend of Zeik's but he's tapped out."

The story shocked Rico as he tried to collect his thoughts. "Well, maybe. I'll need a few days to locate the right buyer. I have friends in Taiwan who could be interested. None of my contacts in Germany are what you'd consider wealthy. Let me make some calls and I'll get back to you. If you can email me the list and prices you'd like to get, that would help me find an interested party."

Ivy quickly provided her cousin with the information. In the days that followed, Rico telephoned several people who he believed had the financial resources combined with an interest in classical art. He eventually reached someone who was both a collector and extremely affluent. After reviewing the array of paintings and estimated prices, they negotiated a deal, including Rico's cut, and settled on a sum. Rico would be responsible for crating the artwork and shipping it to the buyer in Taiwan.

"Ivy, I have a buyer!" Rico announced, then described the figure he agreed to with the buyer. It was lower than expected, but she wanted to be rid of them. Ning gave Rico a time that she'd have them at her condo. She trusted him to deliver as promised. The buyer would wire half of the sum to a private bank account. When the artwork arrived, they'd pay the balance.

Detective Alex Blaine contacted Poole and Kaide when his men gave him the details of another recorded conversation. After thanking their friend, the Interpol partners decided to stake out Ivy's residence. They brought food and water with them in case they had to wait for an extended period. As it turned out, Ivy left her condo later in the day. They watched her drive from her underground parking lot in an SUV.

"Where do you suppose our friend's going in her flashy Mercedes?" Kaide asked his partner.

"We'll find out," Poole replied as she pulled away from the curb to follow. They drove through the streets of Berlin behind Ivy, finally tailing her to an ancient church. "What the hell?"

The Interpol partners parked a distance away and jogged to the rear of the church. The Mercedes was parked next to an open wooden door. They were curious where it led. "Should we follow or wait for her to come out? What do you bet she'll be carrying some famous stolen paintings?"

Several minutes passed. No sign of Ning. Suddenly, she appeared in the doorway, her arms were loaded with three smaller canvases. "Hello, Ivy. I see you're an art connoisseur," Poole quipped. Ivy quickly turned to consider returning to the crypt, but the Interpol officer shouted, "That's far enough. Stop where you are." Ivy froze. Kaide darted to Ning and told her to turn around. She slowly pivoted with tears in her eyes. He took the bundle from her. Poole ordered her to turn around, then placed handcuffs on the prisoner. Ning's body shook with sobs. She screamed in anguish.

Poole went to the back of the SUV and opened the tailgate. Kaide gently laid the artwork in the cargo space. "Watch her," Poole requested, then entered the crypt, cautiously stepping down the worn steps. With the light on, she spotted four more canvases. The masterpieces mesmerized Poole as she pulled away their coverings. *Now I've seen it all*, she thought. When she left the storage cavern, she grinned and told Kaide that it appeared there were seven in all. "You and Zeik must have sold a few of them already, right?" Ivy continued to weep bitterly, shaking her head.

Kaide phoned Detective Alex Blaine and gave him the news of their discovery. "Oh, my! You did it! I'll send a team to bring Ms. Ning in for questioning. What will become of the paintings?"

"When we were here last year, we met a gentleman by the name of Jurgen Kolb at the Wiesenthal Center. His organization has hunted Nazi war criminals and stolen Jewish antiquities for years. He'll be ecstatic to learn that these have been located. I'm sure his group will know what to do. Either return them to museums or to their proper owners. Lots of people are going to be thrilled."

* * *

AFTER AN EMOTIONAL KOLB took possession of the paintings, he couldn't thank Poole and Kaide enough for their efforts. When the Interpol partners left the Wiesenthal Center, they decided it was time to give the good news to Chief Aritan.

"You two have done it again!" the chief bellowed after sipping from a fresh cup of coffee. "I never doubted you'd accomplish your mission."

"Thanks, Chief," Poole replied, as she smiled at Kaide. "We had wonderful assistance from your old pal, Detective Blaine, and his team. We're happy that Kolb will return the paintings to their rightful owners. All's well with the world – at least for a few days." They each shared a hearty laugh but knew there'd be more challenges ahead.

"Yes," the chief added, "as Winston Churchill once said, 'Success is not final. Failure is not fatal. It is the courage to continue that counts.'"

Acknowledgments

While many people provided encouragement in the development of my fourth novel, *Formula for a Felony*, I want to express my deep appreciation to editor and proofreader, Rob Bignell, for his tireless input and feedback. Outstanding contributions were also made by Nicole Conway who designed my covers, and Jennifer Eaton who formatted the interior pages.

Additionally, I would like to thank my parents and grandparents who introduced me to Lake Maxinkuckee. I am also grateful to my wife, children, eight siblings, relatives, and numerous friends who provided positive feedback as I transitioned from one version of this book to the next. Finally, I appreciate the self-publishing gurus who offer excellent tutorials that have given me confidence as an independent author.

I certainly want to credit the following source for information used in the development of this novel: Stephanie Schoppert for *10 Pieces of Art Stolen by Nazis that are Still Missing Today*, 2016.

About the Author

J.T. Kelly gained a love for the European continent while living in Rome, Italy, for a year and traveling extensively. Prior to his writing career, which includes *Fair Ways and Foul Plays, Deadly Defiance, Suite Suspicion,* and now *Formula for a Felony,* he honed his creative skills as an award-winning communications professional.

The author references Lake Maxinkuckee near Culver, Indiana, liberally in his four novels. It is a place that holds many fond memories from as far back as he can remember. The golf course across the road from his family's vacation home also provided hours of entertainment along with moments of exhilaration. While they occurred years apart, J.T. Kelly and his father witnessed each other making holes-in-one at the tree-lined, 160-yard, par 3, number four hole. Decades earlier, the author's father was present when his own father also had a hole-in-one on the same hole. How's that for memorable family coincidences?

An avid reader, J.T. Kelly has enjoyed numerous authors in the mystery, thriller, and suspense categories. As a result, readers of his books will experience the degree of fast-paced excitement that rivals many of the most popular in these genres.

To learn more about the author and to send him a message, visit his website at www.kellyfairways.us. If you enjoyed *Formula for a Felony,* consider leaving a 5-Star review where you purchased it. Thank you.

Made in the USA
Monee, IL
31 March 2022